ELLIE ROLLINS

razOr
bill

An Imprint of Penguin Group (USA) Inc.

Zip

RAZORBILL

Published by the Penguin Group
Penguin Young Readers Group
345 Hudson Street, New York, New York 10014, U.S.A.
Penguin Group (USA) Inc., 375 Hudson Street, New York, New York 10014, U.S.A.
Penguin Group (Canada), 90 Eglinton Avenue East, Suite 700, Toronto, Ontario, Canada M4P 2Y3 (a division of Pearson Penguin Canada Inc.)
Penguin Books Ltd, 80 Strand, London WC2R 0RL, England
Penguin Ireland, 25 St Stephen's Green, Dublin 2, Ireland (a division of Penguin Books Ltd)
Penguin Group (Australia), 250 Camberwell Road, Camberwell, Victoria 3124, Australia (a division of Pearson Australia Group Pty Ltd)
Penguin Books India Pvt Ltd, 11 Community Centre, Panchsheel Park, New Delhi – 110 017, India
Penguin Group (NZ), 67 Apollo Drive, Rosedale, Auckland 0632, New Zealand (a division of Pearson New Zealand Ltd)
Penguin Books (South Africa) (Pty) Ltd, 24 Sturdee Avenue, Rosebank, Johannesburg 2196, South Africa

Penguin Books Ltd, Registered Offices: 80 Strand, London WC2R 0RL, England

10 9 8 7 6 5 4 3 2 1

Copyright © 2012 Paper Lantern Lit LLC

ISBN: 978-1-59514-570-3

Library of Congress Cataloging-in-Publication Data is available

Printed in the United States of America

For my own magical mother.
And also for my grandmother, who
has surely been reincarnated as
a cat by now.

CHAPTER ONE

Zip Zip, Scooting Star

A gust of warm Texas wind rolled over the stage, rustling the velvet curtain door of Ana Lee's dressing room. The wind plucked petals from the flowers on the dresser and blew glittery makeup from the pots crowding the vanity table.

Lyssa looked up as the wind tickled the back of her neck. A film of gold powder settled on her nose and she sneezed, knocking over one of the dozens of bottles of nail polish spread out around her.

"Careful," Penn said. Penn was Lyssa's best friend. She was supposed to be helping Lyssa get ready for her big debut performance. Instead, she was pacing the dressing room on her hands, her skinny legs stretched up toward the ceiling while her brown hair pooled onto the floor. Penn had been going to circus camp since she was six years old. She was more comfortable upside down than she was right-side up.

Lyssa never understood how Penn could get her body to do *exactly* what she told it to, because the only place Lyssa felt graceful was on her scooter, Zip. But her mom wouldn't let her ride it around backstage.

"You look awesome," Penn said, studying Lyssa's toes from her position upside down. "I bet you actually sing onstage today. I can feel it."

Lyssa didn't answer. She looked back down at her freshly painted toes, humming under her breath. She always hummed when she got stage fright—which, so far, had been every single time she'd tried to sing in front of anyone other than her mom or Penn. But maybe Penn was right. Maybe tonight would be different.

"Is that an Athena song?" Penn asked, listening. Athena was their favorite musician—part cowgirl, part rock star. *"You think you're slick, but I know your tricks!"* Penn sang.

"And I'll get there first 'cause I'm quicker," Lyssa finished. She felt her nerves easing up a little. Music was her birthright, after all. Lyssa's mom was the great Ana Lee, headliner in the Texas Talent Show. And when her grandmother had been alive, she had sung opera on some of the

greatest stages in the world, while her grandfather played the banjo. Even Lyssa's dad, Lenny, had a band down in New Mexico, although Lyssa had never heard him play—in fact, she'd never met her dad at all.

Music flowed through her blood like oxygen. It had been passed on to her along with her mother's green eyes and her grandmother's narrow chin. So maybe Penn was right. Maybe tonight was *the* night.

Lyssa looked over her shoulder at her mom as another gust of wind—this one even stronger—whirled into the dressing room.

"Did you guys feel that?" Lyssa asked, trying to pat down her hair.

"Feel what? The wind?" Ana Lee caught her daughter's eye in the mirror and winked. She finished applying her lipstick and pursed her lips together, leaning in to plant a kiss on the middle of the mirror. "Mwuah!"

Ana was already wearing her stage makeup: shimmery blush and dark mascara. Her thick, golden hair was twisted into intricate braids and wound around her head. Watching her, Lyssa fingered her own braids, which stuck out from her head like two yellow sticks. She'd always wished she looked more like her mom, but she was too tall and too gangly, with hands and knees that were far too big for her body.

Maybe that's why Lyssa admired Athena so much.

The famous singer was over six feet tall, but when Lyssa had gone to see her in concert for her birthday last fall, Athena had clomped around stage in her high-heeled cowboy boots, not caring that she towered over everyone around her. Lyssa knew she was extra lucky to have seen Athena perform because right after that concert, Athena's publicist said she'd come down with a bad case of bronchitis and would have to cancel the next show. Nobody was worried . . . until the show after that got canceled, too. And the one after that. In fact, Athena hadn't been seen in public *once* since that night.

"Have I ever told you girls about the winds of change?" Ana asked, pushing one last golden strand of hair back into her braid.

Lyssa and Penn shared a smile. Both girls shook their heads, even though Ana had told them about the winds of change dozens of times. Penn rolled down from her handstand and curled her legs beneath her like a pretzel, sitting on the floor. Lyssa scooted off her chair and joined her. She stuck the end of her braid in her mouth. Her hair tasted like the organic shampoo her mom made using avocados from their garden. It was impossible not to sneak a taste every now and then.

"The winds of change blow through our lives whenever things need to be shaken up a little," Ana said, turning

4

around on her chair. "The wind makes the world spin a little too fast; then all sorts of strange and wonderful things begin to happen. Everyday objects become great and powerful weapons!"

Ana grabbed one of the maracas Lyssa and Penn had made for her out of a packet of tomato seeds and brandished it like a sword. Then she threw the maracas into the air and began to juggle. She was an amazing juggler—if the singing thing hadn't worked out, she liked to say, she could have made it as a circus clown.

Lyssa jumped up and searched the dressing room for other things Ana Lee could juggle. Lyssa threw her mom a few bottles of nail polish, and Penn, joining in, found a rolled-up pair of socks. Soon, it became a contest—who could find the most items for Ana to juggle. A minute later, Ana had over thirty different objects in the air, including one of Lyssa's flip-flops and Penn's wad of watermelon-flavored bubble gum. That was the thing about Lyssa's mom: the stories she told always *sounded* impossible, but when Ana was around, the impossible *did* happen.

"Ana, we need you for sound check."

The new sound guy—Michael—appeared next to the velvet curtain. He was tall, with shaggy brown hair, thick black glasses, and skin the color of skim milk. Ana elegantly caught each object in one hand and tossed them into a basket next to the door. Except for her tomato seed maraca, which she threw to Lyssa.

"Be right back!" Ana kissed Lyssa's head, then danced off past Michael to finish getting ready for her show. As soon as Ana had disappeared beyond the curtains, Penn turned to Lyssa, eyes shining mischievously.

"*Now* can I see it?" she demanded.

Lyssa rolled her eyes. "All right, all right."

Next to her mother's dressing table sat a beat-up trunk. Ana kept everything in this old trunk, and Lyssa was strictly forbidden from rifling through it unless her mom was there to supervise because Ana didn't want anything to get lost or crumpled. Inside were old photographs, like from her first birthday, when Ana had driven a tiny baby Lyssa across Utah. They'd stopped at the Dead Lake, where—rumor had it—a fierce monster lived below the surface. And there were hot sauce packets from that time they searched the entire city of Austin for Tabasco sauce so hot it could make you breathe fire. It was a trunk of mementoes, and Lyssa had been promising to show Penn its contents for ages, especially Ana's collection of playbills from her days as a traveling singer, before she'd had Lyssa. Recently, the trunk's lock had broken, and Lyssa knew it was only a matter of time before her mom had it fixed and she and Penn lost their opportunity.

She tiptoed over to the trunk, accidentally knocking over two more bottles of nail polish. Thankfully, the caps were screwed on tightly. It was hard for Lyssa to know what to do with her long limbs sometimes.

"Um, Lyssa?"

Lyssa whipped around, surprised to see Michael still hovering by the entrance to the dressing room. She frowned—she thought he'd gone off with her mom.

"Hey," she said cautiously, shooting Penn a warning look so she would know not to mention the trunk in his presence.

"I wanted to give you this." Michael took a quick step forward and held out a flash drive. Lyssa hesitated before taking it from him.

"What's it for?" she asked.

"Your mom was telling me you got stage fright. I loaded this up with some recording software. You can download it on your computer and use it to make your own demo CDs. I thought maybe it would help you get comfortable . . . you know, singing in front of people." Michael coughed and adjusted his glasses.

"Thanks," Lyssa said quickly. She thrust the flash drive into her pocket, purposefully avoiding looking at Michael or Penn. Shame stuck to her throat like extra-chunky peanut butter.

She couldn't believe her mom had told Michael about

her stage fright. Lyssa didn't want anyone knowing about that, but *especially* not Michael. He seemed sort of cool. For example, Lyssa and her mom didn't have a computer at home, but Michael sometimes brought over his laptop and helped Lyssa find Athena's concert videos online. Once, he even told Lyssa he thought she was a born musician, just like her mom or Athena. But now that he knew stepping onto a stage made her queasier than riding the Heinous Hurricane roller coaster three times in a row, he probably didn't think that anymore.

Before Lyssa could say another word, her mom bounced back into the room, golden and glowing.

"What do you think, Lyssa?" she asked. "Ready to sing?"

Lyssa's anger at her mom dissipated in a wash of nerves. Her insides tied themselves into knots, then tied themselves into double knots. This was it. Penn stood up next to her and squeezed her hand.

"You're going to be amazing," Penn whispered.

"Good luck, Lyssa," Michael said.

Her mom beamed at her. "Come on, let's go."

Lyssa followed Ana from the dressing room into the dark chaos of the backstage area. She could do it. She *would* do it. Maybe her mom's strange magic would extend to her, just this once, and give her the courage to perform.

Just past the dressing room, the stage curtain whooshed open, revealing white lights and the shadowy silhouettes of hundreds of people waiting to watch the show. The announcer's booming voice echoed across the stage: *"You know and love her . . . here she is, the amazing Ana Lee!"*

Lyssa found she couldn't move. It felt like ice was creeping up over her toes, freezing the bones in her ankles. Her heart pounded against her chest like a zoo animal trying to escape from its cage. Lyssa opened and closed her mouth, trying to force a squeak, a whisper, *anything*—out. But nothing happened.

The crowd roared and cheered. Ana reached for Lyssa's hand, but Lyssa pulled it away, shaking her head. She couldn't do it.

"It's okay." Ana leaned down and gave Lyssa's shoulder a squeeze. "There's always next time. You're going to have so many adventures, Lyssa—don't worry."

Lyssa nodded, but the words rang through her head like a warning. *There's always next time.* As Michael and Penn crowded behind her, she felt suddenly certain, for no reason she could name, that there would not be a next time.

She watched her mother walk out onto the stage. Ana Lee shook the homemade maracas. When she began to sing, the entire audience fell under her spell, growing so quiet that Lyssa could have heard a single kernel of popcorn drop to the ground. Ana Lee sounded wonderful and confident onstage, and as Lyssa listened, she began to feel cold.

She would never sound like that, not if she practiced every single night.

Pushing past Penn and Michael, Lyssa ducked into her mom's dressing room and yanked the velvet curtain closed. She wanted to be alone.

She crawled into the space between her mom's dressing table and the wall, curling her body into a ball. She clenched her eyes shut tight and hummed an Athena song, trying to lift her spirits. This time, the trick didn't seem to work. Lyssa kept humming anyway, louder and louder, until she drowned out the sound of her mother's magical voice and the cheering audience that she just couldn't face.

When she opened her eyes again, it had grown dark. Lyssa could no longer hear her mother singing onstage or the distant crowd clapping. Everything was silent.

"Mom?" Lyssa called. She fumbled her way out from behind the dressing table. "Penn?"

No one answered. Shadows stretched long and dark across the floor.

Lyssa took a step forward and a floorboard creaked beneath her bare foot. She crossed the room, pushing aside the velvet curtain that separated her from the stage. But the stage wasn't there. Instead, a long, narrow hallway stretched out before her.

"Hello?" she called. Her voice echoed off the walls, and when it bounced back to her, it sounded deeper—like it belonged to a stranger.

Lyssa's mind flew to Athena. After Athena's last concert, she had simply disappeared. Was this what had happened to her? Had she woken up one day to find that the stage had vanished? Was that why no one knew where she was?

Something metal gleamed in the darkness. Lyssa got closer and realized it was Zip, her scooter. She wrapped her fingers around the familiar grooves of her scooter's handlebars and, suddenly, she felt a million times safer. Taking a deep breath, she pushed off.

Strange shadows flitted across her path. She squinted and saw a janitor hunched over a broom at the end of the hallway, sweeping the floor and whistling.

"Excuse me." Lyssa rolled toward the janitor. He lifted his head and Lyssa realized it wasn't the janitor at all—it was Melodius, the musician who played his saxophone on the corner of Lyssa's street. He turned toward Lyssa.

"Hey there, Scooting Star," he said in a voice that was deep and slow, like chocolate syrup. He let out a rumbling laugh. "What are you still doing here, girl?"

Lyssa put a foot down to stop rolling. "Melodius, do you know where my mom is?"

"She left a while ago. She told me she had a message for you."

"What message?"

Melodius bent back over his broom. "She didn't tell me. You got to find her."

Lyssa was about to ask, once more, where her mother had gone when she heard a horn honking somewhere in the distance. Melodius grinned.

"I bet that's her now—you better move, girl. Zip zip."

The horn honked again and Lyssa jumped back onto her scooter, pushing off. As she flew toward the corner of the hallway, she thought she heard Melodius's rumbling laugh again, but then the sound became sharper and clearer and she realized it wasn't laughter at all—it was music. She glanced over her shoulder. Melodius's broom had disappeared and in its place he was holding his big, brass saxophone. The music twisted into the air as the notes fell into place and became recognizable: "The Scooting Star," the song Ana Lee had written for Lyssa. Melodius was playing just for her.

Then she was outside. A bright yellow van circled the parking lot, heading for the exit. Her heart leapt in her chest. She recognized that van—it belonged to the Texas Talent Show. Her mom had to be inside.

Lyssa wrapped her fingers tighter around the scooter's handlebars and kicked off harder. She jumped over the stairs leading down to the sidewalk and zoomed out into the street. Tiny rocks shot out from beneath her spinning wheels as she rolled across the parking lot. Ana Lee peeked out of the van's back window and stuck out her tongue. Her eyes sparkled.

"Mom," Lyssa shouted, kicking forward. "Wait!"

Lyssa grabbed the van's back bumper with one hand, holding tightly to her scooter with the other. The van slowed to go over a speed bump and Lyssa bounced up behind it. But the bumper was wet and slippery beneath her fingers. A fat raindrop fell on Lyssa's nose and she looked up. The sky was a rolling mass of gray clouds. Thunder roared in the distance, sounding just like Melodius's saxophone.

"Wait," Lyssa shouted. The ground beneath her shook; there was a flash of lightning. Her fingers slipped off the bumper and she lost her grip . . .

Lyssa opened her eyes.

She wasn't riding Zip across a parking lot on a dark Texas night.

She was lying on her back in the grass, and Mrs. Patel was standing over her, pointing her garden hose straight at Lyssa's face. Water poured over Lyssa's cheeks. In the rays of early morning sunshine, the old woman's silver hair looked almost blue.

"Oh, dear. Lyssa." Mrs. Patel switched off the hose and took a step back, her bright orange garden clogs crunching against the grass.

For a moment, Lyssa couldn't speak. Her dream—part nightmare, part memory—was still so vivid in her head that she could hear the soft strains of Melodius's music. It had all seemed so real . . .

But no. She lived in Kirkland, Washington now, not Austin, Texas. Penn was no longer in the gray house down the street. And her mother was very far away.

CHAPTER TWO

You Think You're Slick

Lyssa scrambled to her feet. Her shorts and T-shirt clung damply to her arms and legs. The dream rattled around in her head like a lightning bug caught in a jar. She'd had the same dream yesterday and the day before that. For the last six months, it was the *only* dream she'd had.

"Sorry," Lyssa muttered, not quite able to look Mrs. Patel in the eye. She'd promised her new neighbor that she wouldn't sleep in her garden anymore, but Mrs. Patel had the nicest flowers in the neighborhood. They reminded Lyssa of the huge sunflowers—some of them as big as trees—that her mom grew.

Well, *used* to grow. Back in Austin.

Ana had always told her that sleeping under those flowers made her dreams sweeter, which was why Lyssa ended up in Mrs. Patel's yard in the first place. She'd hoped that sleeping beneath flowers would help her get rid of her nightmare. No such luck.

Mrs. Patel's eyes softened behind her pink plastic glasses. It was a look Lyssa was getting used to.

"Just try to remember for next time," Mrs. Patel said.

"My mom says . . ." Lyssa started. Then she bit down hard on her tongue, trying to keep the words from jumping out of her mouth.

"Lyssa?" Mrs. Patel said. Lyssa blinked.

"I won't do it again," she said instead.

Before Mrs. Patel could respond, Lyssa ducked out of her garden and wove around the high white fence that separated their houses, so focused on trying to unpeel her wet clothes from her skin that she almost walked smack into a large oak tree.

She used to slip up and talk about her mom all the time, but it made people uncomfortable, so she'd been trying to stop. It was hard, though. Just last week Michael told a funny joke and Lyssa laughed so hard soy milk shot out of her nose. But when she said she couldn't wait to tell her mom, Michael got very serious and they had to have a talk. He told her again that her mom was gone—she wasn't ever coming back.

Lyssa had nodded and said she understood, but secretly, deep down, she didn't believe him. Not entirely. She knew her mom better than anybody. Ana Lee was magic. She'd find her way back.

Lyssa sat down on the cold porch steps and closed her eyes, remembering the day after her grandma Pat's funeral. Her mom had made coffee for a stray cat.

It was a cold day, but Ana had left the window open and chilly morning air poured into their kitchen like icy water from a faucet. A huge gray cat crouched on the window ledge near the sink, its tiny pink tongue licking coffee from a clay mug. Lyssa's mom was at the kitchen table, drinking her daily cup of herbal tea and reading the horoscopes out loud from the newspaper.

"Your grandma Pat is a Sagittarius," Ana had explained when Lyssa slid into the chair across from her. Lyssa looked over at the cat sitting on the window ledge. It *did* have her grandmother's jade-green eyes—the same eyes that Lyssa and her mom both shared. "She came back as a cat to keep me company because she knew how much I missed her."

After that, Lyssa helped her mom make coffee every morning. They put in milk but no sugar, as per Grandma Pat's preferences, then poured it into her special clay mug and left it beside the open window. While the cat drank her coffee, Lyssa's mom read their horoscopes out loud, always reading the entry for Sagittarius first so that the grandmother-cat knew what adventures were in her future.

Lyssa pushed the memory away. She opened her eyes and looked out at her new backyard, which was neat and perfectly trimmed. She stuck the end of her braid in her mouth and chewed at the tips of her hair. But she didn't use homemade organic shampoo anymore, so instead of tasting like avocados, now her braids just tasted like soap. Lyssa pulled her braid out of her mouth and pressed her lips closed. She was trying not to chew on her hair anymore anyway. No one would want to be friends with the girl who ate her own hair.

The back door creaked open and Michael stumbled onto the porch.

"Oh, there you are," he said. He held a backpack the size of a baby elephant in one arm and wrestled his bike out the door with the other. There were so many gadgets attached to it—GPS, mobile phone, calculator—that it looked more like a rocket ship than a bicycle.

"I was looking all over for you. I grabbed your new shoes."

He placed the sneakers next to Lyssa. They were pink and glittery . . . as if a unicorn had thrown up on them.

"I'm allergic," Lyssa said, wrinkling her nose and scooting away from the shoes—wondering if they actually might cause her to break out in hives. Michael raised an eyebrow.

"We talked about lying, Lyssa. Remember?"

Lyssa looked at her knees. This didn't *feel* like a lie. The sneakers made her feet itch, as though she'd just walked through a batch of poison ivy. That was the same thing as being allergic. But Michael said it wasn't safe for her to go barefoot like she often had in Austin.

"Ready for our ride?" Michael asked, patting the handlebars of his bicycle. He was no longer just the new sound guy at the Texas Talent Show or the guy who came around with his laptop so that they could watch Athena videos on YouTube. Over the last year, Lyssa had learned he could eat pizza any day of the week (he'd bought a fancy pizza oven for the kitchen) and hated the taste of coffee. He liked to hang glide and water-ski (he rigged his water skis to be more aerodynamic) but wasn't very good at soccer. And he was obsessed with computers and gadgets. If it was digital, Michael owned it, built it, or bought it and made it better.

He and her mom were married in the hospital a few weeks before *it* happened. In the middle of everything else, moving in with Michael hadn't seemed so bad. Now that her mom was gone, though, it felt uncomfortable. Like wearing too-small clothes. It was because of Michael that she'd had to move, that she no longer lived in a house with a beautiful, tangled garden, that she could no longer sleep under the sunflowers her mother planted or walk down the street to Penn's house when she was feeling lonely. Six months ago Michael announced that they were moving to Kirkland, Washington, where his sister, Nora, lived. He thought Lyssa needed to have a female role model now that . . . now that things had changed.

After they'd moved to Washington, Lyssa had gotten the Nightmare for the first time. The beginning of her dream was always more like a memory: everything was exactly like it had been the night she'd gotten stage fright and refused to sing.

But after Lyssa hid in the dressing room, the dream changed. And never, not once in all the months she'd been dreaming, had she managed to reach the van and find out what her mother had been meaning to tell her.

"I'll get my scooter," Lyssa said to Michael. They went for a ride every day in the early evening. Michael said it was their "family time."

"Hey, you know what? Maybe you should write about the ride in your journal for school," Michael said.

"Um, yeah. Definitely." Lyssa avoided looking at him as she shoved her feet into the pink sneakers. That was another big change. In two weeks, she was starting sixth grade at Kirkland School of the Arts. Back in Texas, Lyssa had been homeschooled by her mom. This would be her first year at a *real* school with kids her own age.

For the longest time, Penn had been the only person Lyssa knew who was her exact same age—all her other friends were performers and animals in the Texas Talent Show. Penn went to school back in Austin and always had funny stories about what happened in the cafeteria and updates about what music everyone in jazz band was listening to (although *Lyssa* had been the one who first introduced Athena to Penn—not that it mattered since Athena was still missing). She'd been excited when Michael first told her she'd be heading to school at the end of August. For a week straight, Lyssa video chatted with Penn every night so she'd know exactly what to expect at school.

But then, two days ago, Lyssa got a package in the mail. Inside she found a journal and an assignment for the first day of school: *Write about your summer vacation.*

There were so many things she wanted to write about: exploring hidden caverns in the woods, spending a night at the zoo, looking for ghosts in creepy old houses. The only problem was that none those things had actually, *technically* happened to her this summer. Those were the kind of things she'd done with her mom, when a normal Tuesday night could turn into anything, from a cross-city footrace to a hunt for buried treasure. But this summer, all she'd done was ride around the neighborhood with Michael. That could be fun, sure. But it wasn't adventurous, the way even ordinary things became around Ana Lee.

So as the first day of school got closer, Lyssa got more and more nervous about what she'd write. Her journal sat upstairs in her room . . . and every single page was blank.

"Ready?" Michael adjusted his helmet and smiled at her from the sidewalk. Lyssa nodded. Zip was leaning against the side of the garage, its yellow paint gleaming in the shadows. Originally, her scooter had been painted sky blue, but when Lyssa had decided that yellow was her favorite color, she and her mom repainted it together. There were still some places where the paint had chipped and you could see the blue beneath, but Lyssa thought that was okay. It was like Zip was a very colorful Dalmatian scooter.

They rode down the same path they always took: through the neighborhood, past the park, and down the road next to Lake Washington. Even though the day was sunny and bright, it still had a damp, cold edge to it, like all the days in Kirkland, Washington. Today the waves in the lake were steel gray and still beneath the clear blue sky. Lyssa pulled to the side of the bridge and stared out over the water as she rolled. Lake Washington probably didn't want to be in Kirkland any more than she did.

A seagull dove into the gray water, resurfacing a few feet away, and she slowed her scooter as she watched it shake the water from its wings.

Maybe, Lyssa thought, her mom was a bird now. Before . . . before the hospital, when Lyssa and Ana used to roller skate around the fairgrounds, she'd watched her mom spin and twist around on her skates, and a few times she swore her mom actually hovered above the ground, as though she was ready to fly off into the sky. Lyssa didn't know anyone else who could make their body move like that. She had always been clumsy, herself. Except on Zip. On Zip, Lyssa could do anything.

She slowed to a stop and pulled the last half of one of her homemade granola bars out of the pocket of her jean shorts. As Michael rode ahead, she tossed some of the granola bar into the water for the bird. Even if Lyssa's mom was a bird now, she wouldn't be able to pass up homemade granola—it was her favorite.

But the seagull squawked at Lyssa, ignoring her granola crumbs and diving back under the waves again.

"Is there a problem with your scooter?" Michael asked. Lyssa looked up, startled. She hadn't realized he'd looped behind her.

"No. I was just distracted by the bird." She felt silly. Of course Ana wasn't a bird. But Lyssa couldn't help feeling that her mom was still out there, circling closer. Sometimes, she even thought she caught glimpses of her.

The same thing happened with Athena, actually. Ever since her favorite singer disappeared, Lyssa kept thinking she saw her. Once, she had followed a woman around the mall for over an hour because she thought she'd recognized Athena's signature cowboy boots. But when Lyssa finally caught up to her, it turned out to be just a really tall man with a ponytail. Athena was still missing, months after the concert that had been her last public appearance. There were lots of rumors about what had happened to her; one of the more popular ones was that someone close to her had died, and that was the reason she'd disappeared from the spotlight so suddenly. Lyssa didn't know if that was true, but it did make her feel even closer to Athena.

"Your scooter's seen some better times," Michael said, jiggling the loose handlebar. "Maybe we should think about getting you a bike."

Lyssa bit down on her lower lip. Her real dad, Lenny, had made this scooter for her. Lyssa had never met her dad—her mom always told her it was because he was a famous musician in Austin and was much too creative to be tied to just one place. Her mom even had a scrapbook filled with all of his old concert posters. Ana had tried to throw it out after she and Michael started dating, but Lyssa rescued it from the trash and stowed it in her sock drawer, where she knew no one would ever look for it. Lyssa thought it was cool that her dad built her a scooter before leaving on his travels. It was like he knew Lyssa would also grow up too creative to be tied to one place. She'd been riding the scooter since she was five, and her mom used to joke that the ridges on the handlebars must be permanently etched into her skin.

"I like my scooter," Lyssa said, pushing off with her back leg. Melodius had always called her scooter *Zip*. He said he knew she was coming when he heard the zipping of those wheels. Lyssa kicked off and soared ahead of Michael on the path, her braids streaming out behind her. She hummed "Scooting Star" under her breath.

The path curved away from the water, heading into a wooded area filled with trees and bushes. Just when Lyssa thought she'd left him behind, Michael panted up next to her, his bike pedals squeaking as he raced to keep up.

"I know you like your scooter," he said between breaths. "But it's getting old. See how the paint is fading? And the back wheel's all wobbly. I have an idea—what if we got you a bike as a birthday present? Your birthday's coming up next month. Didn't you and your mom always do something special to celebrate your birthdays?"

Lyssa's throat seemed suddenly to shrink down to a third of its size, so she could only nod. Ana had done something special for every single one of Lyssa's birthdays. On her very first birthday, during a cross-country drive, they'd wound up in Utah, and Ana had brought her down to the Dead Lake to see the Spiral Jetty, a sculpture that looked like a huge snake twisting out into the middle of the water. Lyssa had heard that story so many times, seen so many pictures of red sand and sparkling rocks, that she almost remembered sitting on the jetty with her mom.

When she was five, she and her mom took an origami class and learned to make paper airplanes and swans. When she was nine, they went to visit real-life cowgirls on a ranch. Lyssa had loved it—loved the hats and the lassos, and the horses, of course. Plus, with their heeled cowboy boots, the cowgirls reminded her a little of Athena.

But Lyssa's last birthday had been the best. That was when she and Ana had gone to see what turned out to be Athena's last concert. Lyssa didn't like the idea that she had to keep having birthdays. Without her mom, without Athena. She'd rather never have another birthday again just so that she could keep that one, perfect memory in her head forever.

"Well? What do you think?" Michael's voice cut through her daydreams. Lyssa blinked, refocusing on his face. She hadn't realized he was still talking.

"What do I think about what?" she asked.

"The bike. We could build it together."

"Oh." Lyssa frowned and pushed farther ahead on her scooter. This time, Michael didn't race to keep up with her. She put her foot down, stopping the scooter to be polite.

"I know it won't be like . . . like when your mom did your birthdays," he said. "But she was special—your mom. She had this way about her. It was like she was—"

"Magic?" Lyssa cut in. Michael beamed.

"Exactly. Did I ever tell you about our first date? She showed up outside my apartment with a couch in the back of that Talent Show van she used to drive and a bag full of the best vegan tacos I'd ever eaten. We drove around for hours, talking and eating, and when we finally ran out of things to say she pulled over and we unloaded that couch. As soon as we set it on the ground and sat down, the sun started to rise."

Michael stopped talking and stared off into the distance. "You know, it was strange. I actually thought she made the sun rise all on her own. That's what it felt like."

Lyssa stared down at Zip's handlebars, not wanting to meet Michael's eyes.

"I don't think I want a birthday present this year," she said.

"Come on. Don't you think it's time for a change? It'll be fun—I used to build bikes with my dad all the—"

"My dad already built me a *scooter*." Lyssa's voice sounded high and squeaky—kinda like the way Zip sounded when she pushed the wheels too hard or took a sharp corner. Maybe her scooter seemed like a piece of junk with faded paint to Michael, but that's because he only liked things with wires and computer screens.

Michael cleared his throat. "Well, we could always do something else for your birthday. We could go out to a really nice dinner!"

Lyssa tightened her fingers around Zip's handlebars and pushed off hard, wishing she could feel the rocky sidewalk through the thick soles of her new shoes. A dinner? She thought about what her mom had always said to her. *You're going to have so many adventures in your life . . .* She wanted to believe that, but it seemed like all of her adventures had ended six months ago.

"I'll think about it," she said when Michael pedaled up next to her. For a second he looked like he might try to argue, so Lyssa kicked off again, rolling faster and faster down the path. She couldn't think about her birthday. The idea that her mom wouldn't be there made her head hurt and her chest ache.

Her mom wouldn't be at any of her birthdays ever again.

Lyssa heard Michael calling to her, but she didn't stop.

She saw a narrow dirt trail beaten into the woods next to her and on a whim, she veered onto it. The smell of evergreens rushed thickly past her as she bumped through the forest, tearing down the hills. She felt a rush of joy. *This* was an adventure. Maybe it wasn't magical and fantastic, like the ones her mom could make happen. But it was fun.

The bushes and trees seemed to jump aside for her, creating a path that was all her own. Her heart was slamming in her chest. The ground beneath Lyssa grew steeper and she started to pick up speed. She didn't even need to kick off anymore—Zip and gravity were doing all the work for her. Far in the distance she could hear Michael yelling after her, but the wind was blowing hard in her ears and she didn't know what he was saying.

Then she saw it.

A few yards ahead of her the ground disappeared, ending in a jagged, rocky line: the edge of a cliff. Far beyond it, a great body of water twinkled, icy gray beneath the wispy cloud sky. Lyssa tightened her grip on her handlebars. Wind stung her cheeks and eyes. She was going too fast. There was no way to slow down. She was going to fall.

Zip bumped over twigs and dirt and pebbles and, when it reached the edge of the cliff, a rock caught its front wheel, causing the scooter to arch upward in midair. Lyssa clung to the handlebars and screamed. A flock of birds in a nearby tree took to the sky, echoing her cry.

Below her was a playground. A few children looked up, mouths gaping open. As Lyssa soared through the air, a tiny blue paper airplane fluttered in front of her—it looked just like the airplanes she and her mom had made in origami class. Lyssa squinted against the sun. For a second, everything seemed to slow down. Lyssa felt like she was floating.

There were words on the airplane's wing, written in curly, slanted handwriting.

There's no place like home, the writing said.

In the next second, the floating feeling vanished.

She was falling—*fast.*

CHAPTER THREE

Perk Up Those Little Ears

Lyssa tore her eyes away from the little paper airplane. She didn't have time to worry about what the message meant. As the playground rushed at her, she concentrated on steering her scooter toward the sandbox with every muscle in her body, every thought and wish.

But no matter how she twisted and turned in the air, she wasn't headed for the sandbox—she was going straight for the twisty tornado slide. Her scooter's front wheel clipped the top of the slide and she barreled down, riding the smooth metal as easily as a surfer rode a wave. A little girl on the slide let out a squeak and threw herself over its side as Lyssa came speeding toward her.

"Sorry," Lyssa called over her shoulder. She shot out of the bottom of the slide and suddenly she was airborne again. She flew across the park, over the sandbox, and toward the sidewalk beyond it. Wind cut into her cheeks. She clenched her eyes shut, certain she was going to crash into the concrete—possibly face-first.

Lyssa grunted; the force of the impact shook her entire body. Zip's front wheel squeaked as they both skidded to a stop. It sounded, for a moment, like the scooter was screaming. Lyssa automatically put one foot down to stop herself from going any farther and a sharp pain shot through her heel and up her leg.

But that was it: no broken bones, no smashed-up face. Her sneaker had absorbed most of the shock—it didn't even feel like she'd hurt her ankle. Lyssa had managed a near-perfect landing. She considered her sparkly pink shoes with a newfound respect, then looked back over her shoulder at the cliff she'd just soared over. It rose high into the air—impossibly high. How had she landed without a scratch?

"The universe," she whispered.

She remembered her mother's stories about wind, and how the world sometimes spun too fast and crazy things—magical things—started to happen. Her breath catching in her throat, Lyssa stood perfectly still, listening. Was the world spinning too fast now?

But all she heard was the sound of paper rustling in the wind. Looking down, she noticed a piece of blue paper wedged beneath her sneaker. On the corner of the page, Lyssa saw the word *home*.

She slid the paper airplane out from underneath her shoe, holding it carefully in her hands so she wouldn't smash it. Bold type covered the underside of the plane, along with pictures Lyssa couldn't quite see. Curious, she slid a finger into the crease just behind the wing and pulled the plane apart.

It was a flyer. She recognized the people in the picture right away: Stumpy and Hank—performers from the Texas Talent Show—were front and center with the trapeze artists, flying monkeys, and strong woman all crowded in behind them. Lyssa flattened the flyer against her leg, rereading the headline: *Austin's Own Texas Talent Show Reunites!*

A hollow space opened up in the pit of her stomach and she almost had to sit down right there in the middle of the sidewalk. The Texas Talent Show had disbanded after what happened to her mom. All the performers agreed it would be impossible to find a replacement—not that any of them wanted to replace Ana Lee.

But now they were performing without her—and without Lyssa too? Who was going to pull the curtain back for the opening performance? Who was going to re-paint the set when it started to look worn? And—the thought made it difficult for her to breathe—were they going to *replace* her mom? Was someone else going to braid her hair and put on motorcycle boots and dance around stage with an accordion made out of paperback novels?

Lyssa looked up from the flyer. Who had thrown the paper airplane in the first place? How had it gotten here all the way from Texas? It's like it had appeared out of thin air. The hair on the back of her neck stood on end.

The wind makes the world spin a little too fast, she thought.

At the bottom of the page there was a short paragraph below the photo:

Join hands with the Texas Talent Show for one last concert protesting the destruction of beloved singer Ana Lee's home. Show the Austin Real Estate Corporation that we're not letting them knock down this community landmark without a fight!

Lyssa clutched the paper so tightly that it crumpled beneath her fingers. Her mom's house—*her* house? Knocked down?

When her mom had first described her plan to donate the house to a charity, for use as community center, Lyssa hadn't liked the idea of giving away their home at all.

"But don't you see? That way we'll always be there," her mom had explained. Even sick, lying back on the pillows of the Austin General Medical Center, she had seemed to glow. "We may travel far away, but we're leaving our roots behind."

Whenever Lyssa remembered this, she imagined standing shoulder to shoulder with her mom in their backyard, toes dug into the earth and faces lifted toward the sun like they were flowers, like they'd been left behind in the garden even after everything had changed.

Now it felt like they were going to be ripped out of the soil, left to wither in the rain and shade. It made Lyssa's stomach turn to think about it.

"Lyssa!"

Michael's voice thundered down to her. He was standing at the top of the cliff, his face bright red. He was clutching his hair with both hands: it stuck out all over his head in awkward clumps.

Michael didn't usually get upset—Lyssa had only seen him like this once before, when she'd tried to plant a flower garden in one of his new speakers (it looked like a planter!) and short-circuited a wire when she poured water over the seeds. The explosion that followed had made Lyssa's braids stick straight out.

She knew she should wait for Michael to get down to

her, but the crumpled-up paper plane was making the hollow feeling in her stomach grow even bigger.

Something rumbled in the distance and a fat raindrop fell onto Lyssa's nose. A storm was coming—just like the storm in her dream. And, just like in her dream, she knew her mother was trying to give her a message.

But this time, Lyssa thought she knew what it was: Go to Austin. Go back home. Stop this, somehow.

Lyssa wiped her nose with the back of her hand and turned away from Michael. Hunching up her shoulders against the chill, she hopped onto her scooter and pushed off, rolling faster and faster, until the evergreens that lined the sidewalk were just a blur of green.

By the time she reached the house, her tank top and jean shorts were soaked all the way through. They clung to her back and shoulders in lumps, making the skin beneath cold and clammy. She pressed her icy blue lips together—trying to keep her teeth from chattering—but her jaw jumped up and down on its own.

All Lyssa could think about was the crumpled-up flyer in her pocket and the horrible words printed across it: *destruction, knocked down.* When she arrived at the house, she leaned Zip against the porch steps and fished the key out of her pocket.

Michael's house was nothing like Lyssa and her mom's place back in Austin. The furniture here was sleek and modern, and Lyssa knew none of it had any stories to tell at all.

The only place Michael's creativity showed was in his love of technology. One or two paper-thin flat-screen monitors hung on every wall. As soon as Lyssa walked into the living room, a frothy wave covered the far wall and came crashing toward her. The sound of water roared in her ears and she jumped, biting back a scream. When she lived with her mom, Lyssa hadn't owned a TV. Sometimes it was hard to remember that the pictures were just images on a screen. They looked so *real*.

Slipping off her sneakers, she raced up the stairs. As soon as she was in her own room, she pulled off her wet clothes and changed into a fresh tank top and new pair of shorts. Her bedroom was the only place in Michael's house that still felt a little like home. She'd programmed her giant computer screen to flash pictures of her old room: there was her painted garage-sale furniture and the flowery silk scarves she hung from her windows, fluttering in a breeze she couldn't actually feel. There was even a mason jar full of sunflowers from their garden sitting on a nightstand.

Usually the images calmed her, but today they just made her feel worse. She dug the wet, crumpled paper airplane out of her jeans pocket and placed it on one of the plain white dressers she and Michael had picked out for her new bedroom. If what was written on the flyer was true—if her house back in Austin really *was* going to be destroyed—then the pictures would be all that she had left of her life Before.

A door slammed open and closed downstairs.

"Lyssa!" Michael yelled.

The sound of his voice made goose bumps spread up and down her arms. With one last look at the blue flyer, Lyssa pushed her bedroom door open and stepped into the hallway.

"I'm right here."

She ran her fingers over the ropy lengths of her braids, trying to keep herself from sticking her hair in her mouth. Michael appeared at the foot of the stairs. Water clung to his black-framed glasses and caused his T-shirt to stick to his skin.

"How could you *do* that?" he burst out. His voice sounded more scared than angry, but Lyssa still wrapped her arms around her chest, wishing she could turn around and flee into her room. She forced herself to stand still.

"You scared me, Lyssa." Michael lowered his voice, shaking his head. "Do you know what could have happened to you?"

"Wait," Lyssa interrupted. She needed to explain. This was about her mom's house—her *home*. "You don't understand . . ."

Michael didn't let her finish.

"I don't want to hear it. You're *never* allowed to go off on your own like that again. Do you understand that? Never."

All of the anger and frustration of the day bubbled up in Lyssa's chest.

"You can't tell me what to do," she fired back, before she had time to think about what she was saying.

"Yes, I can," Michael said. "Your mom left me in charge. It's my job to make sure nothing happens to you—"

"Nothing *happens*?" Lyssa shook her head, her wet hair leaking water onto her tank top. The bubble of anger inside her grew so big that she thought she might pop. "You're making me go to school! You're forcing me to wear shoes— my mom wouldn't have *wanted* those things to happen to me."

Lyssa paused, surprised by her own outburst. She'd been excited about going to school—and the shoes weren't really that bad. But she knew that she couldn't take her words back. She stuck the ends of her braid in her mouth, forgetting that she was trying not to chew on her hair any-more.

"*Those things* are for your own good," Michael said.

"You don't know what's good for me," Lyssa said. The cat that was really her grandmother popped into her mind, and the next few words burst out of her mouth before Lyssa could think about them. "My mom will understand. When I find her, you'll see—"

"Find her?" Michael interrupted. He rubbed his eyes. The red patches on his cheeks had disappeared, and now he looked just like Lyssa felt: cold, wet, and miserable. "But Lyssa, your mom is—"

"*No!*" Lyssa screamed. She didn't want to hear Michael say the next word. "I don't have to listen to you! *You aren't my dad.*"

Before he could react, Lyssa spun around and ran into her room, slamming the door behind her. It cracked inside its frame, sending a loud, booming noise down the hall.

Lyssa paused for a second, taking a deep breath and forcing herself to hum a few bars of her favorite Athena song. But her old trick wasn't working this time. Maybe, Lyssa thought, that's because the time for staying calm had passed.

Now it was time for action.

Suddenly, Lyssa realized what her nightmares were about. Her mom had been trying to send her a message in her dreams. And then, this paper airplane—just like the ones she and Ana had learned to make on her fifth birthday—showed up telling her to go to Austin. It was Ana's special brand of magic. Lyssa knew it in her bones.

Right now, the Texas Talent Show needed her. As for Michael . . . well, there was just so much that Michael couldn't understand. Like how summers should be *exciting*, or that flower planters were more important than fancy speakers, and that shoes and backpacks should be yellow—like the sun—not pink like unicorns. And he wouldn't even let her explain about the flyer, which proved he didn't get her.

Maybe going back to Austin now would bring back some of her mother's magic. Michael might not understand that, but there was still one person who would.

She went to her computer, found Penn's name on her contact list, and hit *Connect*.

CHAPTER FOUR

Paper Airplanes, Peanut Jars, and Plans

Seconds later, Penn flickered onto the screen. She was upside down: her brown curls brushed against the floor while the rest of her body disappeared near the top of Lyssa's screen. Lyssa squinted at the image of Penn's room, realizing that Penn was hanging upside down from her mini-trapeze. She kept it in her bedroom and it was kind of like an old stuffed animal or a security blanket. Penn only used it when she was really upset, because she had a much bigger, professional trapeze in her backyard.

Lyssa's computer screen was so big that the image of Penn was nearly life size. It was almost like Penn was in the room with her, except Lyssa couldn't smell the strawberry shampoo she used or the faint scent of smoke that always lingered in her bedroom because she practiced her fire breathing in the corner.

"Penn!" Lyssa grabbed the sides of the computer monitor. "What's going on? Did you hear what's happening with my mom's house?"

"Lyssa, I'm so sorry." Penn's voice was shaky. "My parents found out last night. A development company bought your mom's land—her house, the garden, *everything*. Lyssa, they're going to knock the house down."

"Why didn't you tell me?" Lyssa thudded down into her desk chair. She couldn't believe it. Penn always told her everything.

Penn's eyes were ringed with red, as though she had been crying. "I—I thought you knew! I thought Michael would tell you."

"He didn't," Lyssa said bitterly. She closed her eyes and opened them again. She needed to focus. "What about the community center?"

"They're saying you can't build a community center in a residential area. It's against some stupid law. Wait—hold on a second."

Penn's head disappeared. There was a whooshing sound and her screen trembled a little. Lyssa had seen Penn dismount from her trapeze a million times and she could picture the perfect flip she'd just performed in her room.

"Okay, are you still there?" Penn swiveled her computer around so Lyssa could finally get a good look at her best friend's face.

Penn's curls looked more like a lion's mane than like hair—they were so big they nearly took up the entire computer screen. Whenever Penn was really upset, she fluffed up her curls.

Lyssa pushed back her desk chair and started to pace. Whenever there was this much nervous energy running through her body, she couldn't sit still. It was as though her body moved without waiting for her brain to tell it what to do. Her mom used to say that's why Lyssa walked into so many tables.

"Still here," she said to Penn. She went to her closet and wrestled down her new backpack from one of the shelves. Michael's sister had given her the backpack as a "congratulations" present since she'd be starting school soon. It even had a blue patch on the front from the University of Washington, where Nora had gone to law school. "But not for long."

"What do you mean?" Penn crouched closer to her webcam, until Lyssa could see the little flecks of gold in the middle of her brown eyes.

"When is the performance?" Lyssa asked, purposely avoiding Penn's question. The fewer who knew about her plan, the fewer people who would try to talk her out of it.

"Less than a week," Penn said. She narrowed her eyes. "But, Lyssa, how did you know . . ."

"I'll explain later. Less than a week, huh? That should give me enough time."

"Time to do what?"

"Don't worry about it." Lyssa pulled open the bottom drawer of her nightstand. There were still a few sandwich bags of homemade granola bars hidden there. She'd made them last week but kept them in her bedroom because if she left them in the kitchen, Michael ended up eating them all. The granola bars were made from her mom's secret recipe. She and Ana used to bake together all the time. Sometimes, when Michael was up in his room working, Lyssa would pull out her mom's old cookbooks and make one of her favorites—black bean brownies or pumpkin soy cheesecake. Then it was almost like her mom was in the kitchen with her.

She grabbed the bags and shoved them into her backpack.

"Lyssa." Penn scooted closer to the screen. Unlike Lyssa's giant computer screen, Penn had only a tiny laptop. She was probably trying to see what Lyssa was doing. "What's going on?"

Penn's tone of voice made Lyssa pause. It was her lion tamer voice—the same voice she used when Lyssa wanted to go scuba diving in the water tower, or put cooking oil on her scooter's wheels to make them go faster, or cut off the sleeves of all of her winter coats because they were too itchy. It was Penn's way of telling Lyssa that she was going a little crazy. Usually, Lyssa listened to her.

But not this time. It wasn't just the dream and the paper airplane that made Lyssa want to get back home. She and her mom left their roots in Austin—roots that were about to be dug up. She couldn't let that happen. Her mother had *wanted* the community center. It was supposed to be a reminder of the beautiful life she had created with Lyssa. This wish expanded inside Lyssa's chest like a balloon. But then she glanced back down at the flyer she was still holding and the balloon popped.

The word *performance* stared back up at her. The Texas Talent Show performers were going to sing and dance and do tricks. Lyssa *couldn't* help out with the protest—not if it meant getting up on stage in front of a bunch of people. After that last night at the Texas Talent Show, Lyssa hadn't even been able to *look* at a stage without getting clammy palms and feeling a little dizzy.

She sank down onto the edge of her bed, feeling deflated. Even if she *could* perform, would it be enough to save her home? Protests had always been her mom's specialty. One time, Ana took Lyssa to protest the destruction of their favorite park. As soon as Ana sat down on the grass in front of the park, a bulldozer accidentally rolled over a rock and broke down. By the very next day a geologist from the community college showed up at the park to examine the rock and declared it to be a rare Morton Gneiss—one of the oldest rocks in the world. The park never was bull-dozed after all—it was turned into a city landmark. Another example of Ana's rare magic.

Then, just like that, two little puzzle pieces inside Lyssa's head clicked together. It was so simple that she almost laughed out loud. Maybe she couldn't sing onstage, and maybe a bunch of Talent Show performers wouldn't be enough to save her home—but a little of her mother's magic *would* be. Lyssa just had to find it.

She had to find her mom.

"Penn," Lyssa said, spinning back toward the computer screen. "Do you remember the stories my mom used to tell us? About the wind?"

Penn nodded, slowly. "But Lyssa," she said. "Those were just stories."

Lyssa took a deep breath. "I'm starting to think the stories were real. Something happened today. It felt like the winds of change. It felt like . . ."

Lyssa let the end of her sentence trail off before she could say the word *magic*. But wasn't that what had happened when she sailed off the cliff? Her mom's magic had found and protected her.

Lyssa knew what she had to do. She'd go to Austin, and everything would be okay. Her mom would make sure of it. She would be waiting in Austin, too—as a bird, maybe, or a cat.

Lyssa gazed at her screen. For a second it looked like Penn was going to say something. Instead, she just nodded, and Lyssa wondered if Penn had guessed that her plan was to come home. Sometimes she and Penn thought the same thoughts at the same time. Maybe Penn was thinking about protests and Morton Gneiss and her mom's magic, too.

"Be careful, Lyssa," Penn said.

"I'll call you soon, okay?" Lyssa closed the browser window without waiting for Penn to reply.

Opening up the top drawer of her nightstand, Lyssa pulled out an old peanut jar. Rolled up inside was all the money she'd made that summer from mowing Mrs. Patel's lawn. It wasn't a fortune, but it should buy her a few meals and a bus ticket.

Lyssa started to push the drawer closed—then hesitated. Underneath the peanut jar was the scrapbook of her dad's old concert posters, the one Lyssa had rescued from the trash. She paused, running a hand along the edge of the book.

Part of her wanted to take the scrapbook with her—but it was big and heavy. Frowning, she pushed the drawer closed and shoved the jar into her backpack, atop the odds and ends that she kept there—from dental floss to her favorite ladybug hair clips. She pulled two pairs of jean shorts off a shelf and stuffed them into the backpack along with a few T-shirts, some extra socks and underwear, and a sweatshirt she didn't like much because of the itchy long sleeves. She looked around the room for anything else she might need and settled on her mom's seed packet maracas, the only instrument of Ana's she'd kept. She grabbed the maracas and stuck them into her bag, too.

Last, she packed her purple water bottle, which she'd covered in band stickers. The Texas Talent Show's sticker was front and center. Lyssa smiled down at it, rubbing her thumb over her mom's grinning face. For the first time in a while, her mom's picture filled her with hope and determination instead of with sadness. Ana would be in Austin waiting to help her. Lyssa was sure of it.

She turned to her computer and clicked on her Athena playlist, blasting it at top volume so Michael would think she was still in her room.

"You're a black cat! You're a lost key! You're a million different things that are bad for me . . ."

Lyssa let the music wash over her as she made a final

survey of her room. Athena's voice always had the power to inspire her, to help her see exactly what she needed to do and do it. Watching Athena dance across stage at that final concert made Lyssa want to perform in a way nothing else had. There was just something about the spotlights glimmering down on her, flashing blue and green and yellow, and the way the entire audience cheered whenever Athena hit a high note. It was an energy that Lyssa craved—it made her realize exactly why she wanted to be a singer.

Maybe Athena was out there on the road too, looking for something she'd lost. Through the thrumming chords, she could hear Athena sending her a message: *Go for it.*

Throwing her backpack over one shoulder, Lyssa pushed her bedroom door open and peeked into the hallway. The house was dark. The only light came from beneath Michael's door at the end of the hall—the bright, blue-white glow of a computer screen seeping out onto the carpet. Lyssa could hear the rapid clicking of his fingers against the keyboard.

A tiny twinge of guilt made its way into her stomach, like an insect tightrope walking along her gut.

Maybe she was wrong. If she told Michael where she was going, maybe he'd help her. She *liked* Michael. When he and her mom first started dating, it'd been like having a new, different kind of adventure. Michael was the one who talked Ana into letting Lyssa have a taste of non-organic, sugar-packed soda (the bubbles kept getting up her nose) and he took her to the movies for the very first time (though Lyssa had a hard time sitting through the whole thing). And the three of them used to take picnics together in the strangest places—backstage at the talent show, in the middle of a shopping mall, in Michael's living room. He would understand . . . wouldn't he?

But then Lyssa remembered his face earlier: cheeks bright red, eyes bulging behind thick glasses. His words echoed in her mind. *"You're never allowed to go off on your own again!"*

It wasn't just their fight. Michael didn't believe that the world could suddenly spin faster or that wind could sweep into your life and set everything out of order. He wouldn't understand that Lyssa needed to be back in Austin to find her mother's magic. He didn't know how it felt when every cell and hair in your body worked together, pointing you home.

If Michael found out about her plan, that was the end: Lyssa wouldn't get to Austin, and any chance that she'd have to save their home would be lost. The thought made Lyssa's throat close right up. This was too important to risk Michael's interference. She'd never forgive herself if the house got knocked down when she wasn't there to stop it or if her mom had come back as a bird or a dog or a cat, like her grandmother had, and Lyssa wasn't there to find her. She'd have to go it alone.

She slipped on her shoes and crept down the stairs, grabbing an apple and half a peanut butter sandwich from the kitchen. Michael would be in his bedroom working for the rest of the night. He probably wouldn't even know she was gone until the morning.

And then . . . well, who's to say he'd even be mad? He was the one who wanted to send her to school, after all. This might be the change they *both* needed.

"He'll be happy," Lyssa whispered to herself.

She crept down the hall into Michael's empty office. She wasn't going to tell him where she was headed, but she would leave him a note to let him know she was okay.

Computer screens glowed at her from every direction, each one flashing the same photo of Michael and Lyssa's mom holding hands at their hospital wedding. They'd turned the hospital room into a chapel and made a couple old hospital gowns into a wedding dress by sewing them together and stitching paper roses to the skirt.

The picture made Lyssa's heart lurch painfully. She remembered the moment, a week before the wedding, when Michael had taken her aside in the waiting room. He told Lyssa that he'd wanted to ask her mom to marry him for a long time, and he even showed Lyssa the ring he'd bought (a giant aquamarine—Ana's birthstone). Before he gave the ring to her mom, Michael said, he wanted Lyssa's approval. He explained that she was an important part of their three-person family, and she needed to be okay with the marriage if it was going to work. At the time it had been easy for Lyssa to give her blessing.

But now Lyssa didn't know what to think. They were no longer a family anymore—not really. It was just her and Michael. She sat down at Michael's desk, facing the largest computer in the room, and thought about what she should write. Finally she opened a Word document and pulled the keyboard toward her.

Dear Michael—

The winds of change are coming and they're taking me with them. Don't come looking for me.

Lyssa

She reread the message to herself in a whisper. *The winds of change are coming*—what Ana had always said. And now the winds of change were going to blow Lyssa back home.

When she glanced back down at Michael's desk, she saw the paper airplane sitting next to the keyboard. Weird. She didn't remember folding it back up into an airplane or carrying it down from her room. She decided it should probably come with her anyway. For good luck.

Beneath the airplane was the journal Lyssa was supposed to write in for her first day of school. She bit down on her bottom lip, considering the journal. If her plan worked, she wouldn't be going to school in two weeks. She'd be in Austin, where she wouldn't have to do that stupid assignment at all. Still, she scooped the journal up and shoved it into her now-full backpack. It could come in handy.

Taking one last look at the place that was had been her home for the summer, Lyssa took a deep breath and headed to the garage. There was one final thing she needed.

CHAPTER FIVE

A Black Cat and a Lost Key

The garage was cold and musty smelling. After stubbing her toe on one of Michael's skis, then nearly tripping over a pair of running shoes, Lyssa took her cell phone from her pocket and held it out in front of her to help light her way. Even though she had left Zip on the covered porch, she found it propped next to Michael's bike. Michael always brought it in from the rain. He said it would rust if she didn't bring it inside. Lyssa ignored the feeling of being watched as the gadgets attached to Michael's bike winked at her in the half dark, like eyes. She rolled her scooter forward.

"Ready to go, Zip?" she whispered. She patted Zip's handlebars and pushed the door open.

A gust of wind blew into the garage, forcing Lyssa to take a quick step back. The rain was driving hard, stinging drops that cut like cool glass. A flash of lightning tore across the sky. She hadn't realized the storm had gotten so bad. She took a deep breath, then shoved her scooter into the rain and down the driveway.

Clouds obscured the moon and stars. Even the streetlamps seemed dimmer than usual. Silver raindrops shot sideways through yellow pools of light, and when thunder rumbled in the distance, one of the lamps flickered and went out entirely. Water gushed down the street next to her, making it look more like a river than a road.

Lyssa had never seen so much rain in her life. One dry summer, she and her mom had tried out this rain dance they read about in a book, but it hadn't worked—in fact, that night in Austin seemed even hotter than usual. Secretly, Lyssa preferred it that way. She loved when the ground was so warm it burned the bottoms of her feet.

She climbed onto her scooter and kicked off. Riding was more difficult than she expected. Water logged her wheels, causing them to skid, and the rain made her handlebars almost too slick to hold on to. She gritted her teeth. She'd never had so much trouble riding her scooter before. She was the Scooting Star! She'd ridden her scooter over the fire breather's bed of coals. She could handle a little rain.

She forced herself to go faster, rolling beneath the tall evergreens, hoping they'd shield her from the wind. While she rode, she fantasized about the warmth of the bus depot. Maybe when she got there, she'd find a place where she could get a cup of hot chocolate.

The bus depot was not far from Michael's. Even so, by the time Lyssa turned the corner into the parking lot, her fingertips were blue from the cold and her braids were plastered to the back of her neck. She had to squint to see just a few feet in front of her. Lightning shot across the sky, illuminating the parking lot.

There wasn't a single bus parked next to the long, squat building. All the windows were dark.

She had never considered that the bus depot might be closed. Buses ran all the time, didn't they?

She started toward the front door and was only three feet away when something large and furry jumped down in front of her. She stopped short, gasping.

It was a cat. Its black fur was wet and matted and two of its whiskers were missing, making its face look a little lopsided. When it saw Lyssa, all the fur on its back stood on end.

Lyssa froze in place. Fear crawled into her gut. Black cats meant the worst luck.

"Easy, kitty," she breathed.

With a final hiss, the cat darted into the shadows. Pushing her anxiety aside, Lyssa ran up to the front door and jiggled the handle: locked.

There was a note taped inside the door but rainwater fogged up the glass, and Lyssa had to wipe off the panes with the sleeve of her sweatshirt before she could read it. It said:

WE AREN'T GOING OUT IN THIS STORM AND YOU SHOULDN'T EITHER! GO HOME! WE REOPEN TOMORROW, 7:00 A.M.

"No!" Lyssa shouted, banging her fist against the door. How could they close the entire bus depot just because of a silly storm? Already luck was against her. It was the black cat's fault!

"Tell me what to do, Mom," she whispered. She wrapped her arms around her chest, hoping for a sign. She'd never been afraid of sleeping outside before—but then again, it never stormed like this in Texas. When she and Ana went camping, they'd gather a bunch of blankets and pillows and head to the fairgrounds, building a tent behind the game stands and watching the lights of the fair and the stars twinkle through the holes in the blankets. The stars always twinkled a little brighter when Ana Lee was around, almost like they were trying to show off. They would build a fire, heat up cocoa and s'mores, and sometimes the circus clowns would join them, telling stories until Lyssa fell asleep.

A fat finger of rain drew itself down Lyssa's back and she shivered. She hopped up and down a few times to try to get warm. She had to move. If she stayed out here all night, she'd get hypothermia — or *drown*. She needed to find a shelter where she could hide out until the depot opened again, somewhere warm and dry where she could get some sleep.

"Think, Lyssa, think," she whispered. She closed her eyes and tried to *visualize a solution*, like her mom had taught her to do. She wasn't far from the Lake Washington, and right next to that was . . .

"The marina," she said out loud, her eyes popping open. Michael had once pointed out all the boats, explaining that people tied them up to the dock at night so they wouldn't float away. Lyssa remembered thinking how much more fun it would be to live on a boat.

She leapt to her feet and jumped on her scooter, kicking off into the rain. There were always hundreds of boats docked by the marina. All she'd have to do was hide below-decks on one of them and curl up for the night. Then, at seven o'clock sharp, she'd board a bus for Texas.

Lyssa sped down the wet sidewalk. Water arced on either side of Zip as the front wheel cut through the deep puddles. Soon, she consoled herself, she'd be dry, rocking to sleep on a boat, dreaming of adventure.

Lake Washington was the color of steel, so dark and

stormy that Lyssa almost couldn't separate it from the angry bruised sky above. The marina was on a piece of rocky land right next to the water. The long arms of the docks stretched out from the shore, and the sailboats and yachts crowded around them like thick clusters of fingers. A few lights blinked on and off from the streetlamps above, flooding the marina in eerie, orange light.

Lyssa slowed her scooter. The wind made twisting spirals in the water and caused it to crash over the side of the docks. Boats rocked on angry-looking swells.

Taking a deep breath, she started down one of the docks, pushing Zip with one hand. There were so many boats here—there had to be at least one she could hide out on.

But every boat was covered in thick tarp and secured with ropes and padlocks. Lyssa scurried onto one of the few uncovered boats and tried to open the door leading belowdecks. Locked.

The wind cut into her skin, letting cold seep all the way to her bones. She hadn't considered that people would actually *lock* their boats. She climbed back onto the dock and wandered past the boats, trying a few more doors to see if, maybe, one of them had been left open. None of them were.

There was nowhere else to go, and nothing to do but return to the bus depot. Lyssa supposed she could curl up near the door, underneath the little ledge that shielded from the rain. It would be cold and miserable—already Lyssa's fingers were numb—but at least she'd be the first person at the depot when it opened. She thought about huddling near the door, holding her sweatshirt over her head to shield herself from the rain. Maybe, if she dreamt of Texas, she wouldn't be so cold.

Then she saw something glitter on the dock, barely visible beneath the water running over the wood. Curious, she leaned over to examine it.

It was a small, silver key—too small to belong to a house, and not quite the right shape for a car. Maybe it was a key to one of the boats? Lyssa leaned over to scoop it up when something small and furry streaked out in front of her. She stumbled backward, landing hard on the dock. Her scooter clattered to the ground next to her.

Sitting on the dock in front of her was the black cat with the lopsided whiskers. Licking its front paw, it cocked its head, as though challenging her.

Goose bumps rose on Lyssa's arms—it felt like someone was pinching her skin with a tiny pair of tweezers. That cat was *following* her. Pushing herself to her feet, Lyssa searched the dock for the key. But it was gone. The cat must have pawed it out of the way when it streaked past her.

"Where did the key go?" Lyssa demanded. "What did you do with it?"

The cat looked at her and blinked, all innocence. It flicked its tail, seeming to point at the frothing water below. Lyssa's heart sank. Even though she knew it was hopeless, she leaned over the side of the dock and thrust one hand in the waves, aimlessly groping around in the water for the key. She leaned over so far that she nearly tumbled into the waves, catching herself at the very last minute.

That's when she heard it—a low rumbling, like a distant car engine. Shielding her eyes with her free hand, she tried to blink away the rain. She pulled her other arm out of the waves, sitting back on her heels.

The noise got louder and she watched as a bright blue remote-controlled boat shot out from between the yachts. Who would be playing with a toy boat tonight, in the middle of a storm?

She looked up and down the dock but saw no one. The little boat swayed in the angry waves, heading for the dock at the very end of the marina. Just before it ducked out of view, Lyssa saw something glitter on its tiny deck: the key.

The boat bobbed on the water, then disappeared behind a sailboat. She jumped onto her scooter and tore after it.

CHAPTER SIX

The Hidden Lair

Lyssa raced after the toy boat, watching helplessly as it disappeared behind the dock near the end of the marina. She sped across the maze of docks until she reached the place she'd seen the toy boat vanish; then, dropping to her knees, she leaned over the side of the dock and searched the water below. The water was shallower here, and it crashed against rocky land underneath the warped wooden planks of the dock. But the boat wasn't there. It and the key had simply vanished.

Groaning, Lyssa sat back up. She'd dropped Zip on the dock next to her and now it was speckled with rain, looking just as miserable as Lyssa felt.

"Sorry," Lyssa muttered to her scooter, patting the handlebars. One of the silver pompoms was missing—it must've fallen off at some point.

Rain beat down on her forehead, and just beneath the sound of the howling wind, Lyssa could almost hear laughter. It was like the universe thought her bad luck was some funny joke.

The laughter started up again, louder this time. It *wasn't* her imagination—it sounded like it was coming from directly beneath her. She crawled back to the edge and peeked over, grabbing the side of the dock to steady herself.

Directly underneath the dock, and sheltered from the rain, the waves gave way to a dry, rocky ledge scattered with furniture: patched armchairs, a coffee table with three legs, and several rows of sturdy-looking army cots. Televisions and speakers were stacked one on top of another, like Roman columns, each showing a different image. Everywhere Lyssa looked, remote-controlled toys buzzed through the air like bees. Toy cars zigzagged among the furniture, toy boats ducked in and out of the waves next to the ledge, and there were even toy helicopters hovering in the air around the television towers. The buzzing sound of all the motors together was kind of like techno music.

Lyssa had to bite her lip to keep from laughing out loud. It was *amazing*. She leaned over a little farther. This place was like a giant secret clubhouse. She craned her neck to get a better look, and that's when she saw them: a group of a dozen or so teenagers scattered throughout the space, each fixated on a different television set.

Lyssa couldn't help grinning. She and Penn used to spy on their old babysitter back when they were little, but she hadn't done anything more interesting than call her boyfriend. Maybe these teenagers were runaways, too.

The girl nearest Lyssa sat in a beanbag chair. She had short, spiky hair, small eyes, and a beaky-looking nose.

"Demo, turn the volume up," the bird-like girl said without looking away from the TV.

"What're those dangly things hanging off your body, Regina? Oh, right—*legs*," a boy—Demo—said, but he walked over to one of the televisions and turned a knob. He had broad shoulders and black hair that he'd gelled up in the center to look like a mohawk. A few of the other kids groaned and threw popcorn at him as he walked between them and the television screens.

Lyssa scooted farther over the edge, wishing she could get a closer look, like when she would wander around the fair, spying on the clowns as they put on their makeup. Just as she was trying to get a good grip on the wood, her fingers slipped and she toppled over the ledge. Waves rushed toward her and she let out a yelp and squeezed her eyes shut . . .

. . . and suddenly she was no longer falling. Easing her eyes open, Lyssa saw that the water was inches from her nose. She was suspended in midair. It was like her mom had grabbed her by her back pocket to keep her from tumbling into the water, just like she used to do whenever Lyssa teetered over the edge of the stage at the fair as a toddler.

But when Lyssa looked up, she saw that it wasn't her mom, but a toy helicopter the size of a bald eagle holding her up by the seat of her jeans.

"Intruder," screeched an electronic voice from the helicopter. "Intruder!"

Regina and the other teenagers stayed facing the televisions, but the boy named Demo leapt to his feet. "Hey—" he shouted, racing toward her.

Lyssa tried to wriggle free, but the helicopter held her tight. Terror clogged Lyssa's throat.

"Don't come any closer. I know karate," Lyssa lied, holding her arms out in front of her so that her hands were straight and flat, like blades. It was a little difficult to do since she was still upside down, but she didn't want Demo thinking she was helpless. "And . . . and my mom's a cop. She knows where I am and . . ."

Demo motioned to the helicopter. It buzzed down to the ledge and deposited Lyssa on the ground. She awkwardly climbed to her feet.

"Cop, huh?" Demo said *cop* like it was a dirty word. "You a rat?"

Lyssa could have kicked herself. If they were runaways, she shouldn't have mentioned the cops.

"No," she said honestly. "I just didn't want you to think I was here on my own. But I am. On my own, I mean. My mom's not really a cop," she added. "She's a musician."

Demo's face relaxed a little, but he still didn't look like he believed her. "Prove it."

Lyssa looked past Demo to where the rest of the teenagers were sitting. It seemed strange that none of them had even glanced up to see what was going on; they all were too distracted by whatever was on television. One of them took a swig from a green water bottle that looked just like Lyssa's purple one, which gave Lyssa an idea.

"Oh." Lyssa tugged her backpack off her shoulder and dug around inside.

"Here," she finally said, pulling out her water bottle. She turned the bottle around until she found the picture she was looking for—the sticker for her mom's old band. "See? That's my mom, with the accordion."

"She does kind of look like you . . ." Demo muttered, squinting down at the picture. Lyssa felt a flicker of warmth in her stomach. Her mom had been beautiful— tall and elegant, with hair the color of sunflower petals.

Except for their height, Lyssa didn't think they had much in common.

"Commercial break," the bird girl—Regina—yelled from her beanbag chair. One by one, all of the teenagers turned around in their seats until everyone was staring right at Lyssa. The television towers flashed bright commercial lights behind them, making their faces look shadowy.

"Who're you?" a curly-haired boy asked.

"What're you doing here?" Regina asked, cocking her head to one side.

Even though Lyssa was sopping wet, her mouth suddenly got very dry. Her mom used to say she could talk her way through anything. Once, at the fair, Lyssa convinced the manager to rig the Heinous Hurricane so that it went at triple speed by claiming that the plan had magically appeared to her in a grilled cheese sandwich. And maybe Lyssa *had* kind of thought the universe was trying to speak to her through her grilled cheese sandwiches for a while. But that wasn't really the point. Either way, now she felt shy.

"My name is Lyssa," she said, finally. "And I'm—I'm going on an adventure."

If the teenagers were impressed, none of them showed it. The boy with the curly hair yawned.

"What kinda adventure?" he asked.

Lyssa frowned, unsure of how to answer his question. "Are there different kinds?"

A few of the teenagers snickered. The boy with the curly hair turned to Regina and rolled his eyes.

"*Of course* there are different kinds of adventures," he said, turning back to Lyssa. "Three, to be precise. There are air adventures, land adventures, and water adventures. Jeez, don't you ever watch *Lotus Island*?"

"Lotus *what*?" Lyssa asked.

"You never heard of *Lotus Island*?" Regina asked, motioning to the program flickering on the television towers. She laughed and shook her head in amazement. "You must live in, like, a cave or something."

Lyssa stopped herself from pointing out that if anyone lived in a cave, it was Regina. The teenagers' lair had a dirt floor and rocky walls—it looked just like the caves outside of Austin Lyssa and her mom used to visit in the summers.

Demo jumped in. "*Lotus Island* is this reality show where they put people together on an island. They all compete to see who can do the craziest stuff."

"In this episode, people dove off cliffs and zip-lined through the trees and went skydiving," Regina said. "It's intense. If you don't do something dangerous enough, you get voted off the island and have to go home."

"So what kind of adventure are you going on?" the

curly-haired boy asked again. Lyssa thought she heard a bit of challenge in his voice.

"Um. A land adventure, I guess. Or maybe the air one?" she started. "Earlier today I—I jumped off a cliff with my scooter. But it could be the water one, too, because I rode through the storm to get here, and the rain was so bad, it was almost a monsoon. Oh, and I fought off a wildcat. That's a land adventure, right?"

Okay, maybe the black cat wasn't *exactly* a wildcat—but it was still pretty scary. Regina raised an eyebrow.

"Was the wildcat missing half its whiskers?"

Lyssa nodded, surprised. "That's it."

"You fought Old Marty?" Demo said, and Lyssa thought he looked impressed. "She lives around here. You know she lost those whiskers in a fight with a bulldog?"

"A fight she *won*," Regina reminded him. "That was Mr. Haddy's bulldog, remember? He *still* walks with a limp. That cat is vicious."

"Go on." The curly-haired boy nodded at Lyssa. He was no longer rolling his eyes or snickering. In fact, he was leaning forward in his chair, and he looked pretty interested in her story. "Start at the beginning."

As Lyssa talked about finding the paper airplane, and deciding to run away from home, and the locked bus depot, the teens grew very quiet. A few of them scooted closer to her, and they all laughed in just the right spots. When Lyssa finished—describing how she tumbled over the side of the dock—a few of them actually applauded.

"You're, like, better than TV," the curly-haired boy said.

Lyssa beamed. For the first time that night, she forgot, for a moment, about her plan to make it all the way down to Texas. She could picture herself curled up in one of the old armchairs, sipping a juice box delivered to her by one of the electronic cars, wrapped up and warm in a blanket, telling her stories over and over. She could be barefoot all day long and no one would say a word about school.

"Tell it again!" Regina said, nearly bouncing up and down in her seat. "How, exactly, did you get past Old Marty?"

"Reg, come on, the girl's tired," Demo said, winking at Lyssa. "Let's get her some blankets and towels and stuff."

Regina gasped, shooting a worried look over at the television. "But . . . commercial break's almost over."

"Never mind," Demo muttered. Putting a hand on Lyssa's shoulder, he said, "Come with me."

He led her over to the cots, where he grabbed some blankets and towels and handed them over. He even dug half a sandwich and an orange out of a blue cooler. Lyssa used one of the towels to wipe the rainwater from her face. She finished drying her hair and, just as she was looking around for somewhere to put her damp towel, a little remote-controlled truck drove up next to her and nudged her leg. She let her towel drop onto the truck and watched as it zoomed off. This place was like some sort of new age hotel. Even at home, Lyssa'd had to put her towel in the hamper on her own. But these kids had rigged things so that they never had to work. All they did was hang out and have fun. No wonder they wanted to stay here forever.

"So that Talent Show thing," Demo said. "What's that all about? Do you perform?"

Lyssa was surprised—the talent show had been such a small part of her story. Everyone else had been more interested in the part where she jumped off cliffs and tried to break onto boats. She nodded, tugging at her sleeves. She didn't want to admit her stage fright.

"That's cool," Demo said. "Me too. I mean, I want to be."

"Really?" Lyssa asked. "You want to be a singer?"

"Actually, I've got my own style." His face lit up. "Wanna see?"

Lyssa nodded, sitting down at the edge of a cot. Demo looked a little sheepish as he stood up in front of her.

"All right," he said. "No laughing."

He hunched over a little, raising his hands to his face. Then he started to spit and hum, making noises into his hands that sounded like nothing Lyssa had ever heard before. It was as though he were an instrument: the sounds he made were crashing cymbals and drums and staticky speakers. As he hummed into his hands, he started to move, dancing in a way that was jerky and robotic at times and smooth and liquid feeling at others.

Lyssa watched in awe. It was such a different type of music from what she was used to. When he was done, she started clapping.

"Like it?" Demo asked.

"I . . ." Lyssa paused, not sure how to express how *much* she'd liked it. She'd never heard someone make music that way before. "It was *amazing*. Your mouth sounded like a garbage disposal!"

Demo narrowed his eyes. "Is that good?"

"Yes. No, I mean, it was like a machine or something." Lyssa felt her cheeks redden. No one wanted to be told they sounded like a garbage disposal. "It was like you had a drum set in your mouth, I mean."

"Thanks," Demo said, a grin spreading across his face. "I practice a lot. Sometimes I hit the street corners in Seattle and put out a hat, ask for donations. I make okay money."

"Demo, will you shut it?" Regina called from the other side of the room. "The show's back on."

Demo stuck out his tongue at Regina. Then he led Lyssa back over to the rest of the group, introducing everyone in the "Lotus Crew," as they called themselves. She waved hi and found a comfy armchair to curl up in with her blanket and dinner. The television show—*Lotus Island*—wasn't half bad. And during all of the commercials, everyone turned their chairs around to face her, making her tell stories of her adventures again. After she'd told them all about escaping from Michael's house, she moved backward in time and described the Athena concert she'd been to with her mom—how amazing it was to be one of the last lucky people who'd seen Athena perform.

"You remind me of her," Regina said after Lyssa finished. "A little bit."

Lyssa opened and closed her mouth, so shocked that, for a moment, she couldn't think of a thing to say. "I do?"

"Yeah. I watched this interview last week with this music historian, and he's like an expert on Athena, right? He said he spotted her in Egypt, riding around on the back of a camel. She's an adrenaline junkie! That's why she disappeared. Music just didn't get her heart pumping anymore, so she had to find her kicks somewhere else."

"I thought she got abducted by aliens or something?" the curly-haired boy muttered.

"Don't be an idiot. She just left it all behind. Sick of the spotlight." Demo shook his head, but there was a tinge of awe in his voice. "Can you imagine walking away from all that money?"

Lyssa thought about telling him about one of the theories she'd read on a website—that someone close to Athena had died and that grief had made it impossible for the singer to go on—but it made her think too much about her own mom, so she decided not to. Instead, she said, "I was there—at her last concert before she disappeared."

Regina's eyes grew wide. "Shut up."

"My mom took me," Lyssa added. "We did lots of cool stuff like that."

She started telling them the stories about adventures she used to have with her mom: how they'd sneak into department stores in the middle of the day and try on all the hats and ties in the men's department, or set up a tent in the living room on rainy days and pretend they were camping in the wilderness.

In exchange, the Lotus Crew told Lyssa about how they all found each other. Demo explained that he used to put up posters with secret codes written into them all over town so that any kid who was lost or scared or alone could find them if he or she really needed to. As long as a kid could figure out the code, he'd know where to go to find the crew. It didn't matter if he was a runway or an orphan or if he just needed a place to hang out when things at home were bad. The crew was there for him.

"Weren't you ever worried that grown-ups would

figure out the code?" Lyssa asked. Demo just shook his head.

"Grown-ups don't pay enough attention," he said with a smirk.

"But all this stuff!" Lyssa continued. She had so many questions that she could hardly keep quiet. She felt like a pot bubbling over with water. "How did you get it?"

"You'd be amazed at what people will throw away," Demo said. "We all go Dumpster diving after dark. And Regina is a whiz with anything electronic—she's the one who rigged all these cars and set up the televisions and everything."

Regina opened her mouth to say something, but then the show started up again and she turned toward it immediately and motioned for quiet. Demo leaned in next to Lyssa, lowering his voice so it would be barely heard over the TV.

"You can stay here, you know," he said. "If you promise not to tell anyone where we are, you can stay for as long as you like. Just because you'd be the shortest, though, doesn't mean you wouldn't have to pull your weight."

"I—I have to think about it."

But excitement was already rising in Lyssa's chest. Stay with the Lotus Crew? It'd be like having a whole new family again, like being home with her mom and Penn and the Texas Talent Show. She wrapped her blanket tightly around her and looked past the edge of the dock. The clouds parted to reveal a beautiful, black sky covered in stars. Something shot across the sky—a shooting star.

Lyssa glanced around to see whether anyone else had noticed, but the Lotus Crew were all focused on their televisions.

Lyssa's throat caught. Her mom would have cared way more about shooting stars than about a television show.

Even surrounded by new friends, Lyssa suddenly felt very alone. She wanted to call Penn, tell her all about the crazy runaways she'd ended up with. But it was getting late and Penn's parents didn't like for her to get calls after nine on weeknights.

Lyssa finally dug through her backpack, pulling out her journal for school.

Dear Penn, she wrote.

I just saw a shooting star and you know what that means—I get one wish. Jealous? What should it be this time? A swimming pool filled with hot chocolate? It's freezing here. Unlimited turns on the Heinous Hurricane? I miss the fair so much . . .

Lyssa paused and looked back up. Another shooting star streaked across the sky, then another and another, until the whole sky was glowing with light. It looked like the sky was on fire, like it was falling all around her. Lyssa watched the stars, feeling guilty.

Of course she couldn't stay with the Lotus gang. She had to get to Texas. She had to find her mom. She had to do whatever she could to save her home.

Fear and excitement clutching her heart, Lyssa watched the shooting stars light up the sky. It hurt to think about leaving the Lotus Crew, but she knew it'd be worth it once she reached Texas and climbed that dogwood tree in her front yard. Her mother would be waiting to guide her and to fill her with her magic, and Lyssa would know what to do about the protest and her home and Michael and school and everything. All she had to do was get there.

Clenching her eyes shut, she made the same wish over and over.

Let me reach Austin in time to save my house. Let me go home.

Lyssa bunched her backpack up, being careful not to ruin her University of Washington patch, and shoved it beneath her head as a makeshift pillow. She tried to get comfortable, but something hard and sharp protruded from the bottom of the bag and kept sticking her. Frowning, Lyssa pulled the backpack open and started looking through the random collection of items that had accumulated there over the months.

Surrounded by old candy wrappers and pencil nubs

were two demo CDs bound together with a rubber band. When Michael had first given her the voice-recording software, she was sure she'd never use it. But she ended up playing around with it one day when she was bored and, actually, it was a lot of fun to listen to her voice on the computer and use all the editing tools to make it sound professional. She had made the demo CDs before realizing she had no one to give them to. Ever since then they'd stayed at the bottom of her backpack, as useless, Lyssa thought, as her own voice.

She picked at the rubber band that bound the CDs together, then shoved them to the very bottom of her backpack so they wouldn't poke her. As she started to fall asleep, she drowsily thought she saw shooting stars dancing inside her eyelids. But then the stars got closer and closer and Lyssa realized they weren't stars at all—they were headlights.

The Texas Talent Show van tore past her and . . . if she squinted . . . she thought she could see her mom staring out at her from its back window, sticking out her tongue.

CHAPTER SEVEN

Twenty-Seven Times You Called Me

When Lyssa woke up the next morning, the sun was already high in the sky. Light zigzagged off the waves, shining into her eyes bright as a flashlight. Her neck was sore and her hair was coming out of its braids.

The boy with the curly hair was asleep in the armchair next to Lyssa's. He was curled up in a little ball and all his blankets had been kicked to the floor. Every few minutes he let out a hiccup-like snore and started muttering in his sleep. Whoever was in the chair on the other side of him was completely buried under blankets, but Lyssa thought she saw a few spiky tufts of Regina's hair against the pillow. No one had bothered getting up to go to the cots in the back.

The remote-controlled toys were lined up in front of one of the television towers (which weren't turned off—only muted), and Demo was nowhere to be seen. Lyssa slid to the edge of her chair, lowering her feet to the cold, rocky floor and nearly tripping on the pink sneakers she kicked off in her sleep. She wiggled her toes, trying to shake the pins and needles out of her legs.

Lyssa glanced up at the sun again, shielding her eyes from its glare. Her mom had taught her to tell time by examining the sun's position in the sky. Lyssa judged it to be at least nine-thirty or ten o'clock. Dread crept into her throat. Uh-oh.

As quietly as possible, Lyssa started looking for the rest of her things. Her polka-dot socks were wedged under the armchair. She pulled them on, then her sneakers, without bothering to untie the laces. She unzipped her backpack, digging around until she found her cell phone so she could find out for sure what time it was.

As soon as Lyssa pushed the button to un-silence her phone, the ring tone began blaring: it was a snippet of an Athena song that Lyssa had downloaded.

"Twenty-seven times you called me. Twenty-seven times you told me you were sorry . . ."

Lyssa frantically searched for a way to control the volume. She hadn't had the phone for very long—her mom had always hated them. Michael made her carry it around for emergencies, but she'd mostly been using it just to send texts to Penn.

The curly-haired boy thrashed around in his patched-up chair.

"Just five more minutes, Mom," he said groggily, the armchair creaking beneath him as he shifted in his sleep.

Desperately, Lyssa started pushing buttons at random. She accidentally pulled up her missed calls log—oh, no.

There were nineteen missed calls from Michael. Lyssa checked the time of the last missed call: nine o'clock that morning. A hard, hollow feeling formed in Lyssa's stomach as she pushed another button—this one taking her back to the home page where she could check the time. For a second she could only gape at the numbers on the screen.

10:34. It was 10:34. Lyssa was over three-and–a-half hours late getting to the bus depot, and Michael knew she was missing.

The phone beeped one more time and Lyssa automatically looked down at the screen: another message from Michael. She opened the message, but before she could read a single letter, the curly-haired boy thrashed in his chair.

"I *said* five more minutes!" He grabbed the phone out of Lyssa's hands and threw it away with a grunt. Lyssa spun around just in time to see the phone splash into the water.

"Much better," the boy muttered, letting out a snore.

"No!" Lyssa shouted, no longer caring whether or not she woke anyone up.

She raced to the edge of the water. A few bubbles floated along the surface and Lyssa swallowed. Her phone had probably reached the bottom of the bay by now. Still, she had to try to retrieve it—even if it would be waterlogged and useless.

She kicked off her right shoe and frantically peeled off her sock, peering over the side of the ledge. The water looked cold. Just as she was about to kick off the other shoe too someone put a hand on her shoulder.

"I wouldn't do that if I were you," Demo said.

Lyssa whirled around, nearly knocking her sneaker into the water. Demo looked worn out—like he'd been running. His skin was bright red and covered in a thin layer of sweat. Even his mohawk was sticking out in strange tufts, looking windblown.

"My phone," Lyssa started to explain, pointing to the water. "That boy thought it was an alarm clock and—"

Demo cut her off.

"You have bigger problems to worry about," he said.

"What?" Lyssa asked, though she wasn't sure she really wanted to know. She thought of the nineteen missed calls from Michael and the text message she didn't even get a chance to read. What if he'd already tracked her down?

"I was just downtown," Demo said. "There are pigs everywhere. They're passing out your picture."

"Pigs?"

"You know, cops? *Police.*"

Lyssa swallowed. *Police?*

Somehow, when she'd first come up with the plan to return to Austin, she hadn't imagined *police*. That was even worse than Michael looking for her.

"Listen," Demo continued. "They'll be here any minute. Someone found this streamer thing that was on your scooter or something . . ."

"Pom-pom," Lyssa said automatically. She looked around for Zip, feeling irrationally angry with her scooter, as though it had deliberately betrayed her. Then she realized it wasn't Zip's fault. The pom-pom had fallen off in the storm. It was an act of nature. It was the universe throwing one big pie in her face.

"Whatever," Demo said. "Listen, I went by the bus station, just in case. No police there, yet. If you hurry, you can probably make it."

Relief flooded Lyssa's chest. No police at the bus depot. Michael must not have guessed she was headed back home. This was good news. If she caught the next bus to Austin, she still might make it.

"Thanks, Demo," Lyssa said. She grabbed her backpack

and her right tennis shoe and crept around the cots to a beaten-smooth dirt path that led up and around the rocky ledge. Crawling up the path, Lyssa reached the top of the dock and saw her scooter lying in the sun. She patted Zip's handlebars.

"We're going to make it," she whispered.

She pulled on her sock and shoved her foot back in her sneaker. She started to reach out for Zip, then immediately ducked her head. There were three men in blue uniforms crowded around the boats near the end of the marina, talking to a shorter man wearing jeans and a sweatshirt. The man gestured to the boats, looking angry. One of the police held up a pom-pom and Lyssa's heart sank.

She'd never been in trouble with the police before. Once, she and her mom slept in a tree overnight to protest a development company that wanted to cut it down. The police had come to get them out of the tree, but they hadn't gotten in trouble. In fact, Lyssa had actually managed to convince the officers that the development was wrong and, in the end, the cops had climbed up into the tree with them.

Lyssa bit down on her lower lip, not wanting to take her eyes off the police officers at the end of the dock. She had a feeling that even she wouldn't be able to talk her way out of trouble this time.

Lyssa heard Demo crawl up behind her.

"Demo," Lyssa whispered. "What should I do?"

"Okay," he whispered back, peering over the side of the dock to where the police were standing. "They know you're around here somewhere, but they don't know where—no one knows where the Lotus gang hides." He gestured to the short man in jeans. "That's Mr. Haddy," he explained, keeping his voice low. "He's the property manager for the marina or something. If he ever finds us, he'll turn us over to the police."

"So what's the plan?" Lyssa asked.

Demo bit down on his lip, looking determined. He picked up a large flat stone.

"Wait for my signal," Demo said. He paused to make sure the police were still deep in conversation with Mr. Haddy and then stood up and chucked the stone.

It landed in the water just past the police. All three men turned and glanced behind them.

As soon as their attention was distracted, Demo darted across the dock, ducking behind a sailboat on the other side.

Lyssa didn't follow him. She crouched next to Zip, steadying her scooter with one hand. She had a feeling they were going to need to be ready to go—fast.

"We just have to watch for the sign," she whispered to Zip, giving her scooter a reassuring pat.

Demo climbed down the other side of the dock, looking a little like a spider monkey as he swung from the wood and darted across the ropes connecting the boats to the marina. Lyssa glanced nervously from Demo to where Mr. Haddy stood with the police. They were heading down the dock now, Mr. Haddy in the lead.

"Hurry," Lyssa whispered.

Demo loosened a rope and a large sail dropped with a thud, already billowing in the wind like the boat too was eager to escape. Then Demo hopped out and unknotted the rope that connected the boat to the marina. When it fell free, he leaned against the side of the dock and pushed the boat away with his foot. The sailboat rocked in the water, then started to drift away.

One of the policemen gave a muffled shout and pointed to the sailboat. Lyssa ducked farther behind the dock as the cops ran toward it. She could still see Demo—his mohawk was just visible above the dock—and it looked like he was swinging from boat to boat, untying ropes and pushing them into the waves. Soon the water was spotted with boats, all floating away, like massive white swans coasting over the bay.

Demo swung onto one final boat, quickly undoing the knot. Then he waved at Lyssa and dropped into the water below.

"Demo!" she called, as loud as she dared. He didn't resurface. She poked her head above the dock and saw the police scattered across the marina, all pointing in different directions.

"She's on one of the boats," an officer called out, and dove into the water. The remaining officers followed until they were all bobbing up and down in the water, trying to swim after the boats. Mr. Haddy stayed on the dock, but his back was to Lyssa now.

"This is it," she whispered. She stood up and climbed onto Zip, wrapping her fingers tightly around the familiar grooves of the handlebars. She kicked off, shooting down the marina, sneaking past Mr. Haddy and over to the road. She chanced a glance behind her when she reached the end of the marina. Mr. Haddy was still gazing across the water at the police officers bobbing up and down in the waves. He had one hand over his eyes to shield them from the sun.

"I think I saw someone moving in that boat," he called out, pointing to a sailboat several yards away. Lyssa threw a hand over her mouth to keep from laughing out loud. No one had seen her escape. Maybe she had inherited a little of her mom's magic after all.

She pushed off again, rolling down to the end of the block. Zip's wheels squeaked excitedly, as though it too was pleased with their bold escape. Demo was leaning against a stop sign, soaking wet. The water had messed up his mohawk and his hair hung down in clumps around his face, making his head look smaller.

"How was the diversion?" he asked, grinning.

"Amazing," Lyssa admitted. She glanced over her shoulder to make sure no one was following her yet. The road was all clear. She turned back to Demo. "I don't know how to thank you."

"Don't worry about it," Demo said.

Lyssa's mom used to tell her that it was good manners to give gifts to show appreciation for someone who had helped you. Making a quick decision, she yanked open her backpack, digging through the worn-down nubs of pencils and her favorite pair of sunglasses for something she could give to him. Her fingers brushed the bound-together demo CDs at the bottom of the bag. Hadn't she made them with the intention of giving them away? Well, now was her chance. Knowing she'd chicken out if she hesitated, she pulled out one of the CDs and thrust it into Demo's hands.

"This is for you," she said. "You let me watch your singing and so . . . so here."

Demo turned the case over in his hands, then glanced up at her questioningly.

"It's a recording of my songs," Lyssa explained. Now she felt embarrassed. She looked down at her feet, resisting the urge to stick her hair into her mouth. "I mean, it's nothing special, and you have to imagine a band would be—"

"I'm sure it's killer," Demo interrupted, and she could tell he meant it. "Thanks a lot, Lyssa." He paused for a second, and the smile stretched across his face started to wilt, like day-old lettuce. "Are you sure you want to leave?"

Lyssa's heart pulsed in her throat, and, once again, she imagined what it would be like to stay. Talking late into the night with the Lotus Crew. Going on adventures with Demo. Singing on street corners during the day—if she could work up the courage.

But then a gust of wind blew past, ruffling the hair on the back of Lyssa's neck and blowing her braids out behind her. If she stayed here, what would happen to her home? She thought again of standing by her mom's side in the garden, their toes wriggling deep into the earth. If Lyssa didn't protect their roots, who would?

"I'm sure," she said with a small smile. "If you're ever in Austin, head to the Texas Talent Show. That's where I'll be."

"You can count on it," Demo said. Lyssa waved to him and headed down the street to the bus depot. Demo called out after her.

"Good luck!"

CHAPTER EIGHT

Goldfish Don't Look for Mosquitoes

The bus depot was crowded with people. Men and women wearing suits and carrying briefcases rushed by Lyssa; teenagers jostled her with their large, lumpy backpacks. Twice, she would have ended up sprawled in a heap on the floor if she hadn't had Zip to hold on to. An old man was swaying in front of the entrance, singing under his breath. As Lyssa walked past him, she wrinkled her nose. He smelled like the clowns at the fair did after drinking their "special" cider.

Some of Lyssa's confidence began to slip away. Everything about the bus station seemed big and strange. She caught sight of a huge, electronic billboard hanging over a row of desks, flashing city names, times, and rows of other numbers that Lyssa didn't understand. The numbers changed quickly—Lyssa had to watch the city names flash by three times before she finally saw *Austin, TX*. There were only two times listed next to the name: 11:35 and 6:35.

Lyssa's mouth went so dry her tongue could have cracked. She looked from the billboard to the digital clock below. It was 11:20 right now—which meant that she had less than fifteen minutes to get that bus ticket or she'd have to wait until after six to leave. She swallowed, stepping out of the way as a man with a briefcase pushed past her. The cops were sure to check the bus depot before six.

"Come on," she whispered, glancing down at Zip. "We can do this."

She pulled off her sweatshirt and tied it around her waist; it was warm enough in the bus station that she really didn't need it. As soon as her arms were uncovered, she felt a little bit better, like she could breathe for the first time all morning. She glanced around the bus depot, trying to figure out a plan.

A line of people snaked away from the ticket counter and twisted around to the back of the station. They looked like they'd been standing there for a while: a few of the men and women were reading newspapers and magazines and there was a group of teenagers sitting cross-legged in the middle of the floor, playing cards while they waited. Their backpacks were piled high around them.

Lyssa watched one of the teenagers stand up and push the pile of backpacks up a few inches as the rest of the line shuffled forward. She'd be waiting for at least an hour if she went to the end of that line. She'd never make her bus.

She needed a plan.

The old man who had been singing at the entrance shuffled toward her. He was wearing an old, patched coat and a baseball cap with a logo for Golden Apples Land-scaping emblazoned across the front. As he got closer, he sang louder, until Lyssa couldn't help hearing the words to the song:

"You think you're slick, but I know your tricks," he muttered, continuing his strange, shuffling dance across the room. A few people making their way to the back of the line dodged out of his way, looking annoyed, but Lyssa smiled wide and sang the last line along with him:

"And I'll get there first 'cause I'm quicker."

The song was Lyssa's all-time favorite, "Tricks," by Athena. She glanced at the ticket counter again. She *would* find a way onto that bus.

As Lyssa pushed her scooter past the old man, toward the front of the ticket line, he lifted his baseball cap and bowed at the waist.

"Rosebud," he said, as though he was greeting her.

Lyssa gave him a tentative smile. Okay, so the man was a little crazy—but the song was still a sign. Ignoring the line completely, Lyssa pulled her scooter right up to the ticket booth.

Her mom always said she could talk anybody into doing things her way. Now was Lyssa's chance to prove her right.

"Excuse me," Lyssa said, trying to look as innocent as possible. The woman selling tickets had patchy skin and her eyes looked tired. She had hair that had been dyed red so many times it almost looked purple.

"I was hoping you might be able to help me," Lyssa continued, winding her braid around one finger. The woman smacked her lips together.

"End of the line," she barked. Then, glancing at the person directly behind Lyssa, she shouted, "Next."

"Wait!" Lyssa held her hand up to keep the next person in line from darting in front of her. "You don't understand: I need to get on the bus to Austin, Texas. It's leaving in fifteen minutes."

The woman in the ticket counter narrowed her tired eyes, leaning farther over the counter.

"We don't sell tickets to minors . . ."

"Of course not," Lyssa said, thinking quickly. "I'm not here on my own."

She dropped her braid and looked back over her shoulder, her eyes darting around the bus depot. The confused old man stumbled up behind her, still singing under his breath.

"I know your tricks, I know, I know."

"That's my grandpa," Lyssa blurted out, turning back to the ticket counter woman. "See, we're traveling together, but he gets confused and only bought one ticket. I need to get another one fast; otherwise the bus will leave without us both."

The ticket counter lady narrowed her eyes even more, until they were just tiny slits. Lyssa licked her lips nervously and turned back to the old man.

"Isn't that right, Grandpa?" she asked.

The old man turned around, his eyes wide.

"George Washington!" he replied.

Lyssa forced a laugh and turned back to the ticket counter, shrugging.

"That's Grandpa for you," she said, trying to give the lady a winning smile. "I told you he got confused."

Rolling her eyes, the ticket counter lady slid Lyssa a one-way ticket to Austin. Lyssa dug around in her backpack for her money. The bus ticket was $60—that only left her with $13 more. Biting down on her lower lip, Lyssa slid the money over, saying a silent prayer of thanks for all those lawn-mowing jobs she'd done for Mrs. Patel over the last few months. Then she grabbed the strange old man's arm and steered him away from the line.

"Hey, thanks a lot," she said when they were far enough away from the counter that the noise of the bus depot drowned out their voices. "I owe you one. Want a granola bar?"

The old man screwed up his face, like Lyssa had just offered him a dirty sock.

"The goldfish don't look for mosquitoes after midnight," he whispered, as though he were telling her a secret.

"Um, okay," Lyssa said, putting her granola bar back into her backpack. "What does that mean?"

"It means the winds of change are coming," the man said. Then, tipping his hat to Lyssa, he stumbled away, still humming under his breath.

The winds of change are coming. A chill swept up Lyssa's arms and legs as she watched the man stumble away. She *was* on the right path. She pulled her backpack onto her shoulder. Then, shoving her ticket into her pocket, she ran for her bus.

CHAPTER NINE

Let's Hear It for the Cowgirls

Lyssa pushed her nose up against the bus window, excitement and nerves rattling around in her stomach like the last two pennies in a piggy bank. It was cool to watch the fields and trees fly past, a blur of colors and growth. Plus—hello!—the bus seats were all covered in yellow fabric. And just a few minutes earlier she'd seen an entire field of yellow flowers that she couldn't even name. These were signs. Good things were coming.

Still, Lyssa couldn't help thinking of her narrow escape from Washington. Would the police still be after her? Would they follow her into Oregon?

She pulled the tangles in her hair apart with her fingers,

then rebraided it, humming some of her favorite Athena lyrics under her breath to calm herself down: *You never know where your life will go. You can never tell where your dreams will take you . . .*

"First stop, Pendleton, Oregon," announced a scratchy voice over the bus's PA system.

Leaning back against her seat, Lyssa popped the last chunk of granola bar into her mouth. It was the second granola bar she'd had that morning, but it was already past two in the afternoon and she was starving. Even though she was still hungry, she needed to save the rest. She only had six granola bars and $13 left and that had to get her all the way to Texas.

The bus turned off the highway on to a narrow service road and then bumped into the parking lot of a rest-stop diner. The smell of waffles and french fries and bacon drifted in through the cracked-open windows, making Lyssa's stomach grumble loudly.

"Forty-five minutes for lunch," the driver announced.

The bus jerked to a stop. Lyssa tumbled forward, smacking her head against the seat in front of her. All around the bus, belt buckles clicked open and passengers started getting to their feet. Lyssa rubbed her forehead and glanced out the window . . .

. . . coming face-to-face with a large, brown nose.

Lyssa let out a strangled "yelp!" and scooted out of her

seat. The nostrils on the nose widened, pushing right up against the glass of Lyssa's window and snorting loudly. Then the nose disappeared. Curious, Lyssa pressed up against the window and looked down.

The nose belonged to a huge brown-and-black horse. It gazed up at Lyssa again, giving a disapproving toss of its head, then trotted off to the other side of the parking lot, its hooves making clip-clop noises against the concrete.

Lyssa stared. She could hardly believe what she was seeing. There wasn't a single car in the parking lot. Instead, there were horses. Chestnut-colored horses with shiny coats munched on the grass next to the highway; spotted white horses that looked like overgrown Dalmatians galloped across the parking lot. There was even a tiny white horse nudging the windows of the diner.

Grabbing Zip and her backpack, Lyssa stumbled off the bus. She was pretty sure they wouldn't let her ride around on her scooter inside the restaurant, but leaving it on the bus didn't seem safe either. Did people steal old scooters? She hid it behind one of the large Dumpsters standing next to the restaurant.

Her eyes fell on a sign just under the diner's windows: *The Wild Horse Diner, home of Chef Louie's secret stew, is proud to sponsor the cowgirls in Pendleton's famous Rodeo Roundup!*

Lyssa excitedly hitched her backpack higher on one shoulder. Cowgirls? *Real cowgirls?* There were cowgirls in the Texas Talent Show, of course, but they were just show cowgirls—their costumes were spotless and white, with leather fringes down the legs, and their cowboy hats were bejeweled with hearts and stars. It was cool to watch them sing and dance onstage, but Lyssa knew they'd never be able to ride a wild horse around in a rodeo or lasso a running bull.

Real cowgirls reminded Lyssa of her ninth birthday, when her mom surprised her with tickets to the Austin rodeo. They'd bought popcorn and watched the cowgirls gallop around on their beautiful horses. After the show, Ana Lee had actually taken Lyssa back to the stables to meet the cowgirls and a few of their horses. One horse—Pablo—was wilder than all the others. Not a single cowgirl could go near him, but Ana sang a few bars in her beautiful, high soprano, and before Lyssa knew it, Pablo was nuzzling her mother's shoulder like an overgrown kitten. He even let Lyssa feed him a few carrots.

Lyssa practically ran for the front doors.

The diner reminded her of an old saloon. Hay and peanut shells coated the floor, and red-leather-topped stools were lined up in front of the counter. Something sizzled in the kitchen and, even though Lyssa knew it was probably bacon and sausage frying up in a pan, she couldn't help picturing a cowboy holding a red-hot branding iron over a bed of smoldering coals.

Just ahead, a cowgirl with a face full of freckles and messy brown hair stood in the middle of a sea of cowboy hats. She put one bright blue cowboy boot up on her chair, causing the metal spurs on her heel to jingle. It was just like the rodeo! Lyssa's heart climbed up higher inside her chest. The cowgirl twirled a lasso, then threw it across the room. It circled a bottle of ketchup at the end of the table. While the people around her clapped and cheered, the cowgirl tugged on the lasso, and the ketchup slid into her waiting hand.

"Woo-hoo!" another cowgirl shouted.

Seconds later an angry-looking waitress appeared. She had bleached-blond hair and earrings that dangled to her shoulders.

"Daisy, can't you just wait until I come over to take your order like a normal person?"

"Don't think I can do that, Sal," the cowgirl said. All around her, the rest of the cowgirls clapped and stomped. Daisy the cowgirl spun around, catching Lyssa's eye.

"Well howdy, little lady," she said, smiling wide. Lyssa couldn't help staring—Daisy's two front teeth were made of shiny gold that glimmered under the bright diner lights.

"Er, howdy," Lyssa said, feeling shy. She shifted her

gaze back up to Daisy's eyes, not wanting to be rude. "That was really cool, what you did with the ketchup."

Daisy grinned wider. "Thanks!" She bent down so that she and Lyssa were at eye level. "You aren't here by yourself, are you, little cowgirl?" she asked.

"Um . . ." Lyssa swiveled her head. Several of the people from the bus were crowded around the counter, ordering cups of coffee and sandwiches to go. None of them were paying any attention to Lyssa. Daisy raised an eyebrow, and Lyssa hurriedly added. "I am, actually. I'm . . . a child star and there's a production company in Austin that wants me to audition. My management arranged for me to travel down to meet them."

It wasn't *completely* a lie. If Lyssa'd had the guts to sing in the Texas Talent Show, it would be kind of like an audition. And Mrs. Patel was the manager at a flower shop—since Lyssa earned all of her money from mowing her lawn, a manager *had* actually paid for her bus ticket. Anyway, Daisy seemed to believe her. She leaned over, patting the chair next to her.

"Well, you're welcome to join us for lunch if you like."

Eat lunch with a bunch of cowgirls? Lyssa felt like her insides might explode. The cowgirls around her cheered again, and a few lifted their cups of coffee in salute.

"Sure." Lyssa slid in next to Daisy. She only had forty-five minutes before the bus left again, but that was plenty of time.

Sal hustled out of the kitchen. When she saw Lyssa, she raised an eyebrow.

"New recruit?" she asked.

As though to answer, Daisy whipped her cowboy hat off her head and placed it on Lyssa's. "That's right," Daisy announced, winking at Lyssa. "She isn't ready to ride the bull just yet, but for now she's with us."

When Lyssa tried to give Daisy her hat back, Daisy just waved her off.

"There's more where that came from," she said. "You keep it as a souvenir, little lady."

Lyssa pulled the cowboy hat farther down onto her head, smiling so hard she thought her face might split apart at the seams.

After ordering a peanut butter and jelly sandwich and split pea soup, she listened to Daisy and the cowgirls tell stories from the rodeo. They showed Lyssa their gnarliest scars and re-created their most horrific falls. After they were done with their stories, Lyssa told them all about the protest and the Texas Talent Show.

Soon her lunch came. Lyssa tried to give the waitress $6 for her sandwich and soup, but Daisy waved her money away.

"This one's on me, little cowgirl. You just eat up and enjoy."

"Thanks, Daisy!" Lyssa shoved her money back into her pocket. A cowgirl had bought her lunch.

While Lyssa tried to eat, the cowgirls climbed up onto their chairs and did a line dance on the table. Their dancing made Lyssa's bowl hop up and down on the table—splattering Lyssa with bright green soup. Her shirt was probably ruined, but so what? Who else could say that the soup stain on their shirt was courtesy of a real-life dancing cowgirl?

Everyone was so busy dancing, singing, and clapping that no one noticed when the television hanging over the counter switched from normal programming to an emergency broadcast. As the announcer started to talk, Lyssa noticed a woman near the counter look up from her coffee.

"Oh, no. Don't tell me it's more hoot-and-holler over that singer . . . what's her name? Alina?"

"Nah, just some kid," the man standing next to her said.

The inside of Lyssa's mouth turned to chalk when the bright red word EMERGENCY flashed across a photo on the screen. The pea soup suddenly felt hard in the pit of her stomach, like it had transformed into rocks and dirt after sliding down her throat.

It was *her*. The photograph was one Michael had taken. She was sitting on the front steps of their new house just a few days after they'd moved to Washington. She was tan and freckly, her blond hair bleached out from the Texas sun. Two bright red words flashed across the bottom of the screen: *MISSING GIRL*.

Suddenly the dancing and singing and clapping sounded very far away. Lyssa pulled the cowboy hat farther down over her face, hoping no one had recognized her. Panic rushed over her like the waves on Michael's computers, only this time the water really was going to crash over her head. She was a *runaway*. The entire country was searching for her. Lyssa would never make it to Austin.

She had to think. She had to get out of here.

Mumbling something about cleaning the soup off her T-shirt, Lyssa grabbed her backpack and Daisy's lasso and stumbled into the hallway. She raced to the bathroom at the back of the diner, hoping she could climb out a window and circle back to the bus, but when she fumbled with the doorknob, she realized it was locked. Turning around, she leaned against the door to figure out a plan. The television blared from the dining room:

Eleven-year-old Lyssa Lee, believed to have been kidnapped and taken aboard one of the sailboats that disappeared from the Kirkland Marina early this morning. Lyssa was wearing a striped tank top and jean shorts and will likely be carrying a yellow-and-blue scooter . . .

Kidnapped? The police thought she'd been kidnapped? But what about the note she left for Michael—hadn't he seen it?

With a sinking heart, Lyssa realized that there were multiple computers in the house. Maybe he'd never even looked at the one she'd written her note on. And now it was too late to go back and explain. She was already in Oregon and she'd spent most of her money on a bus ticket. Plus, she'd lost her cell phone—she couldn't even call Michael and tell him that he didn't need to worry about her.

The sounds from the dining room swelled. Just below the singing and clapping Lyssa thought she heard someone whisper her name and one word: *police*. The cops wouldn't care that Lyssa hadn't meant to worry anyone. They wouldn't care about Lyssa's home. They'd just take her back to Michael and she'd miss the protest entirely.

Feeling desperate, Lyssa pulled on her backpack and looked around for a back exit. She needed to make it back to the bus—then she could just curl up in her seat and wait until they all started moving again.

Halfway down the hallway were two swinging doors. Steam curled out from beneath them, and Lyssa smelled gravy and bacon. The *kitchen*. Kitchens had exits, right? Chefs needed to throw out big stacks of trash. Praying her guess was correct, Lyssa pushed the doors open and ducked inside.

Billowing clouds of steam filled the room, so thick that Lyssa couldn't see through them. She coughed, waving a hand so the steam cleared just a little—enough for Lyssa to see that it was coming from a pot that seemed the size of a bathtub, balanced on top of the massive stove.

In front of the pot was a very round man who looked like a sumo wrestler. His thick neck was bright red, and a chef's hat was balanced on top of his huge, bald head. The floor creaked beneath his weight as he shuffled around the kitchen. He dunked a large wooden spoon into the pot, stirring spices and chopped vegetables into the water.

"That is it," he said with a rumbling laugh. "Let us stir the masterpiece, *il capovoro*!"

Lyssa crept farther into the kitchen, crouching behind a butcher block table covered in vegetables and pasta. She was on the other side of the kitchen from the chef, but the room was so small that he was still only a few feet away. From her angle on the floor, she could see little more than his striped pants and the dangling strings of his apron.

Her heart sank. She didn't see any doors that looked like they led to the parking lot. She scanned the various cupboards, the space between the fridge and the counter—all places she could hide, and think, and wait for the emergency announcement about her disappearance to be over.

The fat chef kept glancing down at the counter. Lyssa leaned around the table, just slightly, so that she could see what he was looking at.

A tiny black-and-white television was balanced on the counter next to the sink, its screen flashing a picture of Lyssa's face. Across the top of the screen was the word REWARD.

"So much pasta we could buy with that money," the chef muttered into the pot, stirring the water with his giant wooden spoon. Something splashed angrily inside the pot and Lyssa felt all of the hair on her arms stand on end.

It was time to move. Lyssa started crawling back toward the kitchen doors, praying her sneakers didn't squeak. She couldn't imagine what the chef might do if he found her.

The chef pulled something out of the pot and slapped it down onto the table. Lyssa watched him grab a heavy butcher knife out of the knife block and slam it down. She didn't see what he'd cut, but a split second later, a fish head tumbled off the table and onto the floor right in front of her.

Lyssa let out a high-pitched scream and leapt to her feet. She took one step forward and slipped on a wet noodle.

Her feet flew out from beneath her and she landed, hard, on the ground. Pain shot through her body, reaching its tentacles up her back and down around her legs.

The chef whirled around. His pudgy face was bright red from the steam and one of his eyes was hidden behind a faded black eye patch. For the briefest second, Lyssa wondered what had happened to that eye.

"*Sciocchezze!*" he said, his good eye widening at the sight of Lyssa. He started laughing. "You! You are the missing one. And *we* have found you!"

Lyssa pushed herself to her feet and raced for the door. With a grunt, the chef hurled his huge wooden spoon across the room. Before Lyssa could rip the kitchen doors open, the spoon lodged itself between the two handles—holding them fast. Lyssa skidded to a stop. How did he *do* that? It was like the spoon had a mind of its own—like it didn't want her to escape either.

Lyssa remembered, suddenly, what her mother had told her about the winds of change and what they would bring: *everyday objects can become great and powerful weapons.*

The chef leapt toward her, his huge belly shaking beneath his grease-stained apron.

"So much money," he said, leering, "so much bread, dough, cabbage."

Lyssa backed up until she felt the wall behind her. She

couldn't help but glance at the giant, bubbling pot on the stove and wonder what was inside. Could the pot become a weapon? Could the stew?

Desperately, Lyssa looked around the steam-filled kitchen for anything she could use to protect herself. There was a bottle of dish soap sitting on the counter next to her, along with some chopped vegetables, onions, and measuring cups. A half-dozen feet away from her, the chef grabbed a spatula so large it could be a rowboat paddle.

"That is it," he crooned to Lyssa. "Stay right where you are, *mi amore*. This is my favorite spatula—Signore Flappy. We are not going to hurt you." His single eye gleamed maliciously.

Lyssa grabbed the dish soap from the counter and squirted half the bottle onto the floor. The chef took one more step forward—and his foot slid right out from under him. His good eye went wide as he flew onto the ground, landing hard on his butt.

His fall sent a tremor through the tiny kitchen. Utensils tumbled from the countertops and produce rolled onto the floor. Lyssa managed to steady herself by grabbing on to one of the countertops and holding tight. The chef would be standing again soon. She needed to think fast.

She still had Daisy's lasso. She quickly looped one end and tied it in a knot and twirled it above her head, just like she'd seen Daisy do. The chef started to pull himself to his feet and Lyssa aimed right for him. "Yee-haw!" she shouted, and whirled the lasso across the room . . .

. . . and watched it miss the chef and loop around the sink faucet.

The chef started laughing as he climbed to his feet. Lyssa tried desperately to yank her lasso back, but it just ripped the faucet spigot off the sink entirely. The spigot clattered to the ground and water shot like a geyser out of the broken pipe.

Lyssa stumbled back a few steps, shocked. She'd never seen so much water in her life. It cascaded onto the soapy kitchen tile. Within seconds there were a few inches of water sloshing around her sneakers.

"Hold still, *bambina*," the chef said. He tried to take another step forward, but the water flooding the kitchen floor caused him to lose his balance again. Waving his arms wildly, trying to steady himself, the chef stumbled backward, colliding with the pot on the stove. Lyssa watched the giant pot of boiling water rock back and forth, then topple over.

"My soup!" the chef shouted. The pot fell to the floor, splashing loudly against the wet tile. Boiling water rolled out, becoming a frothy wave filled with pasta, seasonings, and *live fish*.

As the fish flopped through the boiling-hot waves,

Lyssa pulled herself on top of the counter. She couldn't believe what was happening. The water was nearly as high as the countertops and rising. She glanced over at the rest of the kitchen. The door was still held shut by the wooden spoon, which was now bulging and splintering like it might crack.

The chef finally managed to right himself and started forcing his way through the water—right toward Lyssa. With his bright-red face and one bulging eye, he looked like some kind of fairy-tale monster.

How had things gotten so out of control? She had no time to worry about it. She glanced around the counter, quickly spotting a cutting board even larger than she was. Without another thought, she grabbed it and leapt into the waves of pasta, water, and fish.

Even as Lyssa soared toward the water, she realized what she was doing was crazy. No. More than crazy. Impossible. Still, she kept the cutting board under her stomach, like a body board, clenched her eyes shut, and thought of her mother. She grunted as she hit the water and the cutting board jabbed into her stomach.

Then something *amazing* happened. The water began churning and moving, pushing Lyssa forward toward the kitchen door. She laughed out loud as bubbles popped around her and a few fish swam past, their glassy eyes staring up at her face. As she clutched the cutting board closer, she imagined her mother standing there in the kitchen, twirling around and around, until the water formed a wave that pushed her toward the door.

She'd been right—her mother *was* guiding her, wherever she was.

Lyssa let out a whoop as the waves forced the kitchen doors open—snapping the wooden spoon that barred them—and carried her out into the hallway. There the water subsided. Soaking wet, she scrambled to her feet.

Still a little giddy, she ducked into the dining room, where the cowgirls were still dancing and clapping on the tables, and dashed through to the front door. Once outside, she gulped in the crisp air.

She was just in time to see the bus door snap shut and hear the tires squeal as it pulled away from the curb and drove away.

CHAPTER TEN

Cannibals and Bubble Gum

"Wait!" Lyssa screamed, waving her hands in the air. She knew there was no point in trying to chase after it, but she sprinted for the Dumpster and retrieved Zip. The bus was picking up speed. She wasn't going to catch it on Zip, no matter how well she rode the scooter. For a moment, she flashed to her dream, to the feeling of her fingers slipping from the water-slicked bumper of the Talent Show van.

She looked anxiously around the parking lot, at the horses munching grass and rubbing their backs against the spindly trees outside the diner. The white horse Lyssa saw earlier came over and nudged her shoulder, whinnying in her ear.

Lyssa almost laughed out loud. Of course. She had a whole parking lot filled with transportation right in front of her. She'd ridden horses at the fair, hadn't she? At least, she'd sat on a horse while someone led it around a ring, and that was *practically* the same thing. She was probably an expert at horseback riding and she didn't even know it.

The diner door flew open and Lyssa whirled around. The giant chef was standing in the doorway. His apron and eye patch were soaking wet and covered in bits of pasta, tomato, and carrot, and he was holding half of his broken wooden spoon. A wriggling fish sat on top of his bald head.

"You!" he roared, striding toward her.

With one hand, Lyssa grabbed a handful of the horse's mane and heaved herself up. The horse had looked so small when she was on the ground, but now she realized how big the animal really was. Despite her long legs, she could barely swing over onto the horse's back. The chef was charging furiously toward her, waving his broken spoon over his head like a sword.

"Run!" she shouted once she was mounted, wrapping her arms around the horse's neck. But the horse didn't run—it shifted its weight and pawed the ground lazily.

The chef had nearly reached her. He was six feet away . . . then five . . .

"Come on!" Lyssa bellowed again, squeezing the horse's flanks. The horse trotted forward three feet, then stopped again.

The chef hurled the spoon. It spun through the air toward Lyssa but fell short — smacking right into the horse's flank.

The horse reared high into the air, kicking its front legs wildly. Lyssa threw her arms around its neck, losing her grip on Zip's handlebars. The scooter tumbled to the ground.

"No!" Lyssa shouted. But it was too late. The horse darted forward and Lyssa buried her face in its mane as they tore out of the parking lot and down the highway.

Wind stung Lyssa's cheeks and she bounced up and down on the horse's back as it galloped out of the parking lot. After just a few seconds, her legs were aching and her butt was sore. At least the highway was mostly empty of cars. Thank goodness for that, Lyssa thought, because she didn't know how to steer a horse. She tugged on its mane a little, but all that did was make it speed up. After a few minutes Lyssa's whole backside started to feel numb and her fingers hurt from gripping the horse's mane so tightly.

Once the diner was little more than a dot in the distance, Lyssa tried to get the horse to slow down. She pulled on its mane and shouted *STOP* into its ears and patted its rump with her hand. For a while the horse didn't seem to understand what Lyssa wanted it to do. It trotted backward, then ran around in a circle, then reared—up up up—on its hind legs. Lyssa gasped and threw her arms around its neck, and only then did it thud to the ground and start walking slowly forward.

For the first time in what felt like hours, Lyssa allowed herself to breathe. She was safe . . . for now.

She thought about everything that had happened in the last hour. One thing seemed bigger than everything else: Michael had called the cops. He thought she had been kidnapped. Guilt crept into Lyssa's chest. He must be really worried. Or scared. She thought of his face looking pale and frightened and wondered if she was doing the right thing.

She thought of Zip too, lying abandoned in the diner parking lot, and her stomach turned over. She couldn't go back for it yet. There was too much danger of being spotted by the chef or by someone who had seen the emergency broadcast. The best thing she could do, she decided, would be to ride a little ways and find a place to hide out until it got dark. Then she would return and retrieve Zip. Hopefully, she'd be able to find her way out of town. There was no sign of the bus, and Lyssa doubted she'd ever catch up to it.

She was starting to get the hang of sitting in such an awkward position. She tightened her arms around the horse's neck. She thought about the cowgirls back at the diner and smiled, thinking she must look like she was a cowgirl now, too. She even had the hat.

She adjusted the brim of her cowboy hat and had started humming under her breath, trying to think of an Athena song about riding horses, when the sound of a motor startled her. Lyssa glanced over her shoulder. A black shape was speeding down the highway toward her. At first Lyssa thought the little dot was just a bike, but then blue and red lights flickered to life and a siren started blaring. *Police.* Lyssa whipped back around and dug her heels into the horse's flanks.

"Go!" she shouted. The horse stopped walking completely and looked over its shoulder at Lyssa, as though it was expecting her to give it an apple. Lyssa fumbled in her backpack, looking for a granola bar. Since when did you have to bribe a horse to move?

Before she could retrieve a granola bar, the siren grew louder and a motorcycle whizzed up next to Lyssa. Her face was reflected in the officer's mirrored helmet.

The policewoman pulled off her helmet and climbed off the motorcycle. She fixed Lyssa with a hard look, raising one eyebrow.

"We got a call about a stolen horse," she said. "Do you know anything about that?"

"Um," Lyssa stalled, frantically racking her brain for some kind of excuse as the policewoman's eyes flicked deliberately down to the horse Lyssa was riding, which was currently pawing the ground unconcernedly. "Um . . . okay, there was this man, right? And he stole this lady's purse back at the diner. So I jumped on this horse and tore after him and—"

"Save it." The policewoman held up her hand. "Listen to me, little lady. I'm going to leave my motorcycle here and ride with you back to the station. Then you can give your parents a call and we'll all have a little chat, okay?"

The policewoman climbed onto the horse behind her. She nudged the horse with her knee and made a soft clicking noise and the horse started forward at exactly the right speed. Lyssa felt her face burn with embarrassment. The policewoman made it look so easy. This horse must've thought Lyssa was *crazy*.

It felt like they'd been riding for a long time when a low, orange-brick building came into view. There were bars on all the windows and a line of white-and-blue cop cars parked just outside. In front of the parking lot was a big white sign that read *Gopher Flats Police Station*.

Lyssa clenched her eyes shut—she didn't want to look

at the horrible building for any longer than she had to. Maybe the policewoman hadn't recognized her from the emergency broadcast yet, but it was only a matter of time. Once she got into the police station, someone was sure to figure out who she was with those photographs of her flashing across the television every few minutes.

She couldn't believe she'd stolen a horse and gotten all the way to Oregon only to be picked up by the cops. The memory of Michael's face yesterday—bright red and furious—popped into her head and she shivered. If he was that angry when she'd gone off on her own in their own neighborhood, how mad was he going to be when he got a call from a police station in another state? The thought made Lyssa feel like someone was playing jump rope inside her stomach.

The policewoman stopped the horse right in front of the station's bright blue doors and slid off easily.

"All right, young lady," she said, pulling Lyssa off the horse. "Let's go."

Lyssa followed the policewoman through the doors and into the station. The furniture inside was made of old, cracked plastic that might have been blue a long time ago but was now gray. The fluorescent overhead lights flickered on and off every few seconds. It felt like being inside a giant bug zapper lamp—and Lyssa was the moth.

The policewoman marched her into the front room and pointed to a chair next to an open office.

"I need to call a cowgirl about a horse," she explained. "You wait here. When I'm finished, you, me, and your parents are going to have a little powwow."

"Yes, ma'am," Lyssa muttered. She slid onto the empty chair, shivering at the feel of the cold plastic on her legs. But as soon the policewoman disappeared into her office, Lyssa sat up a little taller, searching the station for a way to escape.

Her heart sank. There were police officers everywhere. Two of them were engaged in an important-looking conversation around a water cooler near the front doors. Another officer sat behind a heavy metal desk just a few feet away. He was eating a sandwich and reading the paper. Pinned up behind him was a large black-and-white photo of an eleven-year-old girl with straight blond hair. *Her photo.* Lyssa swallowed. She hunched down in her seat and pulled her hat down low over her head. Maybe if no one got a good look at her face, they wouldn't know who she was.

One thing was clear: Lyssa needed her mom's help *now*. She squeezed her eyes shut, remembering how she had surfed on a cutting board in the diner's kitchen. She had no doubt that was part of her mom's magic. It had to be.

"Come on, Mom," she muttered under her breath. "It's me. I need you."

But all she heard was the distant crackle of the police scanner and the squeak of someone shifting in their chair. Lyssa eased her eyes back open.

"You'll never make it out of here," said a voice to her left.

Lyssa turned, tugging nervously at the brim of her cowboy hat.

A girl sat down in the chair next to hers. Her hair was two completely different colors—one side was bubblegum pink and the other was bleached blond. It covered her face like two thick curtains, parted in the middle, so that all Lyssa could see was her nose and the corners of her beady gray eyes. The girl rocked back and forth, causing the plastic seat to squeak beneath her weight. When she leaned forward, Lyssa read the spiky black word scrawled across her T-shirt: *Cannibal*.

Lyssa shifted her eyes back down to the backpack in her lap. Fear crawled up her legs and arms, leaving little goose bumps along her skin. She couldn't believe her mom was going to fail her now, leaving her here alone with some creeper. What could the girl be in here for? Was it possible that she was *actually* a cannibal? Maybe the police hauled her out of school for biting people. The thought made Lyssa want to crawl under her seat and hide, but she couldn't do that—she had to look tough or the girl would know she could be pushed around. Lyssa had heard that if you had something to trade with criminals, you could convince them not to hurt you. But all she had was a backpack filled with granola bars, and $13.

Lyssa glanced up again. Not only were the girl's beady gray eyes still looking right at Lyssa, but there were two white balls in her lap and someone had drawn eyes on them with a Sharpie. They were staring at Lyssa too. The girl's hands were bunched near her mouth and she chewed on the ends of her fingers. Lyssa caught sight of one of her fingernails: it was jagged, cracked, and bloody.

That gave her an idea—maybe she *did* have something she could trade with the cannibal girl. Yanking her backpack open, she started digging around inside, finally pulling out a pack of Band-Aids that had been hidden in the bottom of her backpack for months. The Band-Aids were clear and designed to look like tiny tattoos of hearts and swords.

"Here," Lyssa said, handing the box of Band-Aids to the cannibal. "For your fingers. They're pretty torn up."

The cannibal hesitated for a second, then leaned forward and took the Band-Aids. She gave Lyssa a shy smile.

"Thanks," she said, and then gestured to the plastic eyeballs in her lap. "Stress balls," she explained. "I'm supposed to squeeze them so I don't bite my nails. But it doesn't really work."

She wiggled her fingers in front of Lyssa. The nails were bitten down past the skin. Lyssa nodded, trying not to cringe.

"Is that why your T-shirt says *Cannibal*?" she asked.

"What?" The girl glanced down at her shirt, looking confused. "Oh. No, Cannibal is the name of my band. I'm a drummer."

"Oh," Lyssa said, perking up a bit. Maybe the girl was a criminal, but she couldn't be *too* terrible if she was a musician. At least she wasn't an *actual* cannibal. "So, um. What are you in here for?"

"In here?" The cannibal leaned back and laughed, shaking her head. Her stress balls nearly tumbled to the floor. "My dad's one of the detectives. I'm just waiting for him to get off work so he can drive me to soccer."

Lyssa let out her breath. "I was worried you were a . . ." She stopped herself from saying *criminal*. After all, Lyssa was the one who had stolen a horse and run away from home and lied to the ticket taker in Seattle.

The cannibal girl leaned forward in her chair, dropping her voice to a whisper. "See that gumball machine over there?"

She pointed to an old-fashioned gumball machine in the corner of the station. It was red and standing on a wrought-iron pedestal. All of the gumballs inside were bright blue.

"*Evidence,*" the cannibal hissed. "In a poison case. My dad told me all about it."

Lyssa didn't know whether to believe it, but she decided in that instant that she liked the cannibal girl. She reminded Lyssa of the performers back in the Texas Talent Show. There'd been this juggler—Marty—who'd had multicolored hair and little juggling balls just like this girl's.

Lyssa leaned forward in her seat, helping the girl unpeel the Band-Aids and wrap them around her bloody nails. When they were done, the cannibal girl wiggled her fingers in front of Lyssa. It looked like she had tiny heart and sword tattoos on all of her fingertips.

"This *is* better," she said. "Thanks."

"No problem," Lyssa said. She thought about how she was always sucking and biting on the tips of her hair. She knew how hard it was to break a bad habit. Maybe she could stick some Band-Aids on her braids? "I started chewing my hair once my mom got sick, but after she died . . ."

Lyssa stopped short. She'd just said that her mom died. She'd never said that out loud before. Not *ever*. It felt strange, like accidentally saying a curse word or telling a secret. She bit down on her tongue, hard, wishing she could swallow the words that just escaped from her lips. Instead, she hummed a little, hoping the music would wipe the memory of those words from her head.

Cannibal girl raised her eyebrows. "So, what're you in here for?" she asked. She hadn't seemed to notice Lyssa's slip.

"Oh," Lyssa said. "Um. Well, I robbed a bank. With a squirt gun."

The cannibal girl giggled. "Really?"

"Yeah. And it's not just any squirt gun, either. It's a CIA prototype, and now this station is holding it as evidence."

"Oh, okay. Bank robber." She nodded. "So you couldn't be that girl, right?" She pointed to the poster on the far wall and Lyssa felt her blood turn cold. Cannibal girl recognized her!

"That's not me," Lyssa said quickly. "No, you see, I dyed my hair to look like the runaway . . . what's her name, Liza? I knew the police were after me—I had robbed that bank after all—so I decided to take on her identity. See, I figured if the police thought I was just a runaway, they would go easy on me."

Lyssa felt her story becoming more and more real. She leaned forward in her seat, lowering her voice like she was sharing a secret.

"The truth is . . . I have the money buried in a coffee can out in the middle of the desert. If you help me escape, I can cut you in . . ."

The cannibal girl laughed again—so hard that she snorted a little.

"You're real funny, you know that?" cannibal girl said. Lyssa laughed along, shrugging, like she'd wanted to be funny all along.

"Okay, fine. I'll help you," the cannibal said. A glimmer of hope flickered to life inside Lyssa's chest. Escape. The cannibal girl was going to get her out of here.

"Really?" she asked.

The cannibal didn't answer. Instead, she picked up one of her stress balls and rose to her knees on her seat, taking careful aim.

Before Lyssa could say another word, the cannibal pelted her stress ball across the room, where it smacked the fat police officer sitting at his desk right on the nose.

The officer started to choke on his sandwich, spewing chunks of bread and meat across his desk. A tall, skinny officer near the entrance dropped his water glass and hauled the choking officer out of his seat, throwing two arms around the officer's chest and beginning the Heimlich maneuver.

The fat officer finally spit up his sandwich—and it landed with a splash in a policewoman's coffee mug, splattering brown liquid all over her blouse. When the officer she was speaking to pointed at her chest, an offended look spread across her face and she slapped him, hard, across the cheek.

Lyssa turned back to the cannibal girl, her eyes wide.

"What are you waiting for?" the cannibal asked. "Run!"

Lyssa didn't need to be told twice. Grabbing her backpack, she leapt to her feet, stumbling a little as she darted for the door. Chaos had erupted around her—all the officers were fighting and yelling and not one of them seemed to be paying attention to the door. As Lyssa ran, another stress ball came whizzing past her, smacking into the gumball machine. The gumball machine rocked on its pedestal, then crashed to the floor. The glass broke and bright blue gumballs rolled out into the room. The officers trampled over the gumballs until the sticky blue mess covered the floor.

One of the officers glanced up as Lyssa pushed the front door open.

"Wait!" he shouted, "Get back here!"

As the officer reached out to grab her, he tripped over his gum-covered shoes and tumbled to the floor. Lyssa leapt over his arm and out the door.

"Thanks," Lyssa shouted over her shoulder to the cannibal girl as she raced outside to freedom.

CHAPTER ELEVEN

Busking for Bacon

Lyssa burst into the parking lot and immediately let out a cry of pain. She had stubbed her big toe on a big metal something that was leaning against the curb. She hopped up and down in place, trying not to scream. When she looked down, her mouth fell open.

Her scooter.

Bright yellow paint winked in the sun, and wind ruffled the remaining pom-pom so that it waved. A soaring feeling filled Lyssa's chest—like dozens of dizzily spinning kites sweeping through her insides. She pulled her scooter upright—and that's when she noticed a little tag hanging from the handlebars.

Lyssa Lee, the tag read. *Evidence.*

Evidence? Lyssa's throat got dry. The policewoman must've gone back to the diner and found her scooter . . .

Lyssa hesitated. Could she possibly hope to outrun the police? The cops knew who she was. If she went back into the station, the police would call Michael and she would go home. The Missing Person posters could come down and no one would be worried anymore. Lyssa's home in Austin would be torn down—but at least she wouldn't feel so guilty about what she was doing to Michael.

Inside, someone shouted. Lyssa gripped her scooter handlebars tighter. She couldn't give up—not when she'd come so far!

She climbed onto Zip. Time to go.

Two roads branched away from the police station: a narrow, twisty one that led past a field full of tall grass and a road paved in cement headed toward the taller buildings in the distance. Lyssa aimed her scooter down the paved road and kicked off, hoping to find a bus or a train station once she got farther into the city. As she coasted down a hill, she realized Zip's hand brake was broken. The hand brake made a high-pitched squeaking noise every time she touched it. It almost sounded like Zip was crying. Lyssa squeezed the brake three times and still couldn't get it to slow down.

Up ahead, she saw a big intersection: cars whizzed by, a blur of silver, blue, and red paint.

And Lyssa was racing right into their path.

She planted a foot on the ground, but she was going too fast to stop. One of her shoelaces got caught in a wheel and her scooter whirled out of control, spinning around and around like a giant blue top. Lyssa spun out into the street, cars honking as she wove in between bumpers and tires.

She careened through the traffic, bumped up onto the sidewalk, and landed, miraculously, in a heap on the other side of the road. Picking herself up, she tentatively rotated her wrists and ankles, checking for any breaks. Every inch of her skin felt a little bit bruised or bumped, but the only mark Lyssa found was a tiny cut running along her elbow.

"Thanks, Mom," Lyssa whispered. As she sat up, she bumped Zip and her scooter's hand brake squeaked. "Thank you too, Zip," she added.

Her heart still racing, Lyssa pulled her shoelace out of the scooter wheel and wove it around her handlebars, tying her hand brake back into place. She tried the brake again. This time it didn't squeak but gave off a low groan, like Zip was returning her thanks.

"You're welcome," Lyssa said, patting Zip's handlebars. That should hold . . . for a little while.

She lay back in the grass, taking a moment to catch her breath. She pulled her journal out of her backpack.

Dear Penn, she wrote.

I'm officially an outlaw. The cops are after me and I have nowhere to turn. Remember when we ate all those apples from the trees in Mr. Howard's yard? Remember how, when he found out, he chased us around the block and threatened to tell our parents? Well, this is like that. Only a million times worse.

Wish you were here to come up with one of your brilliant ideas.

Sighing, Lyssa closed the journal and shoved it back into her bag, too tired to finish. She'd been running ever since the diner. At the thought of food, her stomach rumbled painfully, like it was warning her a storm was coming. She'd eaten that peanut butter and jelly sandwich and big bowl of soup a long time ago. She only had $13 left in her backpack—barely enough money for dinner, let alone a ticket to Austin.

She stood up and pulled Zip upright, tightening and loosening her fingers around the handlebars.

"What are we going to do, Zip?" she said out loud. Glancing at the sun, she realized it must be at least four o'clock. "How are we going to eat?"

Zip just sat in smug silence. Obviously Zip wouldn't be as worried about the food situation as Lyssa was.

"Lucky," she muttered. Without any real plan she continued along the street, suddenly feeling very weak as she pushed Zip along.

Just a few blocks ahead, Lyssa saw yellow-striped tents and whitewashed stands silhouetted in the late-afternoon sun. Yellow—that was a good sign. Bales of hay stood near the stands, covered in red-and-white-checked tablecloths. When the wind blew, the air smelled sweet: like apple cider and gingersnap cookies. Lyssa's mouth watered. The stands reminded her of the huge farmers' markets in Austin where she and her mom used to buy their fruit and vegetables every Sunday.

The markets in Austin always had free samples to give away. Maybe there were some broken bits of gingersnap cookie or tiny cups of apple cider sitting on those red-and-white-checked tables?

Lyssa climbed off her scooter and wheeled it toward the market. A sign hanging on one of the stands read *Gopher Flats Farmers' Market*. Lyssa reached for her braid and frowned—she was still in Gopher Flats? She'd been going so fast on Zip she was sure she'd passed through four or five cities by now.

There were people *everywhere*. A man wearing a green knit stocking cap stood over a huge metal pot ladling out apple cider to a crowd. Next to him was an upturned crate, which a woman with dreadlocks was piling high with fruit and jars of honey. Across from them were several other stands filled with people selling homemade scarves, clay coffee mugs, and hunks of blue, stinky cheese. A tall woman with brown hair was bending over a cheese stand. Lyssa's heart skipped a beat—she looked just like Athena! But then the woman turned around and Lyssa's heart sank. This woman's face was lined and her hair was streaked with gray. She was much too old to be Athena.

The air around the market was thick with the smell of fresh herbs, cinnamon-flecked cider, and the honey-sweet scent of ripe apples. A line of people snaked around every stand, everyone carrying reusable bags heavy with their purchases. But Lyssa didn't see any free samples anywhere.

She found a vacant patch of dry grass and propped Zip against a tree, watching the people come and go. There was a man with a guitar on the other side of the marketplace, and for a moment Lyssa's spirits lifted. She thought he might sing, but he began to pack up his guitar and she realized she must've missed his show. Before he put the guitar back into the case, he pulled out a thick wad of green bills and slowly counted them.

Lyssa watched him, transfixed. He had made all of that just by playing?

She thought of Demo and how he told her he performed

on the streets in Seattle for money. Lyssa could try that. She still had the cowboy hat; she could set it in front of her and sing for the people walking past. Someone would toss in a dollar or two. She even had her mom's maracas in her backpack.

But a nagging thought pulled at the corner of her brain. Her stage fright. She tried to push the thought away, but it stayed, like a spider in the corner of the room that you tried to pretend wasn't there because you didn't have a shoe to smoosh it.

Maybe, she thought, I've never been able to sing in front of other people before because I wasn't ever motivated enough. She was hungry and she needed a bus ticket to Austin! If that wasn't motivation, she didn't know what was.

Lyssa reached into her backpack and wrapped her fingers around her mom's maracas.

She hesitated. Seconds ago the market had looked small and friendly, but now it seemed like the people had multiplied. And everyone was so tall. They towered over Lyssa like giant, moving trees—all dressed in flannel.

Lyssa swallowed and pulled one of the maracas out of her bag. No one paid any attention to her, and someone even stepped on her toes. She winced. Maybe if she was good enough, they'd all stop moving and listen?

She dropped her cowboy hat onto the ground in front of her. Someone bumped into her and the maraca she was holding went flying. She had to drop down to her knees and crawl between a woman's legs to retrieve it. Standing back up, she wiped the dirt off her jeans and tried to remember the words to her favorite Athena song.

But when she opened her mouth to sing, her throat felt dry and hot. Her head grew hot-air-balloon light. Lyssa closed her lips, frustration bubbling up inside her. She clenched her eyes shut, trying to picture her mom dancing around on the Talent Show stage or Athena belting out the lyrics to "Let's Hear It for the Cowgirls" that night almost a year ago.

Lyssa had *always* wanted to be a singer. This was her chance—so why couldn't she find her voice?

When she opened her eyes again, she had to blink through a film of tears to see an unexpected sight: a fat, pink pig squatting on the dry grass in front of her. The pig snorted, then pawed at the dirt with its hoof.

"What are you looking at?" Lyssa asked.

One of the pig's little pink ears twitched. It looked thoroughly unimpressed with her, and why wouldn't it? She couldn't even sing to a tiny crowd of people at a farmers' market.

"Mabel!" a shrill voice shouted from behind her. Lyssa

whirled around. Charging toward her was the strangest-looking woman she had ever seen in her life.

She was very thin and very tall, almost all arms and legs. Her hair was gray and wispy, like it had been fashioned from dandelion seeds and dental floss, and she wore thick glasses that made her eyes look small as ladybugs. Lyssa wondered if the lenses had been put in backward.

The woman stormed past Lyssa and bent down, giving her pig a rap on the head. "I told you not to wander off like that," she said. Then she spun around to Lyssa, putting one hand on her hips. She smelled strongly of peaches—almost as though she'd bathed in their juice. The smell made Lyssa's mouth water.

"You trying to steal my pig, girl?" The woman shifted her eyes to Lyssa's cowboy hat and glared at it suspiciously, as though she always knew girls with cowboy hats weren't to be trusted.

"What?" Lyssa said, startled. "I mean, no, ma'am. Your peach—I mean your pig—wandered over here. I . . . I was just about to look around for its owner."

Lyssa swallowed. The lie tasted bitter on her tongue. But if the woman thought Lyssa was going to steal her pig, she might call the police. Then Lyssa would be right back where she started.

The woman sniffed and turned around once again

toward the pig. She wobbled a bit when she walked, like a baby giraffe that wasn't quite used to her legs.

"Well, what're you waiting for, Mabel?" the woman said. "Get back to the truck."

Lyssa couldn't be sure, but she thought the pig looked a little embarrassed as it turned to head back to the truck, its curly pink tail tucked between its legs. The strange woman gave Lyssa one last suspicious look, then started to lumber away. She had a strange gait, almost like her knees didn't bend. But Lyssa couldn't get a good look at the woman's legs because she wore a baggy dress that was at least four sizes too big and so long it dragged on the ground behind her. The dress was tie-dyed yellow, orange, and blue. As Lyssa watched, the woman dug into her pockets and produced the largest, juiciest-looking peach Lyssa had ever seen. Lyssa's stomach gave another thunderous rumble.

"Do you work here?" Lyssa took hold of Zip and trailed behind the woman and her pig but kept her eyes locked on the peach. Maybe, just maybe, she could convince the woman to give her a bite . . .

"Do *I* work here?" The strange woman laughed, as if Lyssa had just asked her if the sky was blue or if snow was cold. She took a huge bite of peach and wiped the juice off her chin with her forearm. "I'm Sir See of Sir See's Pigs and Peaches. *Surely* you've heard of me?"

Lyssa had never heard a word about Sir See or her pigs and peaches, but she smiled politely and nodded anyway. Since there were *peaches*—plural—she might even get a whole one to herself.

"Oh, *you're* the famous Sir See? Wow. It's such an honor to meet you."

The woman narrowed her little bug eyes, leaving Lyssa with the feeling that the woman didn't believe a single word she said.

"We're known across the country," she declared. She stopped in front of a red pickup that was large as a whale and so rusted that Lyssa wondered if it still ran. Painted across the side of the truck were the words *Circe's Pigs and Peaches*.

"People come from all over the Northwest to buy my peaches and pork," Circe continued.

The truck's flatbed was filled with snorting pigs and fragrant crates of peaches. Lyssa's eyes trailed over them, and she tried to keep her mouth from watering. There were even a few peach crates stacked up in front of the flatbed, like stairs.

Circe looked down at Mabel and pointed at the flatbed. Wiggling her curly tail, Mabel trotted up the peach crates and into the trunk with the others. Lyssa wanted to climb into that truck and roll around in those peaches, just like the pigs were doing.

"What're you doing out here on your own, anyway?" Circe asked. She patted one of the pigs on the head, then tossed it a ripe, pink peach. "Aren't your parents here with you?"

"Oh—no." Lyssa chewed on her lower lip, thinking fast. Something about Circe was . . . odd. She had a shifty, strange quality, like someone trying to keep a secret. Lyssa had to be careful. She couldn't risk another grown-up turning her in.

But Circe *did* have a truck. And food. Maybe her next farmers' market was down south?

"See, this awful thing happened," Lyssa started. "I was on a school trip and I missed the bus. I need to get back down to . . . er . . . Idaho, but I don't have any money or a phone . . ."

Circe raised one eyebrow and her hair shifted slightly, like it wasn't quite attached to her head.

"School trip, huh? How come you missed the bus?"

"It's a funny story, actually," Lyssa said. She tightened her grip around the scooter's handlebars, and the rubber squeaked a little. She could almost feel Zip warning her to keep her story simple. "My mom owns an organic potato farm back in Illinois . . ."

"I thought you said Idaho?"

"Right, I did say Idaho. See, my mom's farm is in

Illinois, but we just moved to Idaho and she's been researching long-distance gardening methods. I came over here to find out if anyone knew anything about that and before I knew it, the bus had taken off."

Lyssa made her hand swoop through the air, as though to show just how quickly the bus had driven away without her. For a moment there was complete silence. Circe pushed her glasses farther up her nose and shook her head.

"I don't believe a word of that story," she announced.

For a second Lyssa didn't know what to say. *Everyone* believed her. Lyssa had once convinced the stage manager at the Texas Talent Show that *ghosts* were eating sandwiches backstage so that she wouldn't get in trouble for smearing jelly on all the scenery. Lyssa hadn't actually thought that story was so far-fetched. Things were always creaking, and there were always shadows flitting across the walls, even when no one was moving. For a while she'd been convinced there were ghosts backstage, until she'd realized it was only mice.

Circe turned back to the pickup and folded up the latch, closing her pigs and peaches up into the trunk. Lyssa took a quick step backward. She didn't know whether to hold still or start running. Was Circe going to call the police? Lyssa felt like there was ice water running beneath her skin.

But Circe just turned around, narrowing her eyes as she

scanned the now-abandoned farmers' market. Once she was satisfied it was all clear, she glanced down at Lyssa.

"Hold on to my hair for a moment, will you?"

Before Lyssa could respond, Circe yanked the wispy gray hair right off her head and dropped it into Lyssa's hands. Beneath the wig were bright red curls that had been flattened over her ears.

Lyssa could only stare. Circe winked, then leaned over to start gathering up the rest of her peach crates. As she hoisted up the hem of her muumuu, something silver and metallic sparkled where her legs should've been. Stilts.

Picking up a peach crate, Circe looked up at Lyssa, her bright eyes twinkling beneath her too-big glasses.

"You can keep a secret, can't you?" she asked.

CHAPTER TWELVE

Molto Bene!

Lyssa's mouth dropped so far open she could've caught bugs inside it. Luckily, Circe took this to mean that Lyssa could, in fact, be trusted with her secret. She kicked off her stilts and, as she stood in the grass, Lyssa was surprised to see that the strange girl was actually a few inches shorter than she was.

Circe pulled her unruly red hair back into two pigtails. A few stray curls popped out from the sides of her head, reminding Lyssa of a sweater with loose threads. Though Circe was shorter than Lyssa, there was something about the way Circe held her shoulders back and her chin up that made her seem very tall.

"So . . . you aren't really a grown-up?" Lyssa said dumbly. Circe hitched up the hem of her tie-dyed dress, revealing two mismatched flip-flops: one green and one orange. She tossed her stilts into the back of the truck and one of the pigs squealed.

"Nope. I'm eleven and three-quarters," Circe said. She finished packing up the rest of her peach crates and set those inside the truck, too. "I pretend I'm an old lady so I can run my farm in peace. You wouldn't believe how quickly people stick their noses into your business when you're a kid."

"I'd believe it," Lyssa said, thinking of how much trouble she was having just trying to get to Austin.

Circe plucked a leaf of grass out of the ground and wedged it in the corner of her mouth. She leaned against the side of her truck and looked Lyssa over.

"My farm is across the border, in Idaho," Circe explained, rolling the piece of grass over her tongue. "Where are you *really* headed? I might be able to give you a ride part of the way."

"I'm going to Texas," Lyssa said. Circe had trusted Lyssa with her secret, so Lyssa figured she could trust Circe too. Quickly, she explained about her mom and the Talent Show and how she needed to get to Texas in just *three* days.

"That's not a lot of time," Circe agreed. She pursed her

lips. "Well, I can't take you all the way to Texas, but Idaho is on the way. Maybe you can get a bus from there?"

Lyssa couldn't help thinking of the measly $13 she had left in her backpack. How was she going to find enough money for a bus ticket? Still, a ride to Idaho was better than nothing. Maybe she could hitch a ride with someone else once she got there.

"It's a deal," she said. "Thank you!"

"No problem," Circe said. She spit out the piece of grass and hoisted herself into the truck with just one arm.

The truck was old, and it clattered down the road so badly that Lyssa had to hold on to her seat with both hands to keep from bouncing around the cab like a Mexican jumping bean. Lyssa was terrified driving with a kid her own age, but she tried to be on her best behavior. She kept her hands curled around her seat and tried to ignore the braids hanging on either side of her face, taunting her. She would not chew on her hair. She would *not*.

"Do you even have a driver's license?" she asked Circe.

"Oh, yeah," Circe answered, shrugging. "Had one for years. Besides, it's just like steering a tractor. I've been doing that since I was eight."

Lyssa swallowed. She hadn't seen many tractors in the city, but her mom had taken her pumpkin picking out in the middle of Texas one year, and there had been tractors there. Lyssa remembered how slow they moved—like old metal animals looking for a place to take a nap. Circe's truck might be old, but it was *not* slow, and it whipped around the curves in the tiny road so quick that Lyssa had to focus on the dashboard to keep from feeling woozy. Lyssa grabbed for her seat belt, but when she tried to buckle it in, she realized that the buckle was broken clean off. She tied the two ends of the seat belt together in a thick knot.

Trying to take her mind off the terrifying ride, Lyssa pulled out her journal.

Dear Penn, she wrote. She paused, chewing on the end of the pencil. Penn wouldn't like her riding around in a car driven by an eleven-year-old. Penn might be fearless when it came to circusy stuff—like walking across a tightrope or hanging off a trapeze—but she was super-careful about putting herself in other kinds of danger. If Penn knew Lyssa was strapped into an old broken-down truck going eighty miles an hour, she'd be furious.

I found a friend—Lyssa hesitated as she wrote the word *friend.* Could she start calling Circe her friend yet?— *And I'm back on track to Texas. You wouldn't believe how beautiful it is out here, Penn. Remember when we'd climb all the way to the top of the big hill in Mr. Tanaka's backyard and look out over the whole neighborhood? It's like that out here but a zillion times bigger. I'll make sure to take tons of mental pictures for you. Lyssa.*

Lyssa sighed, sticking her journal back into her backpack. She'd need to find someplace to mail all these letters. Otherwise, she'd get to Texas before they did.

Circe and Lyssa drove down a narrow road that wound its way between steep red cliffs. The river and trees below them looked small and far away. Lyssa felt like the whole road had been lifted on giant stilts. The pigs in back squealed every time they hit a bump.

"I always take the back roads," Circe explained. "It's less likely the cops will pull me over that way. And I don't have to worry about traffic."

Circe turned the volume knob on the truck radio and Italian opera screeched out of its staticky speakers. Lyssa perked up. She wasn't a huge fan of opera, but any music was better than no music at all. Circe tried to sing along, but, as far as Lyssa could tell, the only Italian she knew was food related.

"*Molto bene!*" she belted out in a slightly off-key voice. "Fettuccini!"

Lyssa smiled and hummed along with her. Riding in a car with Circe might be scary, but at least it wasn't boring. Circe drove with one foot hanging out of the driver's-side window and the other balanced on the wheel, helping her steer while she tried to brush her red curls off her face. There was a brick propped against the gas pedal since Circe's legs weren't quite long enough to reach it.

"Pepperoni pizza!" Circe sang.

"You aren't even trying," Lyssa said, laughing.

"I think I'm too hungry." Circe leaned over Lyssa's lap and yanked open the glove compartment, pulling out a gooey peanut butter and jelly sandwich. She took a huge bite, then held the sandwich out to Lyssa, leaking a glob of jelly onto her leg.

"Wam thum?"

Lyssa reached for the sandwich gratefully and chomped into it. Mmmm. Peanut butter.

"Thith iv tho good," Lyssa said, swallowing. "What's in here?"

"Secret peanut butter and jelly recipe," Circe said, winking. Lyssa passed the sandwich back. "Want to hear it?"

"Yes!" Lyssa exclaimed. "I love to bake and cook. My mom and I . . ." She trailed off and then coughed to clear the lump that had swelled momentarily in her throat. "Well, anyway. What is it?"

Circe told her the recipe, and she whipped her notebook out and started jotting it down.

Circe took another big bite of her sandwich, steering

the truck with her knees while she ate. There was a big glob of peanut butter smudged across her nose, and Lyssa watched Circe try to lick the peanut butter off with her tongue.

Every time Michael brushed his teeth, he somehow got a glob of toothpaste on the tip of his long nose—just like that. It'd been Lyssa's mom's job to get the toothpaste off before he left for work. After Ana had . . . after, Lyssa had made sure to hand Michael a washcloth every morning at breakfast.

Lyssa's throat felt thick, like she'd just swallowed a rock. Was Michael walking around with toothpaste on his nose right now? Had anyone told him it was there?

Lyssa sighed and leaned back against her seat, pushing the thoughts of Michael out of her head. She pulled her backpack onto her lap and started digging around inside, looking for another granola bar. The peanut butter sandwich had barely taken the edge off her hunger. Her stomach still grumbled painfully, but when she pulled the sandwich bag of granola bars out of her backpack, she saw that they'd been smooshed so badly that they were barely more than a powder of crumbs. Frowning, Lyssa opened the bag and tried to dump the rest of the granola into her mouth.

Circe was licking the final bits of peanut butter and

jelly off her fingertips. She used an elbow to steer the truck over to a wide-open field dotted with red and white daisies, then yanked up on the emergency brake. The truck shuddered to a stop.

"This is the most famous patch of soil in Oregon," Circe said. "We're at the very far edge of the Hood River Valley. You heard of it?"

Lyssa barely heard her. At the bottom of her bag, she felt grainy piles of seeds.

"Oh, no." Lyssa shifted through the other items in her backpack until she found her mom's seed pack maracas. One of the packets had ripped open and there were tomato seeds everywhere.

A lump formed in the back of Lyssa's throat and she swallowed, hard. Her mom used to say seeds were magical: they contained all the beauty and mystery of life in a tiny little package. That's why she and Lyssa liked to use them to make musical instruments. How could Lyssa have just shoved the seed packet maracas in her backpack, where they could get torn up and ruined?

"Hey, are you listening?" Circe asked. She had one hand on the door, like she was about to push it open. "If you're going to ride in my truck, you have to help me with my pigs. They need to graze in this field."

"I . . . I need a second," Lyssa said. She started gathering up the seeds and trying to pour them back into the ripped seed packet. Maybe if she could find some tape . . .

"Hey, what is that?" Circe asked. She reached for the seed packet, but Lyssa held on to it tightly.

"Wait," she started to say, but Circe grabbed the other side of the seed packet and pulled.

Rip!

The seeds were picked up by a gust of wind and flew everywhere—landing between the truck seats and on the dirt road where the truck was parked. The pigs squealed as Circe toppled backward, then somersaulted into the field. Her tie-dyed muumuu fluttered out around her ankles and one orange flip-flop flew right off into the mud.

Lyssa scrambled out of the truck after Circe, but she was too late. All the seeds were already lost in the soil.

"Why'd you do that?" Lyssa could barely keep herself from shouting.

"Relax." Circe pushed herself back up to her feet. "Seeds are supposed to be scattered. You know that, right?"

Circe brushed as much of the mud and grass off her muumuu as she could. Then she collected her lost flip-flop, which had landed right in the middle of a little green pond that was mostly mud and rocks. She walked around to the back of the truck, unlatching the gate to let her pigs out.

Lyssa looked down at her own feet, trying to quell feelings of anger. She and Penn had made the maracas for her mom's birthday one year, as a surprise. They'd been her mom's favorite instruments—and now one of them was ruined. But Circe hadn't known; it wasn't her fault.

There were a few of her seeds lying in the dirt between the flowers and grass and Lyssa leaned over to pick them up, thinking she could tuck them into her pocket and keep a few of her mom's seeds with her.

But as she reached down to pick the seeds up, the strangest thing happened—they burrowed into the dirt like little worms, disappearing completely.

Lyssa straightened up, startled. The ground below her started to rumble. She scanned the field anxiously.

The next second, something green poked up out of the dirt, first timidly—like a rabbit checking to see if a snake was nearby—then faster and faster. Lyssa jumped back as the green shoot grew. Leaves the size of umbrellas unfolded as the shoot soared higher. Something brushed against Lyssa's back and she screamed, whirling around.

"What's happening?" Circe shouted. She was helping her pigs out of the back of the truck, but the ground was trembling so fiercely she nearly dropped the one she was holding. Lyssa shook her head. *She* definitely didn't know. There was an identical green shoot behind her, and another two feet away, and another right in the middle of the dirt road. Lyssa bit back another scream as something began to grow on the shoot nearest her—something that looked like a tiny red button.

The red button expanded like a balloon filling with air until it was the size of a baseball, then a coconut. Hesitantly, Lyssa reached out a finger and touched it. It wiggled on its leaf-covered branch before it broke free, plopping onto the ground and bursting open— spraying red juice all over her face and clothes.

She reached her tongue out to her cheek to get a taste. She could hardly believe it. All of a sudden, she started laughing.

"Tomatoes!" she yelled to Circe. "They're giant tomatoes!"

Lyssa felt giddy. She thought of her mom's garden back home, filled with sunflowers the size of umbrellas. Her mom could coax a plant into growing in any soil. Ana Lee had grown tomatoes in mailboxes and wound giant ivy around her window frames.

And now, here, enormous tomato vines were growing straight up into the air. More and more tomatoes sprouted along the vines and Lyssa watched them in awe, and knew she was getting closer to reaching her mother.

"I *told* you this soil was special," Circe shouted over

the sound of oinking pigs. "Don't just stand there. Grab a crate and start picking."

Lyssa didn't bother correcting Circe. Circe lifted the last pig out of her truck. Already, nearly every inch of her muu-muu was splattered with mud. Lyssa gave Circe a thumbs-up and started picking the giant tomatoes from the vines.

When she'd gathered all the tomatoes she could reach, Lyssa climbed back in the truck and started to eat while Circe guided her now-muddy pigs back to the flatbed. Raw tomatoes were one of Lyssa's very favorite things. Lyssa and Ana used to gather them just as they got ripe and eat them with crackers and cheese, right then and there—sitting in the grass under the shade of their dogwood tree.

These tomatoes were big and juicy and tasted, very faintly, of bacon. They had to be the best tomatoes Lyssa had ever eaten, even better than the ones from her mom's garden.

She ate until her stomach was full and her lips were stained red from tomato juice. The leftover tomatoes were still in crates piled high on the floor of the truck and wedged between the two front seats.

Circe climbed up into the truck and pulled the door shut. She looked just as muddy as her pigs—and just as happy. Lyssa wondered if Circe liked to roll around in the mud just as much as they did.

"All right," Circe said. "Off we go."

As they pulled away from the magic Oregon field, Lyssa felt happier than she had in weeks. It was working. The closer she got to Texas, the more the impossible began to occur. It was like her mom was watching her, sharing just enough magic to let Lyssa know she was headed the right way.

More tomatoes rained down on them, covering the truck's windshield with a layer of red juice so thick that Circe had to turn on the wipers just so they could see the road.

CHAPTER THIRTEEN

I Am Here

While they drove, Lyssa and Circe changed out of their muddy, tomato-covered clothes and into the two spare muumuus Circe kept folded in her glove compartment. Lyssa's muumuu was blue with giant purple flowers. It smelled strongly of bacon. After Lyssa changed, she held the steering wheel while Circe pulled her own clean muumuu on. Thank goodness there were no other cars on the road: Lyssa wasn't too great at steering and the truck rocked and swerved across the road. Circe seemed to think it was hilarious.

"See if you can hit that fence post," she shouted, pointing to the rickety white fence on the side of the road. Lyssa shook her head, trying to pull the truck back into the right lane. Michael had let her steer his tiny Prius around an empty parking lot, once. He'd told her over and over again how careful you had to be with cars.

"You're no fun," Circe pouted, taking the steering wheel back from Lyssa.

Lyssa was noticing that Circe needed everything in her life to be fun. Over the next hour, she told Lyssa all about how she made chores fun by trying to do them while standing on her hands and how she made meals fun by sprinkling marshmallows and chocolate chips over everything she ate. She even tried to sleep hanging upside down from a bunk bed once—so her dreams wouldn't get too boring. Of course, she explained, that stopped being fun when she fell off her bunk bed and woke up with a big bump on her forehead.

It sounded like Circe was always having adventures. But so far, Lyssa observed, she hadn't mentioned any family or friends.

"What happened to your parents?" Lyssa asked.

"They kicked the bucket," Circe said. She glanced up at the rearview mirror and rubbed a smudge of dirt off her forehead. For a second Lyssa was quiet. She was sure she'd heard Circe wrong.

"What did you say?"

"They died," Circe explained. "You know, coffins, graveyard?"

Lyssa couldn't react immediately. She opened and closed her mouth, wordlessly. "I'm sorry," she said finally. Circe was acting like she was talking about an old pet or a grandparent she hadn't known very well—not her own parents.

"Circle of life, right?" Circe said, shrugging. And then, abruptly: "Does that sign say Boise?"

Lyssa glanced at the green sign by the side of the road. "Um, yeah."

"Good." Circe pulled into the right lane. "I need to make some stops."

Circe didn't say another word about her parents as they pulled off the highway and on to a street leading through the city. Lyssa followed her lead and stared out the window in silence.

The buildings in Boise were squat and unimpressive compared to the mountains towering over them. Wide, green parks were tucked between the buildings. It felt like being in the filling part of a taco. If Lyssa narrowed her eyes, the colors blurred together and the buildings became ground beef, the trees lettuce, and the mountains surrounding them on two sides were brown taco shells. It actually made her a little queasy after all those tomatoes.

Circe pulled up next to a huge gray warehouse and yanked on the emergency brake. The truck made an angry grinding sound and skidded to a stop. The smell of burning rubber rose from the tires. Circe tucked her red hair back under the wispy gray wig and shoved the giant glasses onto her nose.

"Welcome to Costume City," Circe said. "Hand me my stilts, okay? And remember to call me Aunt Mabel while we're in public."

Lyssa said, "Aunt Mabel, your wig's falling off."

"Uh-oh." Circe checked herself in the mirror, tucking a curl back under the wig. "Thanks."

It was only August, but walking into the costume shop felt like walking into the world's largest Halloween party. The shop was four stories high and at least one city block long. Plastic skeletons and zombies hung from the ceiling, and brightly colored costumes, wigs, and rubber masks crowded every surface. There were smoke machines hidden beneath the stairs, which filled the entire store with billowing gray clouds of fog. Over the loudspeaker Lyssa heard the sound of creaking stairs, screaming women, and distant thunder.

"Let's start with the makeup and props," Circe said, grabbing a shopping cart. "I need a stronger foundation to hide my freckles. And I was thinking about buying a cast—you know, so it looks like I broke my arm? Could come in handy."

Lyssa decided not to ask how a fake broken arm could come in handy. Instead, she followed as Circe teetered around the supply shop, darting around men dressed like superheroes and two kids engaged in a duel with huge plastic swords. Circe filled her shopping cart, all the while chattering about fake mustaches and the many uses of denture glue. Lyssa was only half listening. There were so many cool things in this shop. She picked up a bright blue wig and sparkly, fingerless gloves—just like the ones Athena wore on stage.

Remembering the measly $13 in her backpack, Lyssa put both items away. She needed to save her money in case of an emergency.

Circe, however, raced around the store, shoving things into her cart without looking to see what they were. The wheels on her cart creaked as she ran and, while coming around a corner, Lyssa's foot caught the hem of Circe's muumuu. Circe stumbled forward, crashing into a rack of plastic noses in all different shapes and sizes and knocking them to the ground with a clatter. Noses rolled everywhere.

A small crowd of people gathered around. They were the strangest-looking people: men with tails poking out from under their business suits and women waddling around in giant, blue flippers. There was even a person— Lyssa couldn't tell if it was a man or a woman—wearing a furry mask that obscured their features. Then again, maybe it wasn't a mask. The person could've just been really hairy.

They all eyed Lyssa and Circe suspiciously, as if *they* were the strange ones.

"My aunt Mabel has polio," Lyssa blurted out, helping hoist Circe back onto her stilts. "She has trouble with her legs."

Circe gave everyone a shaky smile and, one by one, the people scurried off.

"You're clumsier than a bull on a pair of pointe shoes," Circe said. Then she smiled, so Lyssa knew she wasn't mad. "But where'd you learn to fib like that? Awesome."

Lyssa shrugged. She and her mom used to make up identities all the time. When a waitress in some diner asked what her name was, her mom would say it was Nadya and that they were lion tamers traveling with the Russian circus. Or maybe they'd be Gretel and Gertrude, German sisters searching the states for their father, a cowboy from Dallas. It became a game—who could make up a crazier story and get someone to believe it.

Of course, Michael didn't like it when Lyssa lied—he told her that instead of saying her lies out loud, she should write them down in a notebook as stories. Lyssa thought of the journal where she'd been writing to Penn. It had been kind of fun to write her stories down. Maybe Michael had a point.

Circe paid for her things and led Lyssa back out to the truck. Lyssa thought they were going to get back on the highway, but instead Circe circled the store and turned down a narrow alley that led to a large, empty parking lot.

"I have one last thing to pick up," Circe explained.

In the shadows at the edge of the parking lot there was a whitewashed wooden stand with the words FREE OM FIR WO KS written across the top in red block letters. Paint hung from the wood in curly strips, reminding Lyssa of overgrown fingernails. As they pulled up in front of the stand, Lyssa could have sworn she saw something moving in the shadows.

"What are you buying *here*?" Lyssa asked. She had to stifle a yawn. It was getting late, and the last thing she wanted to do was continue shopping.

"Mauve lipstick." Circe pulled up on the emergency brake and the truck groaned to a stop. "Tiresias has the best."

"Tiresias?"

"And maybe we can pick up some cherries, too. They sell the sweetest cherries in Idaho," Circe said. Sure enough, a large wicker basket filled with cherries sat next to a display of Roman candles and sparklers. Compared to the run-down stand, the fruit looked unnaturally red and ripe. The basket held a piece of notebook paper that read *Back in Five*.

"Good, they're gone," Circe said, throwing open her truck door. "The owners can be a drag. Tiresias? You here?"

"That you, baby girl?"

The voice came from the other side of the stand and it was deep and rough, like gravel on sandpaper. Lyssa followed Circe around back.

Sitting on a stool in front of a rickety little table was a large, thickly muscled man wearing a lacy purple dress. There were three silk scarves knotted around his neck, each a different, flowery pattern. He was completely bald, and there was another scarf knotted just behind his ears in a floppy bow. A white–and-blue china bowl filled with cherries sat on the table in front of him. Before Circe had even reached him, Tiresias pulled a tube of lipstick out of his pocket and set it down on the table. Circe put a thin pile of bills onto the table next to it.

"This is Ms. Tiresias," Circe said, slipping the lipstick into her pocket.

"Ms.?" Lyssa repeated. She didn't think she'd ever seen such a large man wearing such a purple dress, but, somehow, it didn't seem strange. Tiresias was more beautiful than anyone Lyssa had ever seen before. He seemed to glow—like there were tiny lightbulbs just underneath his skin. He had high, sharp cheekbones and full red lips; his skin was the creamy color of the hot chocolate Michael sometimes made for her on cold and rainy days.

Circe elbowed Lyssa—she was staring. Lyssa stammered: "Nice—nice to meet you."

"The pleasure's all mine." Tiresias held his hand out to Lyssa and, as she leaned over to shake it, she noticed his cloudy, sightless gray eyes.

"The gods struck me blind for revealing their secrets," Tiresias singsonged, as though he could read Lyssa's mind.

"I didn't mean to—" Lyssa started, but Tiresias waved a large, ring-covered hand, stopping her.

"Don't you worry about it, darling," he said. "Ms. Tiresias is used to people staring. Just because I don't see it don't mean I don't know it happens. Now take a seat."

Lyssa nervously looked back over at Circe. "Um . . . I don't think we're staying."

"Nonsense," Tiresias said. "You need something—you need to *reconnect* with someone. Isn't that right, baby girl?"

Lyssa inhaled, sharply. It was like Tiresias could see through her skin, all the way down to her deepest wish. How did he do that?

"My mom," she whispered. Then, clearing her throat, she said, "I mean, you think I need to talk to my mom?"

"That's right," Tiresias said. "Now sit."

There was an old bucket and an overturned apple crate

sitting next to the table. Lyssa sat on the apple crate, winding her braid around one finger. Circe plopped down next to her like this was a normal part of her day.

"Perfect," Tiresias said, clapping. "Dead people are my specialty."

"Wait," Lyssa started, shocked. "I never said . . ."

Tiresias just waved her words away.

"You tell me everything I need to know without saying a word," he explained. "You're easier to read than a picture book."

Lyssa frowned. She didn't really know what that meant, but if Tiresias knew what happened to her mom without her saying a word, then maybe he was the person she should be talking to.

Tiresias put both hands on the table, his palms facing the sky. He closed his eyes and started to chant under his breath, his voice low and steady like a drum.

Lyssa didn't know what she was supposed to do. She used to meditate with her mom, but they always did it sitting cross-legged in the middle of the living room. There had been no chanting or cherries involved.

Lyssa glanced over at Circe, but her eyes were closed too. Sighing, Lyssa closed her eyes. She pulled her legs onto the apple crate so she could sit cross-legged—but she nearly tumbled off. She unwound her legs, putting them back on the ground as she breathed in slowly—counting to ten like her mom had taught her—and then pushing all the air out of her lungs.

For several minutes Tiresias continued chanting, but nothing happened. She opened one eye to look around.

A gust of wind tickled the back of her neck. The cherries started to tremble.

One by one, the cherries rose out of the white-and-blue bowl and hovered in the air. The edges of the tablecloth fluttered, and the hair on Circe's wig stood up, making her look like she'd been electrocuted. Then the wig twitched and lifted straight off her head, revealing two staticky red pigtails underneath.

"That's my girl," said a voice that was melodic, filled with laughter. Lyssa recognized that voice . . . "Now empty your mind . . ."

Every muscle in Lyssa's body froze and her chest seized up, like she'd forgotten how to breathe. Circe's eyes were still closed and Tiresias kept chanting and neither one of them appeared to have heard anything at all.

"As above, so below," the voice said. Lyssa had to squeeze her eyes shut to keep tears from rolling down her cheeks.

"Mom?" she whispered. The sound of her voice made Lyssa shake. She sounded so close. So real.

"It's like we always talked about," her mom said. "You're going on an adventure."

A cracking, sparking noise sounded in the stand behind them and a firework shot out through the roof, splintering the wood and spitting blue and red and green sparks. As Tiresias continued chanting, a dozen more fireworks shot off, sending glowing stars and hearts and flowers into the twilit sky.

Lyssa lifted her face as multicolored sparks of light rained down on her. She could almost smell the lavender and honey soap her mom always used. She could feel her mom's breath on her neck. For so long she'd been alone, but now, it was like her mom was right next to her.

"Stay," she whispered to her mom. "Please."

Before the words were even out of her mouth, the fireworks faded and the cherries dropped back onto the table. A few rolled onto Lyssa's lap, feeling heavy and awkward as they settled into the folds of her dress.

Circe's eyes popped open.

"Jeez, Tiresias. I thought you knew how to do this," she said, fixing her wig. "I didn't hear any dead people talking."

Tiresias straightened one of his scarves.

"Thought I'd gotten the whole summoning the dead thing down. I guess not. Sorry, baby girl. Now that'll be five dollars. Mama don't work for free."

Lyssa pulled $5 out of her backpack. Now she was down to $8, but she hardly even thought about it. Her mom's words glowed inside Lyssa's chest, like the fireflies she used to catch in mason jars every summer.

Lyssa was quiet as Circe drove the truck out of Boise. It wasn't dark yet, but more and more stars became visible the farther they got from the city. Lyssa kept her eyes on the sky, but for the first time she didn't really notice the stars. All she could think about was fireworks and floating cherries and her mom's voice. *Now empty your mind . . .*

She leaned back against her seat, lost in thought. She felt uneasy. Her mother's magic was fleeting, and it never seemed to do what Lyssa expected it to. What would happen when she got to Texas? Would the magic be sufficient to help her save her home?

Would her mother speak to her again?

Lyssa sighed. If only Circe and Tiresias had heard her mom too; then maybe they could've helped Lyssa sort out what all this meant. But neither of them had said anything about the strange voice, and it made Lyssa feel hollow. Could she have imagined the whole thing?

"Something wrong?" Circe asked, shifting her eyes over to Lyssa.

"Low blood sugar," Lyssa lied.

"You want a peach?" Circe asked.

Lyssa nodded, but she found she had no appetite. She placed the peach on her lap.

After another ten minutes of driving in silence, Circe pulled the truck over to the side of the road and killed the engine.

"Better than any hotel, right?" she said, throwing open her door. They were parked next to an empty field covered in tall grass and scraggly trees. Circe walked around to the back of the truck and pulled two scratchy brown blankets out of the trunk. She tossed one to Lyssa. It was warm and smelled like freshly washed pig and buttermilk and hay. Lyssa lifted it to her face and breathed it in. It reminded her of Sunday mornings when Michael made pancakes and facon for breakfast. Michael was a vegetarian, and facon didn't have any animal products in it, but the smell of pig still made Lyssa feel homey and safe.

They crossed to the middle of the field and spread their blankets out on the ground. The sun was setting in the distance, turning the sky honey gold and orange. Circe pulled off her wig and tossed it to the side. Her red hair was squashed flat to her forehead, and her pigtails stuck out at odd angles. She plopped down on the blanket. Far in the distance, a tiny red plane was flying low over the fields. Lyssa watched, curious, as it got closer and closer, then curved into the air and circled back around.

"It's called a crop duster," Circe said. She too was watching the tiny plane circle through the air.

"What's it doing?" Lyssa asked.

"During the day it covers the crops with pesticides and junk, but when the pilot is done with his jobs, he takes the plane out and practices writing things in the sky. Sometimes when festivals or carnivals come to town, they hire him to advertise for it."

Lyssa and Circe watched as the plane darted in and out of the clouds, writing a message in puffy, white smoke.

I AM HERE, the message read.

"That's a strange thing to write," Lyssa said. Circe shrugged.

"It's just for practice."

For a few minutes there was nothing but silence and the far-off sound of crickets chirping in the grass. Then Circe's low, even snores began to fill the night.

Lyssa didn't sleep. She thought about Michael. Was he worrying about her? Did he still think she had been kidnapped, or had he finally found her note? Lyssa closed her eyes, picturing Michael wandering along abandoned dirt roads, calling out her name.

No. That was silly. Michael wasn't looking for her himself—he'd called the police. And even if he *was* searching for her, he'd probably drive his car.

Still, the image stuck with her, making her feel so guilty that she forced her eyes back open. Surely Michael would find her note soon—if he hadn't found it already—and everything would be fine. To distract herself, Lyssa pulled the journal out of her backpack and grabbed her pencil.

Dear Penn, she wrote.

Do you think you can talk to people after they die? Do you think that anyone lives up in the stars? Do you believe in spirits? Do you think I can get all the way to Texas in just three days? Do you believe in magic? Like, real magic, the kind that can change the world?

Lyssa closed her journal and looked back up in the sky, watching the message fade into the night, slowly replaced by twinkling stars. She wondered if her mom had seen the words *I AM HERE* and if she knew that Lyssa was down here waiting for her.

As above, so below, her mom had said. Lyssa didn't exactly know what she'd meant by that, but she hoped it meant that she was on the right path and that her mom was watching her from the sky, helping her figure out what to do next. She was on an adventure—that was true. She just hoped she'd end up in the right place.

Lyssa stared up at the stars until her eyes grew heavy and she could no longer keep them open. She thought about the crop duster's message: *I AM HERE*. As Lyssa drifted off to sleep, those words stayed painted on the insides of her eyelids.

She dreamed that she was the crop duster, that she was flying the plane across the sky writing loopy letters out of puffy white smoke. As she navigated the plane through the clouds, she kept expecting to find her mom, waiting for her. Then, maybe, they could go home together.

CHAPTER FOURTEEN

Sirens and Storm Clouds

They started out early the next morning, piling into the truck just as the sun was casting dusty strips of light across the grass. Lyssa cast one last look at the field before climbing into the truck after Circe, thinking about all the questions she'd written into her journal the night before. She'd hoped that, by the light of morning, the questions would be easier to answer. But like the words written in the sky the night before, the answers to Lyssa's questions seemed very far away. She slid into her seat and pulled the truck door closed.

Circe navigated the truck over the highway and into the sprawling farmlands of Idaho. She shoved her wig and stilts under her seat, explaining that it was so empty out on the back roads that she didn't really need to worry about staying in disguise.

The land outside Lyssa's window looked like a patchwork quilt. Bright orange and red hills surrounded them on all sides. They drove past towns called Wendell, Jerome, and Rupert. Lyssa couldn't help laughing out loud. She pulled out her journal and made a list of all the town names for Penn.

"See that tree?" Circe said, pointing. "That tree split in two during our last big thunderstorm. And that bale of hay was the one that got lit on fire . . ."

On a distant hill a red farmhouse appeared, sunshine bouncing off the shingles of its roof. Lyssa shifted in her seat, starting to feel nervous. Circe had said that Lyssa would be able to catch a bus once they got to Idaho, but as far as Lyssa could tell, there were no bus stations close by and she still hadn't figured out how to get the money for a ticket. Once Circe got home, Lyssa would be alone in the world—no friends, no money, no way to get to Austin. She stuck her braid in her mouth, deciding it didn't matter if Circe saw her chewing her own hair. Soon, Circe would be gone.

Circe slowed her truck as they got closer to the farmhouse. Dread clogged up Lyssa's throat. She opened her mouth to tell Circe she didn't have enough money for a bus ticket, but before she could get a word out, Circe let out a low sigh.

"Holy hogs," Circe muttered. "*Him* again."

Lyssa sat back up, following Circe's gaze to a figure standing in front of the farmhouse door. He wore thick Coke-bottle glasses and a brown tweed suit. His button-down shirt was pulled tight over his round belly and sunlight glinted off his leather briefcase.

"Who is he?" Lyssa asked.

"IRS goon."

"IRS?" Lyssa repeated, confused.

"A guy who collects taxes—I'll explain later," Circe said as she slammed on her brakes and put the truck in reverse. The dirt road was narrow and lined on either side by a rickety wooden fence, but Circe backed her truck right into it. The wood splintered and the pigs in the back squealed. Circe's tires screeched as she hit the gas pedal and shot forward, making Lyssa's entire body rattle around on her seat. Next to her, Circe had both hands on the steering wheel and one foot propped against the dashboard.

"Hey!" someone shouted. Lyssa looked out her window and saw the IRS goon racing toward them, waving the leather briefcase above his head like a flag.

"I think he needs to talk to you," Lyssa said. The man

climbed into his own car, forgetting his briefcase on the hood as he peeled away. Circe snorted, sounding exactly like one of her pigs. She shook her head and her pigtails came loose, forming a halo of red curls around her head.

"He'll have to catch me first," Circe said. Lyssa watched the man from her window. His car was smaller than Circe's truck, and its back wasn't filled with pigs and peaches. He navigated the dirt road easily, weaving around potholes and broken bits of fence. He'd catch up to them in no time.

Circe must have realized that, too. She glanced behind her, eyes wild. "Find a way to distract him," she shouted.

Distract him? Lyssa's heart was drumming against her chest. She searched the truck for something to use, and her eyes fell on the tomatoes from yesterday. There were dozens and dozens of them, some as large as basketballs. Perfect. Lyssa grabbed the hem of her muumuu and filled the skirt with tomatoes. Then she leaned out the truck window and took aim . . .

Splat! The first tomato splattered against the IRS goon's windshield like a water balloon filled with red paint. The man unrolled a window and stuck his head out so that he could see the road in front of him. Lyssa grabbed another tomato and threw—it splattered across the man's face.

Tomato juice and seeds ran down his cheeks and nose and chunks of tomato got caught in his hair. The car swerved sideways and halted, nearly slamming into a wooden fence by the side of the road.

"We got him!" Circe cheered. She'd been watching from the rearview mirror and when the man ran his car off the road, she pumped her fist in the air triumphantly. Lyssa didn't feel quite so happy. She hadn't meant to cause an *accident*. She watched out the window until the man stepped out of his car, just to make sure that he was okay, and felt slightly better.

"It looks like I won't be going back to the farm for a while," Circe said, sighing. "How's Texas this time of year?"

Lyssa's heart leapt in her chest. Was Circe saying what she thought she was saying? She leaned back against her truck seat. "Really? You want to come to Texas with me?"

Circe shrugged. "If there's a market where I can sell my peaches, then I don't see why not."

Lyssa had to bite down on her lower lip to keep from cheering out loud. Just a few minutes ago she thought she'd be stranded in Idaho with no chance of making it home in time for the Texas Talent Show. Now she had a ride all the way to Austin—and Circe was here to keep her company. Lyssa leaned over and plucked a tomato off the floor, taking a big bite. She felt much better, and lighter, than she had last night. The winds of change were guiding her. They had brought her Circe, after all.

+   +   +

They drove for hours, until they reached a run-down little town just off the highway. Lyssa had dozed off but woke up, startled, to a loud and sudden popping. The next second a cloud of smoke appeared from under the hood of the truck, and the engine sputtered off.

Lyssa caught sight of a sign just before they skidded to a stop in the middle of the road: *Bliss, ID. Population: 250*. Lyssa stared out the window. Bliss didn't look very blissful. There were only a few buildings, and the windows were all boarded up or dark. It didn't seem like the kind of place where anyone would want to stay for long.

Circe turned the ignition off and then on again. The truck didn't make a peep.

"I was worried this might happen," Circe said, tapping her fingers against the steering wheel. "My alternator belt is actually a garden hose."

"Can you fix it?" Lyssa asked. She waved a hand over her nose, coughing. The air smelled like burnt toast.

"Not this time. I'm going to need to find a mechanic. You stay here with the truck—it'll be faster if I go on my own."

Lyssa nodded. Circe pulled her wispy gray wig over her pigtails, tucking a few strands of red hair up behind her ears. She grabbed a fake nose out of her costume supply bag.

"How do I look?" she asked, adjusting her nose in the rearview mirror.

"Fine," Lyssa said, even though she thought Circe looked like a fairy-tale witch. Her chest was already clenched with fear, and not just because Bliss seemed practically abandoned. She glanced at the clock on the truck's dashboard—it was nearly one in the afternoon. She was off schedule already—she didn't even know if it was possible to make it all the way to Austin in two days. "How long do you think this'll take? The Talent Show . . ."

"Don't worry about the Talent Show," Circe said, throwing the truck door open. "You'll be fine. We still have like five days, right?"

"Two," Lyssa called, but Circe didn't seem to be listening. Teetering slightly on her stilts, she started down the street, muttering that Lyssa needed to learn how to relax.

Lyssa sighed and leaned back against her seat, weaving the ends of her hair between her fingers. How could she relax? There was no way Circe would find a mechanic around here. All the buildings were empty. Their windows were covered in cardboard, and jagged pieces of glass carpeted the sidewalks. Lyssa closed her eyes, trying to recall the sound of her mom's voice whispering to her: *It's an adventure . . .*

But the only sounds Lyssa heard were the pigs snorting in the back.

She opened her eyes again and looked out the window. There was a poster taped to one of the storefronts and, for a second, Lyssa just stared at it. She was sure she was imagining things. She blinked, thinking the poster might disappear.

It didn't.

The words MISSING PERSON were written in thick, red letters over a photograph of Lyssa's freckled face. Under the photograph was a row of dollar signs and the word REWARD!

Fear blanketed Lyssa's body and an itchy, anxious feeling prickled along her arms and legs. What if someone walked past and spotted the poster? She would be trapped.

Lyssa peered out the window again. She'd thought the street was abandoned, but now she noticed that there were two men standing at the corner of the sidewalk. The men were both tall and skinny. One had a long, bumpy nose that looked surprisingly like Circe's rubber one, and the other had a bald head so shiny, it seemed like it had been polished. The men were staring at the truck.

Was it Lyssa's imagination, or did their eyes seem to flit back and forth between her face and the poster? She felt as though she'd just swallowed a mouthful of sand. Had the men recognized her?

Broken truck or not, Lyssa knew they couldn't stay

here. She needed to find Circe. But she couldn't just stroll into the street. She needed a disguise.

That was it! Circe had left the rest of her costume supplies in a bag on the truck floor. Lyssa rummaged through it and put on a short, brown wig and a pair of cat's-eye sunglasses, checking her reflection in the mirror. Between the wig, the glasses, and the flowery purple-and-blue muumuu she was still wearing, she doubted anyone would recognize her. If she was stopped, she'd just tell people that she was part of a traveling fortune-telling group. Yeah, that would work. Her name was . . . Ivana. And she could see the future.

Lyssa pushed her truck door open and, grabbing Zip out from under her seat, she headed down the sidewalk, tripping over the hem of her muumuu as she unfolded her scooter and climbed on, rolling off in the direction Circe had disappeared. When she reached the end of the block, she chanced a glance over her shoulder to see if the men were following her.

Her stomach plummeted all the way to her toes. They *were* following her. She turned around just in time to see that she was about to zoom straight into a trash can. At the last second, she managed to jerk Zip's handlebars to the right, narrowly avoiding a collision.

"Hey, kid!" one of the men called out behind her. "Slow down for a minute!"

Lyssa swallowed and pushed off harder. More posters of her lined the broken windows. They all seemed to be tracking her with their eyes. Lyssa tried to ignore them as she flew past on Zip. She wasn't sure what the men behind her wanted, but she didn't want to let them catch up.

"Hurry, Zip," Lyssa whispered.

Her scooter's wheels squeaked, like it was protesting that it couldn't go any faster. Lyssa reached the corner where she thought she'd seen Circe turn, but as soon as she made a left, she knew she had gone the wrong way. Crumpled-up newspapers blew down the sidewalks like tumbleweeds rolling through the desert.

Lyssa bit her lip, her head spinning. She glanced back over her shoulder just in time to see the two strange men round the corner behind her.

"Little scooter girl!" the bald man called after her. The man with the long, bumpy nose laughed loudly.

"We aren't going to hurt you," he yelled at Lyssa. "We just want to take your scooter for a ride."

"Looks heavy for a little girl," the bald man added. "We don't mind taking it off your hands."

Any relief Lyssa would have felt that the men hadn't recognized her was swallowed up in a wave of terror. She wrapped her fingers tighter around Zip's handlebars. How had she ended up here? Had her mom stopped guiding her?

She kicked off again. There was panic sloshing around inside her chest and it was thick and muddy, making her stomach feel like a swamp. She needed to get away—she needed to hide. She didn't slow down to think about which direction she was turning or whether she was heading farther away from Circe. As she tore around another corner, Lyssa almost sobbed with relief. There were lights in the building ahead of her, and lights meant people, and possibly a place to hide.

The building was run-down and shaped, incredibly, like a giant elephant, with gray bricks and a long trunk with two tusks sticking out above the door. The elephant's eyes were circular windows with blue-tinted glass. Lyssa barely registered the sign just below the trunk that read *The Siren Choir: Bliss's Best Burlesque.*

She looked over her shoulder one last time. She could no longer see the two strange men, but the wind snatched up threads of their cackling laughter. They'd catch up to her in no time.

Climbing off her scooter, Lyssa pushed open the front door of the elephant building and stepped inside. The air was smoky and it made her cough. There was only one big, circular room in the club, and it was crowded with velvet chairs and tiny tables all facing a stage. Beneath the smoke, the air smelled sweet—like oranges and cinnamon.

There was a woman onstage, easily the largest person Lyssa had ever seen: at least seven feet tall, with shoulders as broad as tree trunks. Her hair was yellow blond and formed into a beehive. She wore a mermaid's costume, and the green scales on her dress sparkled under the stage lights when she moved. The woman looked weirdly familiar to Lyssa, but she didn't have time to stop and study her. The men were surely catching up.

As Lyssa cast about wildly, looking for a place to hide, two more mermaids pushed open a door on the far side of the room, giggling as they looked out into the audience. There weren't many people in the club right now, but the mermaids waved to a man sitting near the front of the stage, then ducked back through the door. It slammed shut behind them and Lyssa saw a sign attached to it that read *Backstage*.

Backstage! That was perfect. Lyssa grabbed Zip and moved toward that door, weaving around tables and chairs. She stumbled over a chair leg and bumped into a little table but managed to make it across the club just as the front door flew open. She slipped backstage.

Before she pulled the door closed, she peered back out into the main room. The two men entered into the club, craning their necks around. Lyssa pulled the backstage door all the way closed and leaned against it, breathing a sigh of relief. She was safe—for now—but she had no way of knowing how long the men would wait for her outside. Her only choice was to sit it out until she could be sure the coast was clear.

She folded Zip up so that she wouldn't be so noticeable, though the area she stood in was heavily shadowed and so far no one had seen her. The backstage area was crowded with people. Stagehands were gathering props and moving scenery, and there were performers changing into and out of sparkly, feather-covered costumes. The wings were crammed with wardrobes and trunks containing beautiful, beaded costumes and sparkling, sequin-encrusted shoes. Wow, Lyssa thought, Circe would absolutely *love* all this.

Maybe she would bring something back for Circe to wear. Just something small—something that wouldn't be missed. It would be a thank you for everything Circe had done for her.

Glancing around to make sure no one was watching, Lyssa snatched the first thing she saw: a pink-and-green rhinestone-covered bra. She stuffed it quickly into her backpack. For a split second she felt guilty. Chewing on her lower lip, Lyssa pulled her backpack open and felt around inside it until she found her favorite dandelion barrettes. She set those down on the table, figuring it was an equal trade.

As Lyssa debated moving farther backstage, a woman began to sing.

The voice sounded like thunder—deep and rumbling and fearless—and it made Lyssa forget all about the men waiting for her outside and the fact that Circe was wandering around Bliss somewhere with no idea where Lyssa had gone. The voice worked its way into her chest, at once familiar and magical. Before she knew what she was doing, she had started moving through the wings toward the stage, toward the voice, desperate to hear it better. She picked out the lyrics: lost love and pain and how lonely the world was. Despite the sad words, the song made Lyssa feel warm all the way to her bones.

"Once upon a yesterday, I lived far away, oh, so very far away . . ."

Lyssa unconsciously sucked the end of her braid into her mouth. Her mother used to sing her a song like that . . . She sang it to Lyssa every night before falling asleep at the hospital. That had been one of Lyssa's favorite lines: once upon a yesterday . . .

She crept closer, leaning past the stage curtain.

"Being with you feels like home," the mermaid sang. That sounded like a line from her mother's song too.

It wasn't until that moment, as Lyssa was standing behind the stage curtain, watching the giant mermaid sing, that something clicked. There was a reason she recognized that song, a reason she *knew* that voice. She'd heard it echoing from her computer speakers, she'd heard it belted across a stadium filled with hundreds of people on her last birthday. This voice could only belong to one person: Athena.

Lyssa squinted hard at the mermaid. Was it possible . . . ?

Athena hadn't been seen in public in nearly a year—ever since the night of the concert that Lyssa attended with her mom. Then her hair had been a deep, chestnut brown instead of blond, and she'd been wearing her signature cowboy hat and boots, but there was no doubt in Lyssa's mind that the mermaid singing on stage was *her*. She might be wearing platform shoes. She had probably dyed her hair; maybe she was afraid of being recognized.

Lyssa fought the urge to run across the stage. She had a million questions to ask. She wanted to know why Athena had left and when she was coming back. She wanted to ask whether it was true that Athena too had lost someone.

But most of all, she wanted to get closer to that voice. She wanted to suck this new song into her pores, to absorb it, the way her mom had always said music wasn't heard but breathed and felt.

Lyssa looked around, quickly finding the narrow ladder leading to the catwalk above stage. She knew from working with the Texas Talent Show that the catwalk was where the stagehands went to switch out the lights. It was also the best seat in the house, directly above the performers. She tucked Zip behind a heavy velvet curtain for safekeeping, then started up the ladder.

Hanging next to the ladder was a thick length of rope. Lyssa gave it a tug and the cardboard ocean scene behind the singing mermaids shifted ever so slightly. Lyssa looped the rope around her waist before she started to climb. It was a trick she'd learned from Penn, from her early days of circus camp. If she fell (*when* she fell, Penn would say), she didn't want to get hurt. Tightening the rope, she scurried up the ladder.

The catwalk was narrower than Lyssa expected it to be—not even wide enough for her to stand on with both her feet together. She wrapped her fingers around the edges of the wood and rose shakily to her feet, holding her arms out straight on either side like she'd seen Penn do. Nerves clenched Lyssa's stomach, making it feel like a wet T-shirt that someone was wringing out over the sink. She carefully edged forward and the wood creaked beneath her sneakers.

Every inch Lyssa crept forward felt like a mile. She held her breath. The distance between her feet and the stage below terrified her, but she was too scared to tear her eyes away from her pink, sparkly tennis shoes. She'd only ever been up the Talent Show's catwalk with her mom, and it had never seemed quite so high or wobbly. By the time she got to the center of the catwalk, Athena had been joined by two backup mermaids and their voices wove together, growing louder and louder, a wall of sound that made the catwalk tremble beneath Lyssa's feet. Lyssa swallowed, trying to keep her balance by looking straight ahead and thinking balanced thoughts. Clenching her eyes shut, she imagined a bear standing on a ball at the circus or a little kid learning to ride a bike.

It didn't work. This time, when Athena's voice rose into the air, Lyssa tried to drop back down to her hands and knees. On her way down, she stepped on one of her shoelaces and her foot slipped out from under her. All of a sudden she was falling . . .

The ground raced toward Lyssa and she braced herself for a face-first dive into the stage, but the rope around her waist grew taut and she swung forward right at the last second—causing the mermaids to scatter, *screaming*, across the stage. One mermaid leapt into the audience, landing on a man's lap.

As Lyssa swung back and forth, she scanned the stage for Athena—trying to spot her—but the famous singer was nowhere. It was as though, once again, she'd just disappeared.

The ocean scenery rocketed toward the ceiling, breaking into pieces when it hit the catwalk. Lyssa swung forward—

right through a curtain of wooden beads the mermaids had been dancing in front of. Strings of beads tangled against Lyssa and then clattered to the ground, rolling across the stage.

Lyssa swayed back and forth. Her ankle was twisted in the rope above her and she was upside down. The tips of her blond braids brushed against the stage. Uh-oh.

"What in the world . . . ?" A very short man covered in tattoos stomped onto the stage, his face red as a tomato. The name tag on his shirt read *Manager*. Behind him, audience members were yelling and running into one another, as though they were worried the whole theater was about to come down on their heads.

Lyssa looked around once more for Athena. Athena would understand; Lyssa knew she'd be able to explain if she could explain to *her*, but the statuesque mermaid was gone. Lyssa remembered, with a sinking feeling, that just yesterday she'd thought an old woman was Athena. Maybe the mermaid hadn't been Athena after all. Maybe it'd been her imagination playing tricks on her. Again.

"Where are your parents?" the manager demanded, trying to untangle Lyssa's ankle from the rope. "What are you doing here? How did you get in?"

"She's with me," came a shrill voice from the back of the theater. Still swaying back and forth on the rope, Lyssa saw a tall, thin woman wearing what looked like a wig and a fake nose.

Lyssa smiled, weakly, and waved.

"Hi, Aunt Mabel," she croaked.

CHAPTER FIFTEEN

Motel Charybdis and the Whirlpool of Wonder

Lyssa huddled near the club's entrance with Zip, feeling terrible, watching from a distance as Circe argued with the manager in a hushed voice. Circe's face was flushed and she was so distracted that she didn't even notice the bright red curl peeking out from under her wig. She wouldn't meet Lyssa's eyes. The manager said something and Circe groaned and kicked at the leg of a chair with one of her stilts.

"Fine!" she yelled. She tottered out of the club, sweeping past Lyssa without saying a word. A minute later she appeared again, swaying a little on her stilts as she carried a basket filled to the brim with peaches. She dropped the basket onto the floor in front of the club manager. He looked down at the peaches and crossed his arms over his chest.

"And?"

Circe gave him a pained look. Then she stepped off her stilts and kicked them over. The short, tattooed manager immediately picked them up and began strapping them to his feet.

"There," Circe said. "We're even. Come on, Lyssa."

Lyssa followed Circe out of the club without a word. Before she climbed back into the truck, she pulled the rhinestone-encrusted bra out of her pocket. She hoped that it might make up—at least a little—for Circe's lost stilts.

"I—I thought you might need this. For your Aunt Mabel costume . . ." Lyssa trailed off, feeling stupid.

Circe just wrinkled up her nose. "What am I going to do with *that*?" she said, waving away the gift.

Embarrassed, Lyssa balled up the bra and shoved it into her pocket. She walked over to the passenger side of the truck and climbed inside.

Next to her, Circe took a deep breath, shaking her head.

"I can't believe you did that! You know we're trying to keep a low profile. Why couldn't you have stayed in the truck like I told you to?"

Lyssa felt her skin burning. "I couldn't stay there!" she burst out. "There were these guys, and they came after me, and . . ."

"Came after you?" Circe repeated. Lyssa swallowed and stared down at a thin patch in her muumuu that was sure to become a hole, picking at a loose thread with her fingers. She couldn't tell Circe about the Missing Person posters—Circe didn't know she'd run away.

"I—I think they were after Zip," she said, feeling helpless. She'd lost Circe all those peaches *and* her stilts. Lyssa was sure that nothing she could say would make her feel better. "I'm sorry," she added. Circe just shook her head and shifted the truck into drive. A plume of gray smoke escaped from under its hood.

"What are we going to do?" Lyssa asked once they'd been on the road for a few minutes, listening to the truck sputter and spit. Circe shook her head.

"Find a motel."

"Here? Can't we find another mechanic?"

"There's only one mechanic for miles, and he said he'll have the part we need tomorrow morning. We're lucky he got the truck working at all."

Lyssa sighed and looked out her window. She knew they couldn't exactly ride around in a broken truck, but she didn't want to spend the night in this strange, abandoned town either. She turned back to Circe, wishing there was some way she could explain just how sorry she was. But Circe's face was so red and pinched that Lyssa decided to talk to her later.

Instead, she pulled out her journal.

Dear Penn, she wrote.

Remember that one time when I accidentally cut up your tightrope cord and used it to make a jump rope? You were so mad, but I sang every Athena song I knew outside your bedroom window, and soon you started laughing and singing along. I wish it was that easy to stop fights with everyone.

Lyssa closed the journal and shoved it back into her backpack. Circe was still in a terrible mood. As they drove she kept muttering about money and scribbling numbers on spare napkins while they waited at traffic lights. When she stopped for gas, she found a pay phone and spent half an hour looking through the phone book for a motel that would allow her to bring her pigs into the room. While Circe argued on the pay phone, Lyssa watched the numbers on the truck's dashboard clock tick away. 2:45. 3:02. 3:21 . . .

Finally, they pulled up in front of a motel that looked like something out of a horror movie. A vacancy sign flickered at the edge of the parking lot and heavy floral curtains

covered all the motel room windows. In the buzzing fluorescent glow the flowers on the drapes looked like they
were moving. Lyssa swallowed.

"Can't we just sleep outside again?" she asked.

"I want to take a shower, if that's all right with you,"
Circe said in a clipped voice.

A sign in front of the lobby read *Motel Charybdis.*

"What's a cherry-by-dis?" Lyssa asked, stumbled over
the strange word. Circe just shrugged.

"It's ker-*ibb*-dis," Circe corrected her, throwing open
her door. Lyssa swallowed.

"This place looks haunted."

"Do you want to pay for a hotel?" Circe snapped.
"Now come on."

Circe pulled on her wig, and Lyssa followed her inside
to pick up their room key. The motel's lobby was just as
dingy and creepy as the outside suggested. The only spot
of color was a pot of purple lilies sitting on the front desk,
but all the flowers were pointed to the window, their stems
stretched out in odd angles like they were trying to escape.

A young woman with stringy blond hair stood behind
the desk. Lyssa cringed when the woman smiled at them.
Her teeth were very large and very white, and it looked like
there were far too many of them shoved into her mouth.

"Welcome to Motel Charybdis," the woman said. She

had a slight southern accent that made all her words sound stretched out, like an old pair of panty hose. "My name is Kyla. Do y'all have a reservation?"

"Yes, under Mabel Hemmingway," Circe said, lowering her voice to sound older. Kyla gave them both another toothy smile. Circe glanced out the window to check on her pigs, but Kyla kept her eyes on Lyssa. She ran her tongue over those long, white teeth.

"I'm going to wait outside," Lyssa muttered. Kyla gave her the creeps. She stared at Lyssa in a way that made her wonder if Kyla recognized her from all those Missing Person posters.

A few minutes later, Circe came out with the key and they headed over to their motel room. Practically no light filtered through the dusty windows. The carpet was mud brown, and the wallpaper was peeling from the walls. Circe pulled off her wig and tossed it onto the bed. Lyssa huddled near the door while Circe walked into the bathroom and flipped on the light.

"Ugh," Circe moaned, her voice echoing off the bathroom walls. "This won't work at all."

"Is it really that bad?" Lyssa asked, following Circe into the bathroom.

The bathroom was very small. The toilet water was greenish, and there were strips of paint peeling away from the walls. But it looked cleaner than the rest of the motel room.

Then Lyssa turned around and saw the bathtub. Green mold carpeted the bottom of the tub tiles. Three tiny lizards moved around the tub. When Lyssa peeked over the side, their long tongues shot back into their mouths.

"No wonder they'll let me keep pigs in the room," Circe muttered, eyeing the lizards. "Come on."

Lyssa clicked her tongue, hoping the lizards would look up at her. She actually liked lizards—there were always some hanging out by the pond in her garden back at Texas. But there was no point in showering in a mold-carpeted tub.

As Lyssa turned to go, she caught her reflection in the mirror hanging over the sink. Her blond hair was stringy, and it stuck out of her braids in odd clumps, and there were tiny brown flecks speckled across her nose and chin. Lyssa rubbed at the spots on her nose. She sometimes got freckles in the summer when she was outside a lot, but when she leaned in closer, she saw that the flecks were actually tiny spots of dirt and tomato juice.

Lyssa wrinkled her nose. She looked like a creature that lived in the sewers. She and Circe had cleaned off earlier using baby wipes Circe kept in her glove compartment, but Lyssa still had tomato juice inside her ears and in the crooks of her elbows. She needed a bath. *Bad.*

"Are you coming?"

Lyssa peeked out of the bathroom in time to see Circe pull open the motel door and head to the parking lot. She nearly tripped over her own feet scurrying after her, stepping outside just as Circe unlatched the flatbed of her truck. Pigs tumbled down clumsily from the flatbed, stiff from their long time in confinement. One of them rolled up next to Lyssa's feet, grunting and kicking its tiny legs.

"Where are we going?" Lyssa asked, kneeling down to help the pig up.

"Swimming pool. Out back, behind the motel," Circe said. She clucked her tongue and the pigs all trotted up behind her, tumbling into line like fat, pink soldiers. Lyssa had to race after Circe as she led all thirteen pigs to a sidewalk that curved around the side of the motel.

At the back of the motel was a huge swimming pool, encircled by a chain-link fence. Unlike the dirty hotel room, the pool was sparkling and clean. Circe pushed open the gate and followed her trotting pigs onto the pool deck.

"Bombs away," Circe shouted, running up to the side of the pool and jumping in fully clothed. The pigs squealed and leapt into the pool after Circe, their curly pink tails wiggling as they plopped into the water. Lyssa, who had followed the pigs to the edge of the pool, had to leap backward to keep from getting splashed. Lyssa shivered, tucking her arms up into her muumuu. Sure, it was August, but it was late in the afternoon and couldn't be more than seventy degrees outside—which, to her, felt freezing. Circe and her pigs might be okay with bathing in a freezing swimming pool, but Lyssa wanted to take a bath someplace *warm*.

Something gurgled behind her. She turned. There, on the other side of the pool, was a hot tub. The water was golden and bubbly—like the homemade apple cider Lyssa's mom used to make on their stove every fall. Lyssa closed her eyes and could practically smell cinnamon in the air. The hot tub was calling to her. It was a perfect place to take a bath.

Lyssa pulled her muddy clothes out of her backpack and headed for the hot tub. She could kill two birds with one stone—wash her clothes and get clean herself. She dipped one toe in and let out a sigh of happiness. The water felt amazing. It was hotter than a Texas lake in August, and the bubbles made Lyssa's toes tingle. All her worries dissolved like the brown sugar in her mom's apple cider. Lyssa dumped her tomato-stained clothes into the water and splashed in after them.

She waded right into the center of the hot tub and closed her eyes. Her muumuu ballooned around her and bubbles popped on the surface of the water, spraying her cheeks and nose with apple-scented suds. Lyssa spun around, letting all of her doubts and worries spin away.

Then she heard a loud noise: like a car revving its engine or a jet taking off. She opened her eyes and stopped spinning, planting her feet firmly on the bottom of the hot tub. The sound, she realized, was coming from just *underneath* her.

All at once, the water became frothy and wild. What was happening?

Bubbles formed faster and faster, the water churning like a milk shake in a blender. Lyssa's feet were swept out from underneath her. She went under and came up coughing. She was twirling around and around in the water, unable to stop, unable to reach the stairs. This wasn't like her mother's magic. This was something dark and frightening, and Lyssa didn't understand it at all.

Now the hot tub seemed as big as a lake, and Lyssa was a tiny toy boat circling the drain. The water was like a living thing. It shot up her nose and tangled her hair and tugged on her legs and feet, dragging her under. She thrust her hands into the bubbles, grabbing for the first solid thing she could reach. Her fingers enclosed something round and slippery, but when Lyssa tried to pull on it, it oinked.

Lyssa blinked the water from her eyes. She was holding on to one of Circe's pigs. The pig kicked her leg away and disappeared back into the bubbles, just as another pig doggie-paddled past her and a third bobbed in the water ahead.

Despite Lyssa's panic, she had time to think the clearest, simplest, stupidest thing: *How did they all get here?*

"The hot tub calls to them," said a melodic, musical voice behind her. Lyssa yelped just as she once again went under and came up spluttering. There was someone in the hot tub with her. She flailed her arms around in the water, hauling herself back up to the surface.

It was the mermaid from the Siren Choir—the one she had been so convinced was Athena! Or, at least Lyssa *thought* it was the same mermaid . . .

This woman was just as tall, and even sitting on the bottom of the hot tub, her head and shoulders were still well above the water. She wore a polka-dotted swimsuit instead of her mermaid costume and beads of water clung to her beehive hairdo. A pair of rhinestone-encrusted glasses was balanced on her nose.

As Lyssa, still dog-paddling, stared at her, she seemed to fade, slightly, until Lyssa could see the blue sky through her golden skin. But the next second the mermaid snapped back into place—looking just as solid as she had before. Lyssa rubbed her eyes. She must be hallucinating. Was the heat from the hot tub making her imagine things?

Or maybe she'd messed up in some way . . . maybe her mother's magic was going haywire because Lyssa wasn't where she was supposed to be . . .

"What—?" Lyssa started to ask, but just then the water swirled her around until she wasn't facing the mermaid anymore.

The mermaid began singing behind her until her voice rose high into the air. Lyssa wondered if the song was a hallucination too. She was so dizzy . . .

The mermaid was no longer singing words, exactly, just stretching one note out as far as it could go until it rumbled with a sound like thunder.

Under again, and then up, gasping, and still the note hovered in the air, beautiful and inhuman. Through her panic, Lyssa thought about how Melodius's music had turned into thunder in her recurring dream. She craned her head toward the sky. The clouds were purple and black, and they swirled together violently. Lightning crashed down from the clouds and thunder rumbled just beneath it.

Desperately, Lyssa pushed through the water and grabbed for the handrail leading out of the tub, but her hand slipped and she fell back into the waves.

"Help!" she shouted, hoping the mermaid would try to save her. The pigs were still swimming in the water around her. It looked like they were performing some kind of choreographed water dance. They swam in a circle, then ducked into the water at the exact same moment, kicking their legs into the air playfully.

"Lyssa!" she heard someone shout.

"Circe!" Lyssa splashed around in the water, trying to stay afloat long enough to find her friend. The powerful jets sucked at her toes—trying to pull her under. She kept dipping below the surface of the water. Lyssa kicked and kicked, but she couldn't keep her face above the waves. "Circe! Help me!"

She was under again. She opened her eyes and all she saw were bubbles. She couldn't even tell which direction was up.

Then Lyssa felt strong hands wrapping around her arms as someone lifted her out of the water and set her on the edge of the hot tub. Lyssa sucked in a breath of fresh air and everything around her became still. The jets buzzed off and the bubbles disappeared.

Lyssa spit out a thin stream of water. She looked around for the mermaid, or whoever it was who had saved her from the dangerous waves, but the woman was gone. Sitting on the side of the tub was a bright blue cowboy boot, a Crock-Pot, and a pom-pom that looked exactly like the one that had gone missing from Lyssa's scooter.

Still a little dazed, Lyssa reached out and grabbed the pom-pom.

"What happened?" Circe demanded, running toward Lyssa as she struggled to her feet. "I leave for a minute to take the pigs back to the hotel room to get dry and you almost drown! Don't you know how to swim?"

Lyssa rubbed her eyes with her palm. Hadn't Circe seen the crazy bubbles and the jets and the mermaid? Could Lyssa have imagined the whole thing? Was she so tired that she dreamed up a storm? Had the mermaid been there at all?

"How'd you get the hot tub to stop?" Lyssa asked. Circe pointed to a bright red button on the side of the hot tub. A sign above it read *Press in Case of Emergency*.

"Oh," Lyssa muttered, feeling stupid. "Thanks." Circe gave her a strange look and headed back for the stairs.

Lyssa glanced around for her clothes. She knew that she'd thrown them into the water before she got in herself, but they weren't floating on the surface of the hot tub. She was trying to wring out a corner of her wet and cold muumuu, wishing that she had anything else to wear, when she saw her clothes sitting next to the hot tub, clean, dry, and neatly folded.

Lyssa opened her mouth to thank Circe for folding her clothes, but the words died on her lips.

Sitting on top of her clean, dry pair of jeans was the little blue paper airplane. It was crumpled, ripped, and a little water stained, but the message was still clearly displayed on its wing:

There's no place like home.

CHAPTER SIXTEEN

Betrayal Tastes Like Unwashed Socks

After the adventure in the hot tub, the rest of Lyssa and Circe's night at the motel felt like a big slumber party. They watched bad science-fiction movies on television and acted them out, using Circe's costumes to make everything more realistic. Circe showed Lyssa how to make a huge blanket fort using stacked peach crates, pulling the sheets and pillowcases off the beds and stringing them up like a tent. They huddled inside the fort and told each other secrets. Lyssa told Circe that she hated wearing socks that matched, that sunflowers were her favorite flower, and that she was terrible at any sport that didn't involve a scooter. She even told Circe about her mom—how everything she did felt like magic, and how Lyssa still believed her mom was in Austin, waiting for her. Circe wasn't as good at telling secrets as Lyssa was, but she did admit that it sometimes got lonely on the farm with only the pigs to keep her company.

But, after Circe fell asleep, Lyssa's mind kept spinning at a frantic pace, as though she was still being whipped around by the hot tub. The water had seemed almost *alive*. And the mermaid had been there—then gone, just like that. Lyssa felt a gnawing fear in her stomach. She didn't understand it at all. When her mother had talked about the winds of change, they had always sounded like a *good* thing. Exciting and adventurous, sure. But good. The same with her mother's magic. What she felt in the hot tub had been different—scary—and Lyssa couldn't shake the feeling that she had done something wrong.

Finally, Lyssa fell asleep inside the fort, curled up with Circe's pigs, still wearing a fake mustache and huge plastic glasses. The pigs were warm and soft, like wriggly little pillows.

But when Lyssa woke up the next morning, Circe wasn't there. Lyssa sat up and stretched, rubbing sticky gunk from her eyes. A nervous feeling fluttered in her gut. Had Circe left without her? Circe's bag of costume supplies was gone, except for a tube of denture glue that had rolled under the bed, forgotten.

Lyssa crawled out of the fort. Her backpack was wedged beneath a snoring pig's bottom, and another pig was using her sneaker as a pillow. Lyssa sighed in relief. If the pigs were still here, then Circe would be back.

She dropped down to her knees and wrestled her things away from the pigs, who kicked and snorted in their sleep. Just as she was tying the laces on her sneaker, there was a sharp honk from outside. Lyssa jumped up and pulled the curtain aside.

Circe sat behind the wheel of her beat-up truck, wearing her wig and Lyssa's cowboy hat. She leaned out the window and waved.

"Got the part! Listen to this." Circe revved the engine and the truck growled smoothly. Smoke didn't pour out from under the hood, and nothing sputtered or spit.

"Sounds great," Lyssa shouted out the window. She felt a pang of guilt when she thought about how much it must've cost to get that truck fixed. Circe had been so stressed about money the day before. Lyssa only had $8 left, but maybe she should at least offer to pay for breakfast. She was getting a little tired of peaches and tomatoes.

She quickly rebraided her hair, anxious to get on the road again. They only had one more day left to get back to Austin. One day! They couldn't waste another second.

While Lyssa packed up her backpack and put Zip into the truck, Circe tried to round up the pigs. Lyssa finally managed to gather them by luring them into the motel pillowcases with peaches. Carrying pigs in a pillowcase was like carrying a very wiggly sack of potatoes.

"It's going to be a good day," Circe called as Lyssa climbed into the truck. "I can feel it."

Circe's good mood was infectious—but, strangely, it didn't last for long. As they drove away from the town of Bliss, Circe got quieter and quieter. She seemed oddly distracted—even nervous.

"Do you know what happens to runaways when they're caught?" Circe asked Lyssa out of nowhere, after they'd left Bliss and Motel Charybdis far behind.

"I think it's best not to get caught," Lyssa said carefully. Circe was quiet for a moment, chewing on her lower lip. Lyssa wondered whether she was thinking of the man from the IRS. She guessed that Circe was technically a runaway now, too.

"But let's say you—I mean, a runaway—*were* caught. What would happen then? Probably nothing that bad, right?"

Lyssa just shrugged. Circe might not be in trouble if she went home, but Lyssa knew *she* would be. She thought of Michael and a little pang tugged at her heart. Maybe she wouldn't be in as much trouble as she thought she would. Maybe Michael would just be relieved to have her back.

Or maybe not.

After sitting in silence next to Circe for five whole minutes, Lyssa pulled out her journal and tried to write a letter to Penn. She wanted to tell her about the crazy motel whirlpool and the Siren Choir burlesque and the mermaids, but, no matter how many times she rewrote the stories, they always sounded strange and unlikely—almost as though they were something Lyssa had made up. She decided to turn the radio on instead and started looking for a station. An Athena song came on and Lyssa's heart leapt. She turned the volume all the way up.

"Make a splash, this is your chaaance!" Lyssa closed her eyes, letting the music wash over her. Before she knew it, she was singing along.

"Just one life, it's all any of us haaaas."

"Hey! You have a really nice voice," Circe said.

Lyssa felt a whooshing feeling inside her chest. She couldn't believe that she actually sang in front of Circe!

"Thanks," Lyssa said, grinning over at Circe—but when she caught her eye, Circe looked away quickly and started fumbling with the radio dial. She flipped stations so quickly it made Lyssa's head hurt.

"Nope," Lyssa said, swatting Circe's hand playfully,

"we gotta pick a song and stick with it. It drives me crazy if I can't listen to it the whole way through. Deal?"

Circe nodded, but turned the radio off and put both hands back on the steering wheel.

"Is something wrong?" Lyssa asked.

"Guess I'm just a little hungry. You know what I'm thinking? Ice cream for breakfast."

Circe gave Lyssa such a wide grin that she had to agree. Her stomach growled as Circe pulled off the highway and turned down a dusty street leading through a small town. Unlike the town of Bliss, there were people walking down the sidewalks here. There was no broken glass on the streets, and none of the windows were covered in cardboard. A sign by the side of the road read *Bear River City, UT*.

Utah! Lyssa's heart did a little flip. She hadn't realized they'd gotten to Utah already—that was one whole state closer to Texas. She peered out the window, wondering if Utah looked any different from Idaho. It didn't, really. There were the same distant red mountains, the same dusty roads.

Her gaze settled on a poster hanging from a telephone pole—a poster with *her* face on it.

Lyssa immediately forgot her hunger. Instead, her stomach churned and twisted, like there was a giant cobra rolling around her gut. She saw another poster on the next telephone pole and three more attached to the side of a brick building.

"I know the perfect place," Circe announced. Although Circe was smiling, Lyssa noticed that she wouldn't look her in the eye. Circe scooted forward in her seat, scanning the street signs as they passed. There was something sticking out of the pocket of Circe's muumuu—the corner of a slip of paper. Immediately, Lyssa's mind went to the Missing Person posters.

Lyssa swallowed and pushed the thought out of her mind. Circe was her friend—she'd never do that. The paper must be the receipt for her truck repair or something. That's all.

"I don't think I'm hungry for ice cream, actually," Lyssa said, swallowing. It felt like someone had crumpled up one of those Missing Person posters and shoved it down her throat.

"No way," Circe said, scanning the street signs as they passed. "You've never had Helios's ice cream before."

Lyssa didn't bother asking what a Helios was. She couldn't walk around this town. There were pictures of her everywhere—someone was sure to recognize her. She pulled her sweatshirt on and tugged the hood down over her forehead. For once she didn't even mind how itchy the sleeves felt on her arms. She just needed to keep her face hidden.

Luckily, Circe pulled off the busy road and turned down an alleyway that was so narrow there was hardly more than an inch of space on either side of the truck. The alley curved behind buildings and led to a small park filled with trees and picnic benches. Next to the park was a field of green cornstalks that seemed to stretch for miles and miles.

Lyssa stared out the window in awe. She'd never seen so much corn! It looked like a shiny green ocean. There, at least, was *one* difference between Idaho and Utah. Lyssa hadn't seen any corn oceans in Idaho.

Circe threw her truck door open and hopped out, but Lyssa hesitated, still not sure whether she should risk someone recognizing her. The park *looked* safe. There was only one person nearby—a woman sitting on a bench across the street, hungrily devouring a romance novel. She was small boned and bird-like except for her hair, which was enormous and dyed cherry red. Her hair had been ornately curled and sprayed down with so much hair spray that not a single strand of it moved, not even when the wind blew through the park. The woman's fingers were very long, and the way they wrapped around the edges of her novel reminded Lyssa of spider's legs that ended in bright, red acrylic nails the exact same shade as her hair. Lyssa shook herself out of her reverie. She grabbed her backpack and hopped out of the truck after Circe.

"Where's the ice cream place?" Lyssa asked. Circe pointed to a silver truck on the other side of the park bench. Lyssa had been so busy staring at the woman and the field of corn that she hadn't noticed the truck parked directly in front of it. The sign attached to the truck read *Helios's Ice Cream* in swirly, swooping letters. The cornstalks in the field behind the truck rippled in the wind like waves.

Lyssa followed Circe across the street to Helios's. As they walked past the park bench, the woman with the spider fingers looked up and fixed her eyes right on Lyssa. Her face had a pinched look to it, as though someone had accidentally flattened it between two heavy books. Lyssa raced forward, catching up to Circe. When she glanced behind her, the woman had gone back to reading her book.

"Want to see a trick?" Circe whispered, crouching down low so she could sneak past the service window without being seen. Lyssa cast a nervous glance back at the woman on the park bench. She wasn't watching, so Lyssa crouched down too, following Circe around the truck.

The sliding door in back of the truck was wide open, revealing a tiny kitchen. Freezers filled with creamy, brightly colored ice cream lined the truck walls. Lyssa had never seen so many different flavors of ice cream all in one place. The truck was completely empty; its owner must have stepped away.

"Helios doesn't keep a very good eye on his products," Circe whispered, pointing to a little man standing a ways away, by the truck engine. His hair was shiny black, and he held a cell phone to his ear. A twirly black mustache twitched above his lip with every word he spoke.

"But the warranty expired yesterday. *Yesterday!*" he yelled into the phone, pounding a fist against the bumper of the van for emphasis. When Helios turned his back to them, Circe crept into the back of his truck, a giddy grin spreading across her face. She grabbed two waffle cones off a wobbly tower and loaded them up with ice cream— piling scoops of banana, strawberry, and chocolate–peanut butter one on top of another.

When there was so much ice cream stuffed into the cone that Lyssa worried the whole thing might topple over, Circe thrust a hand into the candy jars lined up against the back wall and sprinkled fistfuls of candy on top of the ice cream.

"Here," Circe whispered, handing Lyssa a cone. Lyssa plucked one of the bright red candies off the top of her ice cream cone and popped it into her mouth. Red Hots! They were her favorite candy; she loved how they tasted like someone poured hot sauce on top of them. When you lived in Texas, you ate hot sauce with everything. She picked the rest of the candies off the top of her ice cream cone and stuck them into her pockets. Those she'd save for later.

"How are we going to pay for these?" Lyssa asked, shooting another nervous glance at Helios.

Circe frowned. "You want to pay for them?"

"Well, we can't just *take* them . . ." she pointed out.

"Hey!"

Lyssa jumped, dumping half of her ice cream cone on the ground. Helios was off the phone now, glaring at Circe as she put the finishing touches on her own ice cream cone.

"You looked busy . . . we didn't want to bother you," Circe said. She hopped down from the truck, grabbing hold of Lyssa's wrist.

"This way!" she shouted.

Helios stormed around the ice cream truck as Circe pulled Lyssa into the field of corn. To Lyssa's surprise, a pathway cut through the field. It was narrow—almost hidden—and it twisted and turned around the tall, green stalks.

"It's a corn maze," Circe yelled over her shoulder. "We'll lose him easily."

Lyssa glanced nervously behind her to see if Helios was still on their heels. Feeling guilty, she pulled a few crumpled dollar bills out of her pocket and tossed them behind her. Hopefully that would cover the ice cream cone . . .

They were running so fast—curving down and around

the corn maze paths—that Lyssa couldn't be entirely sure which direction they were heading. Her ice cream hopped up and down on her cone, barely staying aloft, and a few of the candies rained down on the ground like the bread crumbs Hansel and Gretel left behind to guide them home. Lyssa quickly slurped the rest of the candy off her ice cream. Otherwise, the candy trail would lead Helios right to them.

Circe didn't seem nearly as worried about Helios catching up to them. She was laughing hysterically; obviously, this was her version of an adventure. When she saw that Helios hadn't managed to follow their path through the corn, she started running backward.

"Moo!" Circe called, giggling. She took a big bite of ice cream, getting a swirl of strawberry on her nose. "Oink! Oink!"

"What are you doing?" Lyssa hissed. Circe stopped running and doubled over, giggling and oinking.

Lyssa stopped next to her, shifting her weight from one foot to the other. "Circe, he's going to find us."

"He'll never find us," Circe said. She laughed so hard that fat tears rolled down her cheeks. She shoved more ice cream into her mouth and let out another loud "oink!" This time, Lyssa heard Circe's pigs from a distance, snorting back in the truck. It sounded like they were calling to Circe.

"No one will ever find us," Circe said. Her mouth and cheeks were covered in ice cream, but she wasn't laughing anymore. She stood up again, grabbed Lyssa's hand, and squeezed. For a second it made Lyssa feel warm and happy. But when Lyssa looked into Circe's eyes, she saw the strangest expression flashing there—sadness? Regret? An apology?

All of a sudden, Lyssa began to feel cold all over.

"Circe . . ." she started, but Circe interrupted her.

"Take care of yourself, Lyssa," she said.

Then she pulled her hand away and raced through the corn.

"Wait!" Lyssa shouted.

Did Circe think this was some sort of game? Lyssa dumped her ice cream cone on the ground and started running. But Circe was fast, and she evidently knew her way through the maze much better than Lyssa did. In no time at all she had disappeared.

"Circe!" she yelled. No one answered. There wasn't even the distant sound of oinking and mooing to tell Lyssa where her friend had gone.

Lyssa slowed to a walk, suddenly frightened. How had everything gotten so messed up? She didn't know her way out of the maze, and a very angry Helios was likely still following her through the corn. And Circe was gone. She picked her way through the winding paths slowly, trying to figure out her position by looking up at the sun. It was almost like the universe was punishing her. Maybe her mom was angry about the things she'd been doing with Circe: all the stealing and the lying. She swallowed down a lump in her throat.

All she'd wanted was a friend.

Lyssa tried listening for Helios or Circe, but the only sound she heard was the wind gently ruffling the leaves on the cornstalks. She turned another corner in the path—and froze.

The wind wasn't rustling the leaves—it was rustling posters.

Everywhere Lyssa looked, she saw her missing girl posters. Some were taped to the stalks of corn, while others were scattered across the path.

Lyssa's heart pounded against her ribs like a wild animal banging at the bars of his cage.

Someone knew that she was the girl in the poster. Someone knew that she was in this maze.

Lyssa knew that she should start running again, but her feet wouldn't move. And where would she run? She still didn't know her way out of the maze.

Instead, feeling like she was in a dream, she began tearing the posters off the cornstalks, crushing them beneath her sneakers until they were stained with mud and ice cream. Tears pricked the corners of her eyes, but she blinked them away.

Lyssa had reached up to tear another poster down when someone clasped a hand around her wrist. Lyssa whirled around, stifling a scream.

It was the woman with the big hair from the park bench. Her bright red fingernails pinched into the skin at Lyssa's wrists.

"Let go of me," Lyssa said. She tried to wrench her arm away, but the woman held tight.

"Now sweetie pie, that's no way to greet a lady," she said, pulling her bloodred lips into a wide smile. Her teeth were so white, Lyssa wondered if they glowed in the dark. "Don't fight me now. I just got my nails done this morning . . ."

"Who are you? What do you want?" Lyssa continued to struggle against her. The woman's nails felt like talons, and she smelled so strongly of cinnamon perfume, it was like she had bathed in melted ice cream.

"My name is Calypso," the woman drawled. "Let's go, honey bear. You're coming with me."

"Let. Me. Go!" Lyssa gritted her teeth.

Calypso just laughed and held her tighter.

"Let you go?" Calypso leaned past Lyssa and pulled

one of the last Missing Person posters down from its place on the stalk of corn. "Sweet pea, you're worth a whole lotta greenbacks. I'm not letting you go until I get my piece of the pie."

Lyssa screamed as loud as she could as Calypso dragged her from the maze. Now she *wished* the man from the Helios truck would find her.

"Circe!" Lyssa shouted desperately. Her voice was suctioned away by the tall cornstalks on either side of them. "Circe! Help!"

The woman laughed again and yanked on Lyssa's arm, harder. "You might as well save your breath, honeybunch. Your little friend with the wig was the one who told me where to find you."

"You're lying," Lyssa spat out. But almost immediately, she had a flash of doubt. Hadn't Circe been the one who wanted to get ice cream? Hadn't Circe left her alone in the maze?

"The good God as my witness," Calypso said, with that same easy drawl. "Said she'd bring the missing girl right to me and split the reward money, too. Wanted to steer clear of the cops herself. Can't say I blame her. You're worth quite a pretty little penny, honey pie."

A bad taste rose in Lyssa's mouth—like damp, unwashed socks—and tears welled in the back of her throat. She choked them back down as Calypso dragged her around one last twist in the maze. The cornfield opened up and they were right back where they started, near the park and Helios's ice cream truck and a tiny white sports car that Lyssa realized must belong to Calypso. Lyssa looked around for Circe. Her truck was still in the parking lot, but it was empty of both Circe *and* her pigs.

Lyssa fought a rising tide of panic. She had to act—and quickly.

When they reached the sports car, Calypso reached into her pocket to grab her keys. Lyssa shoved a hand into her pocket, finding the Red Hots she'd saved from her ice cream cone. She squeezed her fist around the candy, grinding it in her pocket until a fiery, sticky paste was left clinging to her fingers.

"Hey, Calypso," Lyssa said.

Calypso glanced down at her.

"What's up, sugar?"

"You have something in your eye," Lyssa said, and shoved her hand into Calypso's face, grinding the burning powder-paste into Calypso's eyes. Calypso screamed and threw both hands over her face, releasing her grip on Lyssa's arm.

Lyssa ran.

As she passed Circe's truck, she reached into the truck bed and grabbed Zip.

"Looks like it's just me and you again," she panted. With Calypso yelling and screaming behind her, she hopped onto her scooter and pushed off. Zip gave little squeals of excitement as they tore down the street.

Hot wind stung Lyssa's face. She pulled on her left braid and stuck the end in her mouth. She pushed off, wanting to go faster and put more distance between herself and Calypso, Helios, and Circe. She wanted to ride until every muscle in her body burned and she was so tired that she wouldn't have to think about what her friend had done. Maybe then, when she could barely keep her eyes open, Circe's betrayal wouldn't hurt as badly as it hurt now.

Her mom always said that holding on to anger was like trying to keep a tiger in your backyard—that it would destroy everything you loved if you didn't set it free. But, for the first time that she could ever remember, Lyssa wasn't sure she agreed with what her mom said. It felt like there was a tiger in her *chest*, shredding her to pieces. If Lyssa could figure out how to get it to leave, then maybe she *would* set it free—just like her mom said. But it wasn't like unlocking the gate in a backyard. It was harder, and Lyssa didn't know the trick.

She felt a sudden, painful longing for her mom—she missed her more than she'd missed her since she had first died. Ana Lee would know what to do—Ana Lee would know just what to say to make the anger go away. But her mom wasn't here.

So Lyssa pulled Zip toward the highway. If she rode fast enough, the wind's roar would fill her ears, so loud that she wouldn't be able to think about anything else.

CHAPTER SEVENTEEN

The Dead Lake and the Ugly One

Lyssa didn't stop even after she'd left the small town behind and reached the highway. She rolled along the edge of the road, and in just a few hours, her jeans and hair were stiff with dirt.

Zip wasn't doing so well either. Its hand brake was now held in place with some dental floss and gum, which Lyssa found in the bottom of her backpack when her shoelace snapped, and she'd had to replace one of the handlebars with an empty Coke bottle. She patted Zip's handle. It was her only friend now, and she wasn't treating it very well.

"You just wait till we get to Austin," she whispered. "I'll find someone to fix you up like new."

The scooter groaned, as though it didn't believe her. Lyssa sighed. What they both needed was a place to sit and rest.

But the idea of stopping worried Lyssa. If she stopped, she'd have to think about Circe and her betrayal, or Michael, and how she was starting to miss him. She'd have to think about the fact that her mom hadn't sent her a single sign, not since the séance, and that the magic she'd been finding was more dangerous and unpredictable than she had thought.

When Lyssa was on Zip, she needed to concentrate on staying far away from traffic, dodging roadkill, and keeping her front wheel out of potholes. She just didn't have *time* to think about all that other stuff. So she rode on.

The highway twisted through a field and narrowed, becoming an old, beat-up dirt road, which Lyssa followed to the edge of a lake. Red sand and spiky bushes surrounded Lyssa on all sides, and hot gusts of wind blew tiny dead flies that got caught in the laces of her sneakers. She finally coasted to a stop, too tired to go on. She didn't think she had enough energy to start a letter to Penn, but, if she did, she knew just what she'd write:

Dear Penn,
New friends aren't worth the hassle. When I get to
Austin, it's going to be me and you against the world.

She pushed her scooter up to the shoreline, wrinkling her nose at the strange smell that seemed to be coming from the lake itself. Her eyes settled on something in the center of the lake, and she gasped.

Coiling out into the water was a long, twisting path that looked like a giant sleeping snake. It was made up of packed mud and clay, its edges lined with chalky-gray rocks that lit up like Christmas lights whenever the sun bounced over them. Algae crept up over the sides, turning the dirt green.

It was like remembering a dream. Suddenly, Lyssa knew exactly where she was. She'd heard so many stories, seen so many pictures of the strange path twisting into the middle of the water, that she recognized it immediately. This was the Spiral Jetty, where Ana had taken Lyssa for her very first birthday.

The fact that Lyssa had wound up here, when everything was about to fall apart, felt almost like a miracle.

Maybe the magic *was* on her side. Maybe it was a sign from her mother.

"Mom?" she whispered.

A faint breeze ruffled the surface of the water.

Lyssa took a step closer. Ana had called this place the Dead Lake, which made Lyssa think of bones and bodies hiding below the surface, of ghosts floating over the still waters after dark. Lyssa knelt down and ran her hands over the rocks. Wedged in between them were pieces of glass and salt crystal. That's why the jetty lit up in the sun.

She closed her eyes and the earth buzzed below her. This place was magical—she could feel it all the way to her toes. It was where she and her mom had celebrated Lyssa's first year of life. If her mom could talk to her anywhere, it would be here.

She pushed her scooter forward and started walking. She hadn't been able to tell from the shore, but the path stretched far out into the middle of the lake. The packed dirt was exactly level with the lake itself, making Lyssa feel like she was walking on water. When she reached the middle of the coil, she dropped to the ground and rolled onto her back. It even sounded a little magical out here, with the buzzing flies and lapping water forming a strange kind of music.

"Mom?" she called.

White clouds moved slowly across the sky, and wind whistled as it blew over the lake. But no one answered. Even the buzzing flies near the shore seemed distant and quiet.

"Mom!" Lyssa shouted again.

Only her voice echoed back to her. Come on, Mom, she thought. Please be here. "It's important," she said, ignoring the fact that her voice cracked—just a little. "Mom,

I need your help. I have questions. You should be here. I need you *here*!"

Lyssa squeezed her eyes shut and waited. The sun warmed her face, and water lapped soothingly against the path. Lyssa opened her mouth to call out again—and yawned instead. She was so tired . . .

Her eyes fluttered, then closed, and she was drifting, drifting into sleep.

When Lyssa opened her eyes again, the sky above her was dark and roiling with steel-gray clouds. Lyssa groaned and pushed herself off the ground. She must have fallen asleep. Water dotted her cheeks and wind roared around her head, blowing her hair over her face. A sliver of lightning appeared on the horizon, spiderweb thin and so far away that she could barely hear the rumble of thunder. The shock of light illuminated the jetty and the rocks appeared to move, like an animal shifting in the darkness.

"Time to go, Zip." A storm was coming.

She yanked up her scooter and started walking, then running. Water crashed over the rocks and flooded the path, soaking her mud-encrusted sneakers. Another bolt of lightning shattered the surface of the lake.

In the growing darkness, Lyssa could swear the path shifted and stretched, like an animal uncoiling. Fear rose in her chest. She told herself she was imagining things. Rocks didn't move on their own. Sculptures didn't turn into monsters.

Bits of rock and mica glinted every time lightning crashed above her. Lyssa could almost hear her mom's voice, telling of a creature that waited for tired travelers.

"The Ugly One," Lyssa said aloud. That was the monster's name. It lived in the Dead Lake, waiting for someone to fall asleep on its shores . . .

No. It was just a story. She was remembering a story and making herself afraid.

Then the path beneath Lyssa rumbled again and she lost her balance, dropping to her knees in the dirt. The skin along the back of her neck tingled like someone—something—was watching her.

"It's just a story, it's just a story, it's just a story," she said out loud. This couldn't be real—she and Penn would laugh about how silly she was being later.

Swallowing, Lyssa turned and looked over her shoulder.

The path itself shuddered, then lifted from the lake, water streaming off the jagged rocks and shards of glass that lined what looked like a long neck. Two rocks set in the middle of the path gave the impression of eyes. It reminded Lyssa of the komodo dragons at the Austin Zoo, but a thousand times bigger.

As the path lifted higher out of the lake, the ground beneath Lyssa grew steep and she almost fell over. Instead of green scales, the path monster was covered in bleached-gray dirt, salt water, and algae-encrusted rocks.

Lyssa opened her mouth and screamed.

The Ugly One stretched its long neck and opened a mouth filled with razor-sharp shards of glass and rock, releasing a growl that sounded almost like thunder. Flecks of spit landed on Lyssa's face and hair.

She leapt onto her scooter. The creature swiveled its long neck toward her and snapped at her heels as she pushed off and flew down its back, her blond braids streaming behind her. The Ugly One's rocky, muddy back grew steeper every time the creature lifted farther out of the water, so that Lyssa and Zip rolled faster and faster down its back.

Lyssa clung to her scooter's handlebars. She was going faster than she'd ever gone on her scooter before—but she couldn't slow down. She didn't know whether she was riding or falling.

Somehow, she managed to stay on her scooter as she wove around shards of glass that looked more and more like giant scales while the Ugly One twisted and lunged at her heels. She yanked the scooter to the left, barely avoiding a rock.

She could feel the creature's hot breath on her ankles. The shore was just ahead.

Lightning crashed into the Ugly One's back, only a few feet from where Lyssa rode, and the wheels of her scooter skidded out beneath her. She fell, half rolling, half falling down the monster's back, over rocks and scales and glass.

When she looked up, the creature's face was directly above her. Its rocky eyes flashed; its teeth glinted in the darkness. Lyssa screamed again and the creature lunged right for her.

She rolled to the side and its mouth closed around her scooter, crushing Zip between sharp, rocky teeth.

"No!" Lyssa yelled. Various metal parts, handlebars, and a pom-pom fell from the Ugly One's mouth like crumbs. But Lyssa couldn't stop to mourn her loss. She pushed herself up and leapt to the shore.

Wet sand crumbled beneath her sneakers and she dropped to her knees. Her heart felt heavy and cold inside her chest, like a last little bit of muddy snow that wouldn't melt. But she was safe. She knew, even before looking back over her shoulder, that the monster wouldn't be able to follow her onto shore.

Sure enough, the Ugly One hovered behind her, water still pouring from the rocks lining its back. It growled, low and deep, and somewhere in the distance lightning struck again. The storm was passing.

Lyssa stood up, gasping for breath. Her broken scooter was crushed to pieces a few feet away. But at least she was alive.

She watched the Ugly One settle, disgruntled, back into the water, then grow still, until it was nothing more than the twisting Spiral Jetty once again. Beneath the howling of the wind, Lyssa heard something familiar. It was a voice coming from the air and the sky and all around her:

"That's my girl."

"Mom?" Lyssa spoke into the wind-whipped air, her heart beating fast inside her chest. "Is that you?" She didn't wait for an answer; she couldn't stop the words from spilling out of her mouth. "Mom, I've been looking for you. I've been waiting for a sign, but I don't know how to find you, and I don't understand how to use your magic. Mom?"

The wind roared, blowing all traces of her mom's faint voice away. Lyssa took a step forward and something crunched beneath her. She looked down—it was one of Zip's pom-poms, shredded on the sand.

Tears pricked the corners of Lyssa's eyes. This time, she didn't try to stop them from rolling down her cheeks.

She felt like someone had taken an ice cream scooper and hollowed out her chest. Everything was wrong. Zip, her best friend, had been destroyed. Her mom was supposed to be watching over her, but Lyssa couldn't find her anywhere. The magic she'd been putting so much faith in was turning out to be powerful and strange and even frightening. She was cold.

She was alone.

The tears came quickly now, smearing the dirt on Lyssa's face and clogging her throat. She hiccupped, then sank to her knees. She no longer cared about being strong. She cried because she was scared and hungry and because Circe had betrayed her. She cried for every day she'd had to live without her mom, and every day that she would still have to. She cried because it felt like she would never be able to go home again.

Then, just when Lyssa thought she was done crying, she thought of Michael searching for her along the abandoned highways that stretched between Utah and Washington, a glob of toothpaste stuck to his nose. She thought of Penn poofing her hair up while she waited for Lyssa to call and tell her that she was safe, and the Real Estate Corporation getting their wrecking balls ready—waiting for the day they could knock down her home. Tomorrow. Lyssa would never make it in time.

She cried until no more tears would come. Then she curled up, and slept.

CHAPTER EIGHTEEN

Leonard the Bard and the Angry Cherry

While Lyssa slept, she dreamed.

She was back home, in Texas, lying on her back in the garden. Sunflowers towered over her, swaying lazily in the wind, and ladybugs jumped from the ground to the leaves to the tip of Lyssa's nose, making her sneeze.

She sat up, brushing the bugs from her face. Her mom was kneeling in the dirt just a few feet away, her back to Lyssa. Her hair hung over her shoulders in two thick braids, and she had a wide-brimmed straw hat perched on top of her head. She was digging in the dirt with a spade and humming under her breath.

"Mom," Lyssa called. She pushed herself to her feet and

started walking toward her mom. The garden was bigger than she remembered it being, filled with twisting vines and jagged rocks that made her stumble and trip. "Mom," she called again.

But her mom didn't look up. She jammed her spade into the dirt a little more forcefully. The song she was humming seemed sad now. Lonely.

"Mom," Lyssa said. She started running, her bare feet kicking up dirt. When she reached her mom, she grabbed onto her shoulder and forced her to turn.

But the face that stared back at her wasn't her mom's— it was Circe's.

Circe was wearing a wig with braids and Lyssa's mom's big straw hat. She held up a handful of tulips that she'd dug up by the roots.

"The flowers we cut are fleeting," she said. She opened her hand and the dead flowers tumbled off the ends of her fingers. "But the roots we plant are for life."

Lyssa woke in the middle of the night to music: smooth and velvety, with notes that rose into the air and ended in a squeak, like a whistle. The tune started off wild, then became slow and soulful.

She sat up. She didn't know where the music was coming from, but she felt something stirring deep inside her. She didn't know where else to go. She was going to follow it.

She stood and wiped her nose on the sleeve of her sweatshirt. She gathered the pieces of her broken scooter and shoved them into her backpack.

"Don't worry, Zip," she whispered. "I'll find someone to fix you."

She followed the music around the shore of the lake and came upon a dirt road. In the moonlight, she could see that it was crisscrossed with train tracks.

An unmoving train curved along the tracks. One of the boxcars stood wide open, and there was an old man sitting inside it, his bare feet swinging over the edge of the car. He was playing a harmonica, and the sound was deep and sad and lonely. Exactly the way Lyssa felt.

The man had long, tangled gray hair and eyes that were so blue it made Lyssa wonder if he had a bit of sky stuck inside them. His face was wrinkled and open and kind. It reminded Lyssa of her grandmother's old leather handbag: soft to the touch and creased from years of adventures. The man wore a flannel shirt and corduroy pants covered in patches.

"Where's this train going?" Lyssa asked, shifting her backpack in her arms. The man lowered his harmonica and gave her a shy smile.

"Where ain't it going? That's the question." The man

blew into his harmonica again, sending a beautiful chorus of notes up toward the moon, which was high and full, like a spotlight. "I think it ends up in New Mexico."

"New Mexico," Lyssa repeated. The words made her think of sunshine and clay houses and turquoise jewelry. Hadn't her mom told her that her dad had moved to New Mexico to pursue his music? Maybe he could fix Zip up— he was the one who put the scooter together in the first place. Besides, New Mexico wasn't far from Texas. The talent show was tomorrow, but Lyssa could get lucky. Maybe the winds of change were blowing in her favor again. Bus tickets were probably cheaper down here—maybe $8 would get her a ride . . .

Wait—not $8. She was down to $6 after paying for that ice cream.

"Why don't you let me help you up?" the man said, setting his harmonica down on his lap. Lyssa handed him the pieces of her scooter; then he grabbed her arm and hoisted her into the boxcar.

"We should be taking off anytime," he said kindly. He held out one hand. "The name's Oscar."

"Lyssa," she said, shaking his hand. He sat back down and started playing his harmonica again, staring into the night sky. The notes rose up toward the moon and disappeared among the stars.

Lyssa pulled her sweatshirt out of her bag and bundled it up in a ball under her head, using it as a pillow. By the time the boxcar started rocking on the tracks, carrying her south, she was fast asleep again.

When Lyssa woke up, for a second she didn't know where she was. It wasn't until she pushed herself into a sitting position that she remembered she was in a boxcar. She looked around for Oscar, the man with the harmonica, but he was gone. She stared up at the sky outside and determined from the position of the sun that it was around ten in the morning.

The boxcar was parked just inside a huge, adobe train station with whitewashed walls. Outside the station were streets filled with organic grocery stores, coffee shops, and jewelry stands. The air, Lyssa was relieved to find, was toasty warm and dry—just like Texas.

She tied her sweatshirt around her waist and put her backpack on. The scooter was a little too big for her backpack, though, and a few metal pieces stuck out of the top and jabbed Lyssa, painfully, in the neck.

Lyssa sighed, her stomach rumbling. "Well, Zip," she said to the broken bits of scooter sticking out of her backpack. "We should probably head out."

Out of the corner of her eye, Lyssa saw a flash of white.

There was a poster attached to the outside of the boxcar, fluttering in the wind.

Lyssa felt as though she'd been dipped in ice-cold water. But when she scrambled out of the boxcar and pulled the poster down, she saw that it wasn't a missing person poster at all. It was a band flyer. It looked a lot like her dad's old band flyers, but it was for a musician named Leonard the Bard. She couldn't help examining the lead singer's face just a little closer. There was something familiar about the line of his jaw and the way his nose drooped a little at the tip.

Her heart started beating faster. Musicians changed their names, right? When Lyssa's dad and mom were together, her dad had been called the Great Lenny. And Lenny was short for Leonard . . .

Lyssa shuffled around in her backpack, finding her purple water bottle. She had a sticker from one of her dad's bands on the water bottle and, even though it was faded, she could still see his face. She held the water bottle right next to the poster and, as she examined the two photos side by side, tingles shot through the tips of her fingers and scurried into her arms, like there was a team of ants racing through her veins.

The man in the poster might have been a bit older and weighed a little more than he did in Lyssa's band sticker, but it sure *looked* like the same man.

This was fate—a sign. Yesterday she'd felt so lost and alone, ready to stop believing in magic and the winds of change entirely. But today the universe—her mother?—had led her to her father. According to the flyer, he played at a coffee shop called the Angry Cherry every Wednesday night. If Lyssa could find out where the Angry Cherry was, she'd just explain who she was to the coffee shop manager and ask him for her father's phone number. Her dad would want to know that she was here. He'd want to meet her. He'd probably even offer to fix her scooter!

Folding the flyer back up, Lyssa stuck it in her pocket and headed toward the coffee shops and jewelry stands across the street.

Even though Lyssa had never actually met her real dad, she knew all about him. Her parents had met during a Texas Talent Show performance. Lyssa's mom had been dancing around onstage with her tambourine, her braids whipping around and around as she spun. Lyssa's father, Lenny, was in the audience, and he fell over the moon in love with Ana Lee before she sang a single note. He ran up onto the stage in the middle of her song and kissed her—right in front of everyone.

After the performance, Lyssa's mom and father walked around the fair hand in hand, talking about their dreams. Lenny, Lyssa's mom told her, had wanted to be a famous musician. But at that point in the story, Lyssa's mom always got quiet. She'd lean over and kiss Lyssa on the forehead, like the story was over.

"What did you wish for?" Lyssa would ask. Her mom looked down at her and smiled.

"I wished for you," she said, every time.

Lyssa's dad had stayed with them for a few years—he even built Lyssa her scooter, although she was too young to remember it. Then he'd had to follow his dreams and become a famous musician.

Lyssa thought she understood that. Dreams were important. But by now, he had to be famous. Maybe he'd let Lyssa stay with him and they could play music together. And he'd definitely want to know about the demolition. He'd probably even offer to drive Lyssa over to Austin so they could protest together.

Lyssa stopped people on the street, asking if they knew where she could find the Angry Cherry coffee shop. She had to stop twelve different people before someone could direct her. A man wearing an enormous sun visor told her to keep going straight and turn left at the third stoplight.

The Angry Cherry was at the end of the block.

Lyssa lugged the bits of scooter all the way to the coffee shop, barely noticing the extra weight in her backpack. Her mouth was dust dry, but her palms were sweating. She was going to meet her father. She could hardly believe it.

The coffee shop was tiny and there was a large cherry stenciled on the door. Lyssa pressed her face against the window and looked inside. She couldn't tell if it was open. She hesitated there for a long moment.

"Can I help you with something, little miss?"

The voice came from a large, silver trailer parked in the street just next to the coffee shop. A man leaned out the front door. He had shaggy, graying hair that hung over his face, but, when he pushed it away with the back of his hand, Lyssa saw that he was, unmistakably, Leonard the Bard.

His nose looked a lot like the one she saw in the mirror every morning. He had ears that stuck out from his head a little—just like hers. She walked toward him, her heart thudding in her chest. Her father. It was him. It had to be him.

"Hi," she said. Her voice cracked and she bit down on her lower lip and fought the urge to put her braid in her mouth. "I mean, hello. My name is Lyssa."

Lyssa had assumed her father would recognize her immediately, but he just narrowed his eyes and for almost a minute there was complete silence.

"Lyssa?" he said, finally. "Ana Lee's daughter?" He shook his head, causing a few gray strands of hair to stick to the sweat on his cheek. "Well, now. Wild."

Lyssa shifted her gaze down to her feet. The way her father looked at her made her feel uncomfortable, like her skin was too small or like the air was pressing in on her. Something was wrong and she couldn't quite pinpoint what it was. Didn't he know that he was her dad? Didn't he *feel* it?

"So, um, you're my dad," Lyssa said.

"That's right," her dad said, leaning against the doorframe. "Hey, now. I was sorry about what happened to your mom. I heard about it. That's awful." He paused. "You look pretty tired. Want to come in and put your feet up for a second?"

"I'm actually here because there's an emergency," she said, so fast that her words tumbled over one another. "See, my mom's house was supposed to be turned into a community center, but there was a law that it couldn't be and now they want to build condos so I need to get to Texas by . . ."

Lyssa paused, counting back the days in her head. Then she counted them again and one more time after that. Every inch of her skin felt suddenly cold.

"Today," she croaked out, as the realization hit her with the force of a concrete wall. "They're knocking down our home today."

Her father chuckled under his breath and shook his head. "Slow down there," he said, running a hand through his hair again. "Why don't you come inside and sit down for a minute?"

"But we don't *have* a minute," Lyssa protested. "Please. We have to go *now*."

"How about we get you a bite to eat first?" her dad said, still smiling. It was as if he wasn't listening to her at all.

"But—" Lyssa tried again.

"Come on in," he said in a lullaby voice, as though she was five and not eleven. "And then you can tell me all about it, okay?"

Lyssa didn't see what other choice she had. So she swallowed and tried to give him a little smile. "I *am* a little hungry," she admitted.

The man who was supposed to be her father nodded. "Alrighty then. We'll find you something to eat."

Lyssa followed Leonard up the stairs and into his trailer. It was dark inside, even with the light on, but there were plants everywhere—hanging from the ceiling, crowded around the furniture, and even sitting on the countertops. The effect, Lyssa thought, was like being in a dark, cool jungle.

The trailer was small, though, and despite the fact that there wasn't much furniture, it felt cramped—probably because of all the plants. The front room held only one chair, a lamp shaped like a beer can, and a turned-over milk crate that was being used as a coffee table. The carpet was orange and shaggy, and wood paneling covered the walls.

Lyssa looked around, confused. Was this where her father lived? Was this what his dreams had brought him?

Her father crossed the room and pulled open his refrigerator. Immediately, Lyssa was hit with a strong, pungent smell—like feet. She glanced over her father's shoulder and saw that there were only a few things in the fridge: a hunk of moldy-looking cheese, some jars of mustard and ketchup, and a few cases of beer. Her father scratched his head, then shut the fridge door.

"How's about I just grab you some water?" he said. "And then maybe we can order some pizza or something."

We don't have time to order pizza! Lyssa wanted to scream. But she knew it would do no good, so she just nodded, tight-lipped.

Lenny pulled a glass out of the sink and rinsed it out, filling it halfway up with cloudy-looking water. Lyssa awkwardly set down her backpack, filled with the pieces of her broken scooter, and took the glass from him. When she looked into the glass, she saw there were bits of dirt floating on the surface.

Maybe she wasn't thirsty after all.

She perched on top of the milk crate, balancing the

water glass on her knee. Her father sat down on the chair across from her. For a moment neither of them spoke. Lyssa turned her water glass to make the liquid inside swirl.

"I still have the scooter you made for me," she blurted out after a minute, motioning to the silver pieces sticking out of her backpack.

"That thing?" her father asked.

"Well, it got a little broken," Lyssa explained. "Maybe you could help me fix it? Since you made it and all . . ."

Lenny started laughing. "Sweetheart, I can't even put together an Ikea coffee table! Your mom built that scooter. She used to come home every night after work and put that thing together. I thought she was crazy, but, well . . . you know how she can be. She gets those nutty ideas in her head. Got, I mean."

A hard, tight ball formed in the back of Lyssa's throat.

"No," she said, slowly. "You built it. Remember? Mom said you knew I'd be an adventurer, just like you."

"Your mom said that, did she?" Lyssa's father looked away, fixing his eye on a crack running through the wood paneling on his wall. "Well, she always did have quite an imagination."

"*No,*" Lyssa said, more insistent this time. What was Lenny saying? Her mom didn't have crazy ideas—she didn't have "quite an imagination." She made things happen—she filled the world with magic. Lyssa could feel the skin on her face turning red, could feel a headache building just behind her eyeballs. "You built me the scooter so it would remind me of you . . . so when you became famous and traveled around the world—"

"Famous?" Lenny interrupted. He had stopped laughing. Now he just looked sorry. He just shook his head. "Lyssa, where did you get an idea like that?"

"But . . ." Lyssa reached the end of her sentence, realizing she didn't know where she expected it to go. She looked down at the pieces of scooter in her bag.

Her mom had been the one who said her dad built the scooter. Her mom had been the one who told her that her dad had left them to become famous, but here he was, sitting alone in a smelly little trailer in New Mexico.

Lyssa shifted her eyes to her feet, not wanting to meet this man's eyes. How was *this* better than living in Texas with the rest of his family, in a big house surrounded by flowers? How was this better than waking up to the smell of Ana's herbal tea in the morning and kissing Lyssa before she fell asleep at night? If he hadn't even gotten his dream, then what was the point of leaving in the first place?

It suddenly hit Lyssa: her father wasn't famous. He hadn't left to make music. He just left, for no good reason at all.

Lenny leaned forward, resting his elbows on his knees. Lyssa could hardly bring herself to look at him.

"Listen," he said. "It seems like you're a far way from home. Didn't your mom get married again? You know, before . . ." He cleared his throat, awkwardly. Apparently he didn't like talking about what happened to Lyssa's mom any more than she did. "Maybe you should give your step-dad a call and let him know you're okay and tell him where you are. What do you say?"

Lyssa's throat felt dry. She knew that she should object, that she should keep going—she was *so* close to home. But all she had to do was look around the trailer and a feeling of disappointment and loneliness swept over her like a wave. Everything she thought she knew was a lie. If it was magic that led her to her real father, it wasn't trying to help her. Lyssa didn't have any way of stopping the wrecking ball. She couldn't possibly save her home.

Everything she'd thought she knew about her family, about the universe, was just wrong.

Maybe it was time to give up.

"You look a little nervous, kiddo," Lenny said, smiling. "You worried your stepdad's going to be mad? You want me to call for you?"

"Okay," Lyssa said in a very small voice. "Make the call."

CHAPTER NINETEEN

Kung Pao Wow

Her father—no, *Lenny*—gave her a small smile. He stood up, walking down the cramped hallway and into a room at the very back of the trailer. The room didn't have a door, but there was a wooden partition that slid, accordion-like, across the hallway. Lenny had to wrestle it closed.

Lyssa shifted and the old wooden milk crate creaked beneath her weight. Her eyes settled on the red digits of the clock on the microwave. It was almost noon—and the demolition was scheduled for noon today. As she listened to the low rise and fall of Lenny's voice on the phone in the other room, she watched the numbers on the clock change.

11:58. 11:59. 12:00.

Something inside Lyssa crumbled. She could almost hear the sound of the wrecking ball swinging into the big white porch that wrapped around her house, knocking down the dogwood tree in the front yard. Lyssa pictured the big tree's roots being ripped from the earth. It felt like the same wrecking ball had swung into her chest. She hadn't made it. She had failed.

I'm sorry, Mom.

There was a shuffle outside the trailer, then the sound of footsteps. Lyssa stood up, almost knocking over the milk crate. Was someone here for her already? She shifted her eyes over to the far room, where Lenny was still talking on the phone. Wasn't he even going to come out and say goodbye before they took her away?

A piece of paper slid beneath the front door, and Lyssa heard footsteps again—this time running away. Curious, Lyssa walked over and scooped the paper off the floor.

It was a takeout menu for the Lucky Sun Dragon Chinese Restaurant. The pictures of kung pao chicken and crab wontons made Lyssa's stomach rumble. She couldn't remember the last time she'd had a full meal. Lyssa and her mom used to eat pineapple stir-fry all the time—they'd get it so spicy that it burned the tips of their tongues and, for the rest of the night, they could barely talk. Sometimes her mom would even make little paper puppets using spare chopsticks and napkins and they'd have a puppet show after dinner. Her mom could make the puppets talk without ever moving her lips . . .

Lyssa felt another pang. She couldn't think about her mom now. Not after Lyssa had failed her so badly.

Something slipped out of the folded menu and dropped onto the toe of her sneaker. She bent down to pick it up.

The little blue paper airplane. Its wings were broken and torn, and there was so much dirt smudged over the paper that it hardly looked blue anymore.

For a second Lyssa just stared at it, shocked. She checked the back pocket of her jeans, where she thought she'd been keeping the airplane all along, but the pocket was empty. She ran her thumb across the message on the airplane's wing.

There's no place like home.

Home. Even if her home had been demolished, it was still *hers*—that little piece of land belonged to her mom, belonged to both of them. If her mother's magic was anywhere in this world, it was in that land, not in some old motel hot tub off the highway, or at the Spiral Jetty, or here. Maybe there was darker magic in the world—but only good magic could come from that little patch of ground in Texas.

Lyssa looked down at the paper airplane and, suddenly, it felt like someone had adjusted the color on a television set. Everything around her looked brighter and felt clearer. This tiny airplane had been through just as much as she had—it too had been lost and forgotten, it'd been through thunderstorms and whirlpools and that fight with Old Marty the cat. But even though it had been nearly destroyed, the plane was still trying to make its way home.

And Lyssa was just sitting here. Waiting for the police to come and take her back to Michael.

She had to go home, even if her home was nothing more than a pile of dirt by the time she got there.

Lights flashed blue and red through the thin curtains covering the trailer windows. Lyssa stood, brushed away the curtains, and peered outside.

There was a police car parked at the curb, and a man with little hair and a lot of stomach eased his way out of the driver's seat. As he headed toward the trailer, everything about him bounced, from his stomach to his cheeks to the bad, blond toupee.

Watching him approach, Lyssa had only one thought: I could outrun *him*.

She swallowed and backed away from the door. Maybe she had missed the Texas Talent Show's performance and her chance to do anything to stop the demolition, but she couldn't give up on reaching Austin or seeing her mom's garden again. Maybe all the flowers would be covered with rubble, but the garden would still be there, hidden beneath the wreckage. *Though we travel far away, we leave our roots behind,* her mom had said. Roots were buried far beneath the ground. They couldn't be destroyed with a wrecking ball.

"Lyssa?" Lenny called.

Lyssa ducked behind a chair as he forced the partition back open and walked into the room.

"Lyssa, I called Michael and get this—he's in Utah looking around for you right now! Someone spotted you along the way and called in a tip. He told me to call the police to come pick you up . . ."

Lyssa picked up her backpack, searching the room for an escape route. There was an open window on the other side of the trailer. Someone knocked on the trailer door and the floorboards creaked as Lenny stepped forward and pulled it open.

"Thanks for getting here so quickly," Lenny said, stepping aside to let the policeman through the door.

While he was distracted, Lyssa raced across the room. She pushed her backpack through the window and pulled herself up onto the sill. Holy cow—it was *a lot* smaller than it looked from across the room. Lyssa wriggled and pulled, but her bottom half wouldn't budge. She was stuck tighter than a hand in a pickle jar.

She wanted to scream. She'd gotten all the way across the country—escaped monsters and thunderstorms, bad friends and surprise whirlpools—and the cops were finally going to catch her stuck in a trailer window.

Just when Lyssa was certain she was done for, Lenny slammed the trailer door. The sudden jolt helped Lyssa wriggle loose. She toppled out of the window and landed in a prickly bush growing in the alley next to the trailer. Sharp burrs and twigs dug into her arms and legs, leaving angry red marks on her skin. She clenched her mouth shut to keep from crying out. She leapt to her feet and pulled the base of her scooter out of her bag. Dropping it to the sidewalk, she jumped on, hitching her backpack over her shoulders. The base wobbled at first, but Lyssa gritted her teeth and kicked off, riding it down the street like a skateboard.

The policeman stumbled out of the front of the trailer just as Lyssa rounded the corner.

"Hey!" he shouted. "Wait!"

Lyssa nearly tumbled off her makeshift skateboard. She needed something—a distraction. She fumbled in her backpack, and her fingers curled around fabric. When she withdrew her hand, she realized she was holding the pink-and-green rhinestone bra she'd stolen for Circe.

"Stop!" the officer called again. He was getting closer. Lyssa twisted around to face him, pulled one strap of the bra back—like a slingshot—and fired. The bra whizzed through the air and flew at his face. The wind whipped it up over his eyes like a blindfold. The officer stumbled backward, giving Lyssa just enough time to push off and gain speed down the sidewalk. As she tore around the corner, she thought she heard Lenny call her name, but she didn't stop to check.

"We need a place to hide," she said to Zip, or what remained of it. She was heartened to hear a squeak of agreement. Zip too was still fighting.

The block Lyssa had turned down was crowded with tiny boutiques and restaurants, but she rolled past them without stopping. Her father and the policeman would check inside places like that for sure. She needed to hide somewhere no one would think to look for her.

On the next street there was a tiny smoke shop wedged between a deli and a dry cleaner. The smoke shop's windows were dark, and when the door opened, a smell like unlit matches and heavily oiled wood wafted out.

Lyssa coughed, waving her hand in front of her face. Her mom always said that smoke made your lungs shrivel up and turn black until they were tiny, wrinkly raisins. And Lyssa hated raisins, even when they were baked into cookies. She certainly didn't want them inside her body.

Still . . . the smoke shop would be the last place anyone would ever think to look for her. She slowed her skateboard and hopped off. Taking a deep breath of fresh, clean air, she pulled the door open and snuck inside. Her eyes watered. Breathing the air inside the smoke shop felt like trying to inhale cotton. Stinky, dirty cotton.

The shop's countertops were all heavy and dark, and they shone like someone just rubbed them down with baby oil. Smoke floated near the ceiling in miniature gray clouds. At one end of the shop, a man with a heavy Russian accent and a skinny little mustache held a box filled with cigars, motioning wildly with one hand as he spoke. Two men—or maybe they were still just boys—stood in front of him, wearing tight jeans and brightly colored eyeglasses. They had the craziest hair Lyssa had ever seen: it was gelled up on the sides in strange waves and crests.

Lyssa crouched behind a display of old-fashioned wooden pipes, watching the boys lift cigars out of the box and sniff them. Lyssa wrinkled her nose and fought the urge to cough. She was so focused on the strange-looking people that she didn't even notice there was someone sitting cross-legged on the floor only inches away.

"Hey there, ladybug."

The voice shocked Lyssa so much that she leapt up, biting back a scream. She whirled around, smacking the pipe display with her backpack. The display rocked back and forth, then tumbled over and crashed to the floor. Pipes rolled across the dark wooden floorboards of the shop.

"What is this?" the man with the Russian accent demanded. He snapped the cigar case shut and crossed the room in three large strides. "This is little girl? Little girl is not to be in cigar store. You know these things, Scarlett."

The girl sitting next to Lyssa stood and started gathering up the spilled pipes. She wasn't dressed like the two boys. She was very tall, with broad shoulders and long, curly blond hair held back in places by tiny butterfly clips. She wore high-waisted shorts, a T-shirt with a picture of an old-fashioned bicycle on it, and a heavy fur coat that looked way too warm for late summer in New Mexico. She looked familiar, although Lyssa couldn't immediately place her face, which was bare of makeup.

Then it came to her: If the girl had had a beehive hairdo and sparkly, rhinestone-covered sunglasses, she'd look *exactly* like the mermaid from the burlesque show.

Like Athena.

Had she found Athena at last?

Lyssa pushed away the thought and her excitement. She'd thought she'd seen Athena at the grocery store and the market, the burlesque club and in the whirlpool, and she'd been wrong every time. And why on earth would Athena be here, in some cruddy cigar shop?

"Alek, this is my sister, little Ladybug," Scarlett said, giving Lyssa a wink. "Haven't you ever heard me talk about my little sister? Come on, Alek. You've known my family for years!"

Alek harrumphed, but he seemed to soften a bit. Shrugging, he turned back to the boys, opening the box of cigars again. "You clean up mess, yeah?"

"Yeah," Scarlett promised.

Lyssa knelt down on the ground to help Scarlett gather the pipes.

"Thanks," she whispered once Alek had his back turned.

"No sweat, Ladybug," Scarlett said with a wink.

Lyssa swallowed. She couldn't stop looking at Scarlett and visualizing her onstage, in a bright beam of spotlight. "This might sound kinda weird . . . but do I know you from somewhere?" she asked finally.

Scarlett froze with one hand poised over a pipe. She raised an eyebrow. "You think you've seen me somewhere?"

"I—I don't know," Lyssa stuttered, and tugged on one of her braids. "You look like . . ." She lost her nerve. "Like this mermaid I saw at a burlesque show once."

Now Scarlett's lips curved into a smile. "What were *you* doing at a burlesque show?"

"Oh, you know," Lyssa said, trying to keep her voice casual. "I was just there for the music."

Scarlett laughed, but there was a glimmer of curiosity in her green eyes, and she didn't look away from Lyssa.

"So what are you doing here?" she asked. "Hiding out? On the lam from the police?"

Lyssa swallowed and shifted her eyes to the ground. Scarlett had no idea how close she was to the truth. And Lyssa couldn't admit to the truth, could she? The last time she'd trusted someone was Circe. And that hadn't turned out well at all.

Then again, Scarlett had helped her by lying to Alek. Lenny and the policeman couldn't be far away, and if Lyssa were thrown out of the shop, they'd catch her for sure.

The thought made Lyssa's arms and legs feel heavy, like someone had filled them with sand. She was tired of running, she was tired of lying. She was so tired.

"Come on, Ladybug," Scarlett said gently, sliding the very last pipe into place. "I won't rat you out."

"Well," Lyssa started. "I'm heading to Austin, Texas. There was this protest . . ."

And she found herself telling the whole story, from the Texas Talent Show, to her mom's will, to Michael and how he called the police when she went missing. She even admitted that her father and a policeman were roaming the streets of New Mexico right this minute, searching for her.

"And it doesn't even matter anymore," Lyssa said once she got to the end of her story. "The house has already been destroyed. I missed everything."

For a second there was complete silence. Then someone sniffled.

"This is beautiful tale of adventure," came a voice from behind Lyssa.

She turned around and saw that Alek and the two boys with the strange hair had come closer to listen to her story. Alek wiped a tear from his cheek, and the skinny little mustache twitched above his mouth. The boy wearing purple sunglasses and a motorcycle jacket shook his head.

"You aren't talking about that singer's house, are you?" he asked. "Ana . . . something? They were going to do a big show to protest and everything?"

"That's it," Lyssa said, nodding, excited. "Ana Lee's my mom."

"Whoa," the other boy said. His curly red hair had so much gel in it that the curls stuck out like coiled copper wire. "I mean, wicked. It was on the news and everything. They were expecting a huge turnout—like, hundreds of people or something? But there was this storm moving in—like crazy lightning and wind and everything. They delayed the demolition and the show till tomorrow."

"*What?*"

Lyssa felt her entire body start to hum. It wasn't gone? Her house, the garden, everything—*it was still there?*

Suddenly, it felt like everything was moving in fast motion. Lyssa had to move—she had to get to Austin! She hadn't missed anything at all! Her home was still there. She just hoped and prayed she was right about her mother's magic; she knew she wasn't strong enough to stop the demolition on her own.

"Is there a bus station nearby?" she asked, tucking the scooter-base skateboard under one arm. "I have to go!"

Scarlett glanced at the two boys and smiled.

"I don't know about a bus station," she said, looking back at Lyssa. "But I know where to find a bus."

CHAPTER TWENTY

Balloon Wishes and the Sunflower Muse

Scarlett and the two boys from the cigar shop led Lyssa down a narrow alley to the parking lot out back. There was a bright yellow school bus parked next to the Dumpsters, its chipped paint gleaming in the New Mexico sun. Lyssa didn't think she could be happier to see that bus if it was made entirely out of gold.

"It's amazing," Lyssa breathed.

"Wait until you see the inside," Scarlett said.

Inside the bus were more odd-looking people. There were girls with shaved heads and boys with hair so long they could sit on it. The bus driver—a girl who looked like she was still in college—had more tattoos than the illustrated man at the fair. Not only were her arms and back covered in colorful pictures, there was a tiny trail of stars curving along the side of her face.

"Scarlett, you're late," a girl with a mohawk yelled. "We were just about to go and find you."

"Sorry! Got distracted at the smoke shop," Scarlett shouted back. Then, to Lyssa, she said, "Welcome to the family! Are you ready to go?"

"Where are you all going?" Lyssa asked as Scarlett led her down the aisle.

"We travel here and there," Scarlett said with a shrug. "Today, we're headed to Austin."

Lyssa grinned. She could hardly believe it.

As she took a seat, she couldn't help but gaze in admiration at everything around her. The bus seats had been reupholstered in striped, polka-dotted, and flowery fabric and someone had painted the ceiling a swirly purple and blue, speckled with sparkly stars like the night sky.

And there were photographs *everywhere*. Polaroids and strips from old photo booths were stuck to every inch of the walls and windows, held in place by band stickers and Scotch tape. Lyssa leaned in to take a look. There were pictures of people climbing trees and having picnics and making silly faces at the camera. There was even a picture of Scarlett standing on top of a mountain in the middle of the night, a black-and-purple sky of stars spread out behind her.

Who *were* these people?

"Are you hungry?" Scarlett asked, sliding into a seat next to her and pulling a plastic cooler onto her lap.

"Do you have any peanut butter and jelly?"

Scarlett wrinkled her nose. "Peanut butter is an allergen, so we don't keep it on the bus, but I do have this."

She flipped open the cooler and pulled out a sandwich wrapped in brown paper.

"It's sunflower spread and raspberry preserves," Scarlett said, handing the sandwich to Lyssa.

Lyssa wasn't so sure about sunflower spread—she preferred to look at sunflowers, not eat them—but she was so hungry that she unwrapped the sandwich and took a bite anyway. The sunflower spread was too salty, but the raspberry preserves were gooey and sweet.

Still, Lyssa thought, the sandwich wasn't nearly as good as the strawberry and peanut butter sandwiches Michael used to make for her. He knew how to apply the peanut butter and jelly in exactly the right ratio. Lyssa stopped chewing.

Even though she had been struggling not to admit it, she realized she was actually starting to *miss* Michael. She missed their afternoon rides by the Puget Sound and how the house always smelled like Downy fabric softener and microwave popcorn. She even missed the way he laughed whenever Lyssa told a joke—he always snorted a little, and if he was drinking something, it'd come out his nose.

There was a low, roaring noise as the engine started and the bus rocked forward.

"So Ladybug, are you nervous about singing in the show?" Scarlett asked.

Lyssa took another bite of her sandwich so that she wouldn't have to answer right away. Back at the smoke shop, she'd made it sound like she was going to sing for the show. But now she couldn't help imagining all those people who'd be in the audience—and the way her throat would close right up when she saw them.

Scarlett and her friends had said there were *hundreds* of people at the protest. How was Lyssa going to sing for all of them when she couldn't even sing for a pig at a farmers' market?

She frowned, swallowing her sticky sandwich. She was better off with her original plan. She couldn't risk ruining the protest by getting stage fright in front of all of those people.

"I don't know if I'll actually perform," Lyssa said, stuffing the last of her sandwich in her mouth. When Scarlett raised an eyebrow, Lyssa reluctantly explained about her stage fright.

"I always thought I'd be like my mom," Lyssa said. "She could sing in front of anyone. But I just get choked up and worry that they won't think I'm good enough. My stepdad even got me this voice recorder software stuff so that I could make demo CDs, to practice. But I still can't sing in public."

For a long moment Scarlett was quiet. Then she gave Lyssa a sad smile.

"I know *exactly* how that feels," Scarlett said.

"Do you get stage fright too?" Lyssa asked.

"I never used to," Scarlett said. Scarlett looked down at her fingernails, studying them carefully. "But now . . . well, I don't know. The thought of facing all those people—it's just like you said. It's like my voice just dries up."

"So you *are* a singer?" Lyssa asked. Her mind flashed again to the mermaid at the burlesque show, to Athena dancing across the stage at her last concert. She tried to shake the thought away. Their resemblance was a coincidence. Wasn't it?

"I was," Scarlett answered. "I mean, I used to be."

"What changed?" Lyssa asked cautiously.

"Life," Scarlett said. She clenched her hands together and placed them in her lap, like she was forcing herself not to look at them. "It's hard to sing, sometimes, when the most important people aren't there to hear you."

Lyssa felt a flood of understanding.

"My mom died," she blurted out. "She died before she could hear me sing onstage. You're right—it is hard to sing when the important people aren't there."

Scarlett looked down at her, a strange mix of emotions flickering across her face. "My mom died, too," she said, her voice quiet.

"Really?" Lyssa knew it was a long shot, but she couldn't help thinking about those rumors she heard about Athena . . .

"I have an idea," Scarlett said, and her face became cheerful again. "Let's make a pact, okay? Instead of worrying about what other people will think of our music, we only worry about what *we* think? After all, we don't sing for other people. We sing for the muse, and the muse comes from within."

"The muse comes from within . . ." Lyssa repeated. "Hey! That's a line from an Athena song."

Scarlett turned to look out the window. "Ooh! Look."

She pointed to the blue-ribbon-colored sky just outside the bus window. Floating in the air between cotton candy clouds were red, yellow, green, and blue balloons. It looked like someone had spilled a bag of M&M's across the sky.

"It's beautiful," Lyssa breathed. She leaned over Scarlett's lap to get a better look out the window. Her breath fogged up the glass.

"It's a balloon fiesta," Scarlett explained. "This year, there's a big race across the sky. People came from all over the world to compete. When I was little, my mom used to tell me I got one wish for every balloon. Want to try?"

Scarlett pointed to a bright green balloon floating through the air above them. "There's your balloon," she said. "Maybe you could wish for courage? So that you can perform during your show."

Lyssa watched the green balloon bouncing among the clouds. "Do you believe in that?" she asked. "Wishes, and . . . and magic?"

"Of course I do!" Scarlett said. "What about you?"

Lyssa frowned. "I used to," she said slowly. "Now I'm not so sure. My mom—my mom could always make special things happen. Magic things." She swallowed, knowing it sounded crazy, hoping Scarlett wouldn't make fun of her.

Scarlett put a hand on her shoulder. "You've got to understand, Ladybug, that magic is like love. You can't force it. It's unpredictable. It can be fierce and dangerous, or calm and wonderful. Magic doesn't do what you tell it to do. It just is."

That made sense to Lyssa. She realized her mom had never used magic to change the way things were—she just let it float through her life like a breeze. She turned back to the balloon and made her wish. She wished that she'd actually be able to perform at the show, that she wouldn't be scared onstage, and that somehow, her song would help save her home.

"Good job, Ladybug," Scarlett said. "You know why I'm calling you Ladybug, right?"

Lyssa shook her head.

"My mom used to say that if you found a ladybug, it meant good luck was coming your way," Scarlett explained, ruffling Lyssa's hair. "And I have a feeling you're going to be pretty lucky for me. Hey, you don't have one of those demo CDs with you now, do you?"

"Well, I do, but . . ." Lyssa pulled off her backpack and shuffled around inside, pushing aside sandwich bags filled with granola crumbs and a few handfuls of spilled seeds until she found her demo—the last one she had with her. Nervously, she handed it over to Scarlett. "But it's not very . . ."

Scarlett didn't seem to be listening. She grabbed the CD and bounced out of her seat.

"I have a great idea," she said. Before Lyssa could say a word, Scarlett raced down the bus aisle. Lyssa followed, careening into the people still sitting in their seats. By the time she reached the front of the bus, Scarlett had the CD out of the case and was talking to the bus driver—the girl with spiky black hair and star tattoos running up the side of her face.

"Lyssa, this is Euma," Scarlett said. "She has a CD player we can use."

Euma lifted a hand from the steering wheel and waved at Lyssa without taking her eyes off the road.

"Hello," she said. Her voice was tinted with a British accent that made the word sound like "allo."

"This is what we're going to do," Scarlett explained. "Euma and I are going to listen to your CD and give you some pointers. That way you'll be prepared for the show. Euma's a performer, like us. She does slam poetry and spoken word performances."

Lyssa glanced down the aisle at the rest of the people on the bus. "They won't hear?"

"Are you kidding?" Euma said, her accent making her words crisp and light. "This bus is so loud they can barely hear the people sitting next to them. You'll be fine."

Lyssa took a deep breath, then nodded. Scarlett inserted her CD into the player sitting on the bus's dashboard.

A second later, Lyssa's voice blasted throughout the entire bus.

"Hi, y'all. My name is Lyssa Lee and I'm here to sing some songs for you."

A few people started to cheer and whoop—one even catcalled. Lyssa's knees went weak. She threw both hands over her mouth.

An anxious crease drew itself between Scarlett's eyebrows. She dropped to her knees and started fumbling with the CD player.

"The play button's jammed," she muttered. "I can't get it to stop. I thought you said this wasn't connected to the bus's sound system, Euma."

"The bus doesn't *have* a sound system," Euma said, looking just as bewildered.

Lyssa looked up at the bus's ceiling. There were no wires, no speakers, nothing that could possibly play her CD. Yet her voice floated above the other riders, crooning out the words to her favorite Athena song, "Tricks." It was like the bus itself was singing, like the funky painted ceiling and flowery fabric-covered seats had found their voice.

Lyssa buried her face in her hands. It felt like a wildfire was sweeping over her face, she was blushing so badly.

But, after a few seconds of listening, the humiliation faded—just a little bit. Lyssa realized she didn't sound so bad. Her voice was clear and strong and she was perfectly on key.

"*I know your tricks, I know, I know . . .*" she sang over the speakers.

Lyssa lowered her hands from her face and saw that people were actually *listening*. They nodded along with the sound of her voice, smiling. Someone started singing along and before Lyssa knew what was happening, everyone on the bus was singing with her. They all seemed to know the words. As the song reached the final verse, Lyssa's voice soared higher and higher, hitting the same difficult high note Athena always hit. The people on the bus cheered!

"Wow," Euma said, running a hand through her spiky black hair. "That was killer."

"Thanks," Lyssa said. She felt a little dazed.

"Have you ever taken singing lessons?" Euma asked.

Lyssa shook her head. "I learned everything I know from my mom."

"Your mom was Ana Lee, right?" Euma asked.

Lyssa nodded.

"Well, don't take this the wrong way, but you should think about taking some voice lessons," Euma said. "You're really good, but you could be amazing. You don't want to just stop learning, right?"

Lyssa glanced from Euma to Scarlett. Scarlett was twirling a strand of blond hair around her finger and beaming down at Lyssa. She was the only person on the bus who hadn't sung along. Lyssa wondered why.

"What do you think?" Lyssa asked her.

"Euma's right," Scarlett agreed. "You're going to be a great singer—with a little work, you could go all the way."

Euma looked away from the road for just a second to give Lyssa a shy smile.

"I really feel like I found myself in my first writing class," she said. "It was an amazing experience."

Lyssa chewed on her lower lip, thinking about that school Michael had enrolled her in. She'd been so excited to start at first, but she'd let her fear grow and grow as the first day approached, until she was dreading it—just like she'd let her fear make her think she wasn't cut out to be a performer. Maybe the school thing really was a good idea. They probably even had singing classes.

She stared out the window, watching the last of the hot-air balloons drift into the clouds and thinking . . .

CHAPTER TWENTY-ONE

Gertie from Berlin

The ride from New Mexico to Austin was long and gave Lyssa plenty of time to get to know the rest of Scarlett's friends. They reminded Lyssa of the Lotus Crew, except they were actually *doing* things.

First she met Igor, who liked to knit scarves and mittens and sell them online, and Carolina, his girlfriend, who was a vegan chef in Albuquerque. They both had shaggy brown hair and wore funky knit hats even though it was eighty degrees outside. Lyssa spent a long time talking to them about how to make the perfect peanut butter and banana brownies. Lyssa pulled out her journal and jotted the recipe down. Maybe she and Penn could make those together—when Lyssa got to Austin.

Then Lyssa met Varsha, a beautiful Indian flutist who was practicing in the very back of the bus. She invited Lyssa to play with her, so Lyssa dug around in her backpack for her mom's other maraca. But when she pulled it out, there was a huge rip down the side and half the tomato seeds were already gone, lost somewhere along her journey. Lyssa ran her thumbnail over the rip, wondering where all of her mom's seeds were by now.

"That can be fixed," Varsha said when Lyssa gave the maraca a sad shake, spilling a few tomato seeds onto the seat between them.

Varsha pulled a stick of watermelon-kiwi gum out of her pocket and made Lyssa chew. When the gum was good and sticky, she had Lyssa plug it into the rip, sealing the maraca shut. There weren't as many seeds left over, but the maraca still sounded great when Lyssa shook it. She played along with Varsha's flute as the bus rumbled toward the hills in the distance.

When Lyssa woke up, it was late afternoon and she was leaning against Scarlett's shoulder. A small pool of drool had collected on the faux fur collar of Scarlett's jacket. The sun was just peeking over the distant hills, turning the whole world greenish gold.

"Time to get up, Ladybug," Scarlett said. Lyssa sat up and wiped her drool away from the side of her mouth. She pulled her sweatshirt down over her palm. Scarlett leaned over and gave one of Lyssa's braids a gentle tug.

"Are we stopped?" Lyssa asked groggily.

"We're not stopped," Scarlett said. "We're here."

Lyssa pressed her face to the bus window. Afternoon sunlight danced over the grass, but once Lyssa's eyes adjusted, her heart began to beat against her chest like a jackhammer.

There was Mrs. Henderson's backyard, with the inflatable pool that was always half filled with water and dried leaves. And just across the street were the pink blossoms on Mr. Tanaka's cherry trees, which he had specially imported to Texas from Japan. And right next door was Penn's house, with its stained glass windows and mailbox shaped like a bullfrog.

Lyssa was home!

She leapt from her seat, so excited that she tripped over her own shoelace as she started down the bus aisle. Scarlett grabbed her arm to steady her so that she didn't land face-first on the sticky bus floor.

"Come on!" Lyssa shouted. She was home. She was *home*.

The corner of Scarlett's mouth hitched up into a sad smile.

"This is where we drop you," she said.

Lyssa shook her head, confused. "Wait, what? Drop me?"

"We have some things to do, Ladybug . . ." Scarlett paused, biting her lip. "And I'm not sure I can face a whole crowd of people just yet."

"But . . ." Lyssa knew she was being childish, but she couldn't imagine singing onstage without Scarlett and her friends in the audience. She searched for a compromise. "Promise me that you'll come if you change your mind?"

"I promise." Scarlett crouched down so she was Lyssa's height and could look her in the eye. "You know what? This isn't goodbye. You and I, we're going to see each other again real soon."

Lyssa nodded. Her throat felt thick, like it was slathered in honey and peanut butter, and she wasn't sure she could say a word without bursting into tears. She shifted her eyes away from Scarlett and dug what was left of her scooter out from under her seat.

When she looked back up, Scarlett was staring out the window, her jaw clenched like she might burst into tears. Unable to help herself, Lyssa threw her arms around Scarlett's neck.

"Thank you so much," she whispered into Scarlett's ear.

"You remember what I said about your performance," Scarlett whispered back to Lyssa. "You sing for the muse, not anybody else."

"And the muse comes from within," Lyssa said. She pulled away, quickly swiping a tear from her cheek with the back of her hand before Scarlett could see it.

Scarlett smiled at her. "Good luck."

As Lyssa ran down the bus, everyone waved and smiled, calling out words of encouragement.

"Sing your tongue off," Euma yelled.

"You work those maracas, girl," Varsha called, blowing Lyssa a kiss.

How was she supposed to say goodbye to people who'd become such good friends in such a short stretch of time? She couldn't. She had to think of this like Scarlett did—it wasn't goodbye. They'd all see each other again.

Lyssa leapt down to the sidewalk, pushing all the tears and thoughts of goodbye out of her head. Penn's house was less than a block away. The thought of seeing Penn filled Lyssa with jittery excitement, like someone was cooking popcorn inside her chest. She was finally standing on the same block as her best friend.

As the school bus pulled away, Lyssa ducked beneath Penn's living room windows and snuck into the backyard. Neither she nor Penn had ever waited for each other on the front porch or rung the doorbell. They had their own system.

Lyssa darted across Penn's neatly mowed yard, gathering dewy wetness on the toes of her sneakers. On the far side of the yard was a huge, twisty tree that she and Penn named the Grandfather Oak because it was so knobby and gnarly they were certain it had to be one hundred years old. Penn's dad had built her a tree house in the Grandfather Oak, and she and Lyssa had made it their secret clubhouse when they were younger. Lyssa grabbed the rope ladder hanging from a thick branch and scurried up the tree like she'd done one million times before, loving the scratchy, familiar feel of the rope beneath her fingers. When she reached the top, she flipped open the trapdoor and crawled inside.

The tree house was exactly as Lyssa remembered it. Squishy pillows covered the floor, and potted plants sat on the ledges of the cut-out windows. Even the air smelled the same—like graham crackers. Lyssa and Penn weren't allowed to toast marshmallows in the tree house, but they'd discovered that s'mores were amazing even when they were cold.

Lyssa crouched near the far window, shuffling around in the pillows until she found the heavy metal flashlight that Penn kept hidden there. Even when it was sunny out, the giant tree cast shadows over Penn's bedroom. Lyssa lifted the flashlight and directed it at Penn's window. Lyssa switched the flashlight on and off three times. Lyssa paused, counted to three, and switched it on again.

For a long moment, nothing happened. Then someone ripped aside the curtains and Penn's face appeared at the window. Her hair was a frizzy halo mess around her face.

"Lyssa?" Penn called, squinting, as though she wasn't sure whether what she'd seen was a dream or reality. Lyssa flicked the flashlight on one more time. Penn squealed. She scrambled out of the window and onto the clothesline that was pulled taut between her room and the tree house. The white sundress she wore billowed around her knees as she stood and walked easily across the thin rope.

"I told you I'd—" Lyssa started to say, but before she could finish her sentence, her friend threw her arms around her, nearly knocking her off her feet.

"I knew you were going to come home," Penn said. "Everyone thought you ran away or were kidnapped or something, but I *knew* you were coming home."

"I couldn't miss the performance," Lyssa said, hugging her friend back just as tightly. "Or the protest."

Penn pulled away. "But everyone's looking for you, Lyssa. There are police stationed all around your mom's house. They'll see you."

Lyssa chewed at her bottom lip, thinking. She'd worked

too hard and traveled too far to be caught by the police now. But she couldn't stay away from the protest, either.

"I need a disguise . . ." Lyssa muttered to herself. She dropped to her feet and started digging through her backpack. She pulled out the short, brown-haired wig she'd borrowed from Circe. There were a few seeds stuck in the tangles and one or two strands of hair poked out at odd angles, but it would have to do. Lyssa pulled it over her head and tucked her blond braids up under it.

"Well?" she asked Penn. "What do you think?"

"I don't know. Your face still looks pretty Lyssa-ish. You need something else . . ." Penn pursed her lips, considering. "Wait! I know."

Penn was out the window before Lyssa could blink, racing back over the clothesline to her bedroom. Lyssa groaned. Penn did this sometimes. She'd get some great idea, then rush off without explaining a thing. It was like her arms and legs worked faster than her mouth.

Minutes later Penn appeared at the window again. She made walking across the clothesline look so easy . . .

"What's all of this?" Lyssa asked as Penn dumped the clothes she was carrying onto the floor of the tree house. Lyssa picked up a pair of cat's-eye sunglasses.

"Stuff my sister outgrew," Penn explained. "Here, put this on—it doesn't look like you at all."

Penn handed Lyssa a flowery dress and a pair of combat boots. Lyssa grinned as she took them from her. The dress wasn't something she normally would wear—but with the boots, it looked kind of cool.

"Your name is Gertie," Penn said. "You're a foreign exchange student from Berlin."

"Berlin?" Lyssa pushed the cat's-eye sunglasses up her nose. "Ve vill eat frankenfurters, den! Und sauerkraut."

Penn twisted a scarf around her own brown curls, frowning. "What?"

"That was supposed to be a German accent."

"Oh. It sounded like you accidentally bit your tongue. Now hurry. The performance doesn't start until five, but people have been lining up all day."

Lyssa quickly changed into her costume, and Penn decided to try out one of her older sister's dresses and a pair of rhinestone-covered sunglasses. When they were all ready, Lyssa realized she didn't feel like herself at all. She felt a little older, a little more confident. Maybe she really was the kind of person who could sing onstage in front of all those people; maybe she *was* her mother's daughter. The flowery dress and combat boots reminded her of her mom's stage costumes: all those flowing, gauzy tunics and heavy, leather motorcycle boots. Lyssa smoothed down her brown wig and adjusted the frames of her sunglasses. She was ready.

She and Penn scrambled down from the tree house and hurriedly walked the block and a half to Lyssa's house. The closer they got, the harder Lyssa's heart began to beat against her chest.

Home. She was finally here.

They entered from the garden. Sneaking under the loose fence post, they found themselves suddenly surrounded by sunflowers that stretched above Lyssa like giant, yellow windmills, with petals wavering in the light wind. Lyssa's heart swelled. This was what she'd been looking for all along.

This, right here, was her mother's magic.

She reached a hand out to touch the stems and leaves. They were just as she remembered them. Just down the rocky stone path was the bench that Lyssa and her mom had built themselves. It was rickety, and one of the legs was attached with bubble gum and rubber bands. But Lyssa and her mom had scratched their names into the wood with kitchen knives and, somehow, the bubble gum and rubber bands had held up for years. Lyssa knelt down next to the bench and found their names. They were faded, worn down by wind and rain and storms. But they were still there.

"*Though we may travel far away,*" her mom had said, "*we leave our roots behind.*"

"Lyssa, look," Penn breathed.

Lyssa tore her eyes away from the flowers and her breath caught in her throat. There were protestors *everywhere*— hundreds of them, thousands even, crowded around the house and spilling onto the sidewalk and street out front. Lyssa tried to count them all, but there were just too many people—people she recognized and people she'd never seen before.

Tears pricked at the back of Lyssa's eyes. These people had come for her home. These people had come for her mom.

The big backyard just beyond the garden was set up to look like a fair. Every few feet there was a different food vendor selling fried peanut butter and jelly sandwiches, sugar-dipped gumdrops, or chocolate-chip-filled cotton candy. There were rainbow-colored tents and game stands and even a tiny carousel that glinted in the sunlight. Music poured out of the stands—Ana Lee's recordings. Some of the songs were ones that Lyssa hadn't heard since before her mom had died.

"Wow," Lyssa breathed. It was like going back in time, like being at the fair again. She almost expected her mom to appear at the Skee-Ball stand to play a quick round before her performance, just like in the old days.

"Come on," Penn said. Lyssa adjusted her sunglasses, suddenly nervous. If she was going to be recognized anywhere, it would be here—in a yard filled with the people who'd known her and Ana best. She didn't see any police officers around, but that didn't mean they weren't there.

Keeping her head down, Lyssa followed Penn through the crowd. She was so busy trying not to step on anyone's toes that she didn't notice when she walked right into a pair of blue-uniform-covered legs.

"Whoa, there. What's your hurry, young ladies?"

The legs belonged to a tall man with hair so shiny and blond that the sun bounced off it like a mirror. Lyssa's eyes wandered down to the badge attached to his chest.

A cop.

Her mouth went dry and her eyes grew wide behind her own cat's-eye sunglasses. The cop leaned over and adjusted the frames of his glasses, like that would help him see through Lyssa's disguise.

"Not a lot of children running around here without adult supervision," the cop said. Lyssa swallowed. She wasn't sure whether or not that was a question, but she shook her head anyway.

"No, sir."

For a second the police officer was quiet. There was a piece of grass in the corner of his mouth and he chewed on it, lazily.

"We're on the lookout for a girl about your age. Can I ask what you ladies are doing here?"

Though her mouth felt as dry as the desert, Lyssa forced words through her lips.

"We're . . . we're reporters. For the school paper. We're here for a story."

"Yeah, that's right," Penn added quickly.

"Don't you need notebooks? Cameras? Recorders?" the cop asked.

"Oh, um . . ." Lyssa said. She shoved a hand into the pocket of her dress, but the only thing she found was a tube of old lipstick that must have belonged to Penn's sister. She pulled it out and held it up for the officer.

"You know how technology is these days," she said, smiling. "This *is* a recorder."

"That's right," Penn said. She pulled a pack of gum out of her own pocket and waved it in front of the cop. "And, and this is a camera! See."

She held it up to her face and pretended to take a photograph. Lyssa bit down on her lower lip to keep from laughing out loud. The officer frowned. Since Lyssa couldn't see his eyes behind those glasses, she had no idea whether or not he believed her.

"Did I hear someone say *reporter*?"

A short, round man, like a beach ball with arms and legs, shouldered his way past the cop. Despite the fact that he was dressed casually, in a T-shirt and jeans, he also wore a battered-looking top hat and a monocle, which he fumbled with anxiously.

"You'll *need* to interview me! My name is Henric. I discovered Ana Lee," the man said. He rocked back and forth between his heels and the balls of his feet.

"You'll vouch for these girls, Mr. Henric?" the cop asked. Henric nodded his head and waved the cop away.

"Yes, yes, yes. Don't be ridiculous," he said, waving his hands at the cop dismissively. He wore white gloves that came just to his wrists. There wasn't a single smudge or speck of dust on them.

The cop gave Lyssa and Penn one last look, then stalked back into the crowd.

"The stories I could tell you about Ana," Henric said. He stretched out Lyssa's mom's name, so that it sounded like *Aaaahnaaah*.

"What kind of stories?" Lyssa asked. Her ears perked up. He had *discovered* her mom? She held the tube of lipstick up to Henric's face. For a second, she forgot that it didn't *actually* record a thing.

"The first time she came out on that stage, she couldn't utter a single sound," Henric said, laughing so hard that his big belly shook back and forth. Inexplicably, he switched his monocle from one eye to the other, then straightened his top hat with the tips of his gloved fingers. "That girl looked like she'd seen a ghost. Eventually she could sing like a bird, but that first time on the stage I thought she'd pass out from fear."

Lyssa almost dropped the tube of lipstick. Her mom had never told her that she had stage fright, too! In all the stories she told about how she got her start, she made it sound like she was never as comfortable as she was onstage—like she could have been born there.

Huh. Knowing that her mom had been scared gave Lyssa a little more courage. Maybe she'd be able perform tonight after all . . . but her stomach clenched and she had to push the thought away.

Henric led Penn and Lyssa around the yard, introducing them to more of Lyssa's mom's old friends. There was Carl, a short but thickly muscled man who explained that he'd been the bouncer at the first jazz club Ana Lee ever sang at. He told Lyssa that Ana used to have bubble-gum-pink hair and a piercing in her nose. Despite his small size, he said, he'd been one of the best bouncers in the business.

"I'm a good kicker," he whispered to Lyssa, winking. Then he showed off a few roundhouse kicks for good measure.

Then there was Louise, an energetic old woman with white hair and a big smile. She used to live next door to Ana Lee when she first moved to the city.

"She loved my oatmeal butterscotch cookies," Louise said. Lyssa smiled. *She* loved oatmeal butterscotch cookies too.

Lyssa met Careen and Cora, a pair of twins with long, glossy black hair and lips as red as cherries. They used to sing in the chorus with Ana Lee, and they had a bad habit of finishing each other's sentences.

"Men, they loved Ana Lee," Cora said. "They all wanted to whisk her away to Morocco, or Iceland. But she always said—"

"Not a chance," Careen cut in. "She had that lovely daughter, you know. She always had to make sure to do what was best for Lyssa."

"What about Michael?" Lyssa piped up. She knew she was supposed to keep quiet, but she couldn't help herself.

"Michael!" Careen smiled, looking at Cora. "Do you remember when she met Michael, Cora?"

"Oh, yes! He showed up at the Talent Show on that bright green Vespa he'd rebuilt himself. She fell head over heels. She called us right up," Cora said. "She was so excited . . ."

Lyssa chewed on her lower lip. She remembered that Vespa. Michael had taken her on ride after ride around the parking lot on it. He had traded it in and bought a Prius after he started dating her mom.

"'Wouldn't he be a great father,' that's what she said on the phone," Careen continued, shaking Lyssa from her memories. The woman beamed down at Lyssa. "Ana was so excited to have found a man who loved her daughter."

As Lyssa and Penn walked away from the twins, Lyssa felt a hard rock forming in her gut. She'd never thought about it that way before—that maybe her mom had fallen for Michael because he was the kind of guy who came over with a laptop just so that Lyssa could watch Athena clips. All Lyssa had focused on was how much things had changed—how they'd had to move to Kirkland and how she'd have to go to school and eat different foods and live in a different type of house. She never really thought about the good changes. Like all of the bike rides Michael took her on, and how he was always bringing home new peanut butter foods (peanut butter broccoli! fried peanut butter bananas!). And he'd taken the time to install that music software into her computer so that she could record all those demo CDs.

Lyssa reached into her pocket and her fingers curled around the tiny airplane. She pulled it out and—for the first time—she noticed that there was a message written on the other wing too.

The winds of change are coming.

"Change," Lyssa whispered aloud.

In that moment, she finally understood. Things had changed. Home had changed.

Home could be a place, but home could be a person, too. It could be a moment, a memory, or a feeling. This house, this garden, it would always be Lyssa's home. But Michael could be her home, too. If she let him.

CHAPTER TWENTY-TWO

Roots and Moonshine

The garden was filling up. If it had felt crowded before, now it was like a pillow so stuffed with feathers it was bursting at the seams. Everywhere Lyssa looked, she saw people huddled together, munching on fried peanut butter and jelly sandwiches, laughing, and playing the carnival games.

Penn leaned over and said something that Lyssa couldn't hear over the roar of the people talking all around them. It sounded like "my scream luck," which didn't make any sense.

"What?" Lyssa asked. Penn cupped a hand around her mouth.

"Ice cream truck," she yelled, pointing just past the

house. Lyssa gave Penn a thumbs-up and led the way, winding through the people and slowly making her way to the front yard.

The front yard didn't have quite as wild a garden as the back did, but there was the big, wild dogwood tree growing just next to the white porch that wrapped around the front of the house. There were daisies scattered across the grass. It looked like someone had taken flower seeds and thrown them every which way, paying no attention to where they landed. Which, Lyssa knew, was exactly how her mom had planted the flowers.

She turned to ask Penn where she'd seen the ice cream truck—but Penn wasn't behind her. Lyssa was hemmed in on all sides by strangers.

Nervous now, Lyssa decided that she needed to make her way to higher ground. She stopped next to the front porch and hoisted herself up onto the old, wooden banister—just like she used to do when she wanted to see a storm approaching from miles away. Her hands and feet instinctively found the worn-down grooves in the wood where she'd pulled herself up a million times before.

The first thing Lyssa saw after crawling onto the banister was a fat, gray cat with jade-green eyes. It was sitting on a porch swing that swayed slightly, back and forth, as though the cat was making it move through sheer force of will.

"Grandma," Lyssa called. She wanted to throw her arms around the big gray cat but had to keep perfectly still so as not to lose her balance on the porch banister.

The cat narrowed one eye, as though to ask, *"What took you so long?"*

"I had a long way to travel," Lyssa explained. The cat shrugged and bent down to lick her paw. Lyssa looked past the cat, to where the big, gnarly tree was growing next to the porch. There were already people sitting on its large branches. Lyssa considered joining them to stage the sit-in so that the construction company couldn't knock the house down, and pray that her mom would send a miracle to save their home. But she couldn't keep her eyes from traveling from the tree to the porch beneath it: the stage.

A lump formed in Lyssa's throat, but she ignored it. Scarlett's words flickered through her head: *We sing for the muse, and the muse comes from within . . .*

Lyssa looked back out into the crowd, scanning for Penn's big brown curls. Instead, Lyssa saw something else.

Scattered across the yard were all of the people Lyssa had met along her journey. First she saw the cowgirls from the diner huddled next to a pear tree, twirling their lassos and cheering. Daisy smiled wide and the sun glinted off her gold front tooth. Lyssa felt a rush of joy and gratitude at the sight of her friend. Daisy must've remembered when Lyssa told her about the protest just days ago. How amazing she traveled here all the way from Oregon!

And there, parked on the street just behind the cowgirls, was Helios's ice cream truck. A long line of people snaked away from the service window, watching as Helios tossed an ice cream scoop high in the air. It spun up toward the clouds, then fell back toward the truck; he caught it behind his back and made the girl he was serving scream with glee. Lyssa watched them, amazed. The last time she'd seen Helios, he'd been chasing her through a corn maze for stealing some ice cream and candy. How had he ended up at the protest, giving his famous ice cream away for free?

She scanned the line of people waiting for ice cream, hoping to find Penn. To her surprise, Calypso was third in line—her ornately curled hair and bright red fingernails were instantly recognizable. Fear crawled into Lyssa's chest, and she started to climb down from the banister. Calypso *couldn't* find her now. Lyssa was so close—everything would be ruined.

Then the woman started to turn, and Lyssa realized that something about her was off. She was shorter than Calypso had been, and when she turned, her hair slid down over her forehead, covering up one of her eyes. In fact, it wasn't until "Calypso" had turned all the way around to face Lyssa that Lyssa realized it wasn't the cruel woman from the cornfield staring back at her.

It was Circe.

Lyssa froze. Circe was wearing Calypso's curly wig, and she had glued acrylic nails to the tips of her fingernails; she still wore the same tie-dyed muumuu, though, only now there were too-big high heels poking out from under the hem instead of stilts. Circe started across the yard toward Lyssa, her heels poking holes in the grass.

Lyssa wasn't sure she wanted to talk to Circe now, or ever again. But she couldn't move. All too soon, she and Circe were separated by only a few feet of space. Lyssa clambered clumsily down from the banister.

"Nice disguise," Circe said.

"You too," Lyssa said. Her voice was thin and hollow, like an echo. Circe just shrugged.

"I stole the wig off Calypso," she said casually.

Lyssa just stared at her, her face wooden. "What are you doing here?" she asked.

Circe shifted, uncomfortably, on her too-big heels. "Well, you made it sound like it a lot of fun . . ."

"I mean *how could you* come here? After what you did to me?" Lyssa felt tears sting the corners of her eyes, but she blinked them away. "You were my friend."

Circe frowned and crossed her arms. "Listen, kid. I

don't have any friends, okay? I have to look out for myself. I *needed* that money."

"But I trusted you," Lyssa said in a whisper.

For a second, Lyssa thought she saw an expression of regret pass over Circe's face. But it was quickly replaced by her usual look of hard defiance. "Everyone leaves you in the end, Lyssa," she said. "You should just accept that now."

Lyssa couldn't immediately respond. She gaped at Circe.

"You don't really think that, do you?"

Circe shrugged. She'd always been so confident, so carefree, but now she seemed uncomfortable. "It's the way things are," she said.

Lyssa frowned. She'd always admired Circe for having all the answers, but now she saw that Circe was mistaken about the most important thing of all. The people you loved—the people who loved you back—*never* truly left you.

"You're wrong," Lyssa said to Circe. "Friends are more important than pigs or peaches or broken-down trucks. Real friends—real family—stay with you no matter what."

She took a deep breath and added, more softly, "I feel sorry for you, Circe. Take care of yourself, okay?"

Circe opened and closed her mouth a few times, and then

turned and stormed off into the crowd. Lyssa felt another throb of pity for her. Circe had never had the joy that Lyssa knew here, in this moment, surrounded by all the people she knew. Lyssa hoped that Circe could find it someday. The gray cat came and sat next to Lyssa. Lyssa stroked its head absently.

On the other side of the yard, next to a pair of apple trees with a hammock strung up between them, Lyssa saw the one-eyed chef from the cowgirl diner. She swallowed hard and pushed her sunglasses farther up her nose, hoping he wouldn't recognize her.

But the chef didn't look quite so scary anymore. A little boy sat on his shoulders, giggling. Lyssa smiled. The chef looked happy, even if he hadn't gotten his big reward. Maybe he'd figured out a new secret ingredient for his special stew. Either way, Lyssa was glad he'd come.

She was so glad everyone had come. *This* was the miracle Lyssa had been hoping for. It was magic. Now if only Lyssa could find her mom . . .

There were hundreds more people crowded across the front lawn—too many people for Lyssa to count. They spilled onto the sidewalk and into the driveway where the Texas Talent Show's bright yellow van used to park.

But in the street just beyond the protestors was a less welcome sight: men in hard hats and bright yellow vests standing next to construction equipment. Lyssa gulped. There was even a wrecking ball. It was silhouetted in the setting sun, and she could only see its outline.

The demolition crew. Lyssa hadn't considered that she might actually have to watch the crew knock her home down. Parked on the street behind the wrecking ball was a white news van. There were cameramen unloading equipment and reporters fixing their hair. The news van wouldn't be here if the demolition crew was just going to knock the house down, right? The reporters were here because of the protest—because they knew the protesters were going to put up a fight. Lyssa looked back out at the people who'd come to stand up against the demolition crew. She tried to be strong. Next to the thousands of people here for the protest, the construction workers looked small and insignificant.

"Everybody's here, Grandma," Lyssa whispered, reaching a hand out to scratch the cat behind the ears. "They all came through for me. For mom."

The grandmother cat began to purr beneath her fingertips, and Lyssa closed her eyes, feeling so light, so happy that she could almost float away. As she ran her fingers through the cat's soft fur, she thought about how she'd believed her mom might be waiting for her, just like the grandmother cat.

But now that she was home, Lyssa just couldn't picture her mom as a cat or a bird. Ana Lee was too *big* to be contained by something so small. That thought made Lyssa feel proud and sad at the same time, like the two emotions were puppies wrestling around in her stomach.

"See, I *told* you it was her," said a girl's voice near the front porch steps. Lyssa whirled around, nearly falling off the banister. Demo and the cannibal girl from the Oregon police station walked up the stairs. Demo's hair was gelled up in his signature faux mohawk. He wore skinny black jeans and an oversized T-shirt covered in a huge picture of a dinosaur. He looked like a rock star, complete with lemon-yellow sunglasses shading his eyes.

"You guys—hi!" Lyssa hopped down from the banister. She gave the cannibal girl a quick hug, then she threw her arms around Demo. Demo grinned down at her—he seemed so much taller than he had back at the marina in Washington. It was like he'd grown two full feet in just a few days.

"What are you both doing here?" Lyssa asked. Then, furrowing her eyebrows, she said, "Wait—how do you even know each other?"

"I just met Chloe a few minutes ago," Demo said, motioning to cannibal girl.

The backs of Lyssa's ears started to burn. She'd never even asked cannibal girl what her name was.

"Anyway, Chloe asked me if the girl in the brown wig and silly glasses was you," Demo continued. "What's with the disguise?"

"The cops still after you?" Chloe asked, raising her eyebrows. Her formerly pink hair was now neon green, but she still wore her Cannibal shirt. There were even drumsticks peeking out of her back pocket. She had two brand-new stress balls clenched between her fingers—they looked like miniature soccer balls.

"Hey—your fingers are better," Lyssa said. The skin around Chloe's fingernails was all pink and healthy—nothing like the ragged, bloody fingers Lyssa had seen when she first met her.

"Those Band-Aids helped a lot," Chloe said, wiggling her fingers at Lyssa. "And look—check it out."

She stuck the stress balls in her pockets and pulled out the Band-Aids Lyssa had given her at the police station—the ones designed to look like tattoos. She selected one Band-Aid from the box—a skull surrounded by a circle of flowers—and peeled it off, sticking it on Lyssa's arm.

"You can't go to the big house without getting some ink," she said, winking.

"Thanks!" Lyssa said, laughing.

"I listened to your CD, you know," Demo said while Chloe was pressing the edges of the Band-Aid down with her fingers. "It was fantastic! I even wrote some backup music for you."

He passed Lyssa a CD. Before Lyssa, stunned, could say thank you, more members of the Lotus Crew headed up the stairs and spilled onto the porch.

"It's so good to see you," Regina said, shaking her hand in a fast, awkward wave. The boy with the curly hair was just behind her. He cuffed Regina on the shoulder.

"Tell Lyssa your news, Reg," he said. Regina looked a little sheepish, but she grinned.

"I have a tryout—to be a contestant on *Lotus Island*," she said.

"That's fantastic," Lyssa said. Regina nodded happily.

"You inspired me, you know," she said. "You went on all those adventures all by yourself. If you can have adventures, well, then I want to have them, too."

"Who's that?" someone yelled, and the crowd suddenly erupted in hoots and catcalls. Lyssa and the Lotus Crew strained to see what was causing the commotion in the street. A long white limousine with darkened windows pulled up in front of the house. A sign strung across its back windows read *Make Art, Not Real Estate*. Everyone began to murmur and whisper excitedly.

The door of the limo flew open, and Tiresias stepped out.

He wore a full-length, white ball gown and his bald head was covered in a curly, blond wig. He strode across the yard and the crowd of people parted to let him through, as though he were a celebrity.

He paused when he approached the porch. It was as though he could sense Lyssa's presence.

"Still trying to speak to the dead, baby girl?"

"I never stopped," Lyssa admitted. Behind him, more people spilled out of the limousine: the mermaids from the Siren burlesque! They were no longer in their mermaid costumes; instead, they wore matching silver glittery cocktail dresses that glinted in the late-afternoon sun. She watched for the mermaid with the beehive hairdo and the voice like thunder, but she wasn't with the others. Lyssa felt vaguely disappointed.

"How do you know the mermaids, anyway?" Lyssa asked.

Tiresias laughed. "You don't think I tell futures full time, do you? I'm a regular performer at the Siren club. One of the girls . . . well, let's say she *heard* about this little protest and we just had to come check it out."

Tiresias patted Lyssa's shoulder and leaned down to whisper into her ear. "You know, I think I know why we couldn't talk to your mom that day."

"Why?" Lyssa asked, breathless.

"I think she's alive in you." And with that Tiresias strutted back into the crowd.

Lyssa once again felt her throat squeeze. She turned back toward the house. She noticed a man hobbling across the porch, peeking in through the windows. It was the old, crazy man from the bus station in Washington! When he was done looking into the windows, he came across the yard to Lyssa, doing his strange, shuffling dance.

"Never touch the moonshine on the patio," he said.

Lyssa found herself laughing. "I'll try to remember that."

The man winked at her and danced away. Lyssa saw the hobo from the train—Oscar—duck into the crowd. His ragged clothes had been replaced with a nice flannel shirt and crisp blue jeans, and his hair had been combed away from his face, but Lyssa would recognize that harmonica anywhere, sending its velvety music up to the heavens.

A tiny, stick-thin man in a white tuxedo hurried up the steps to the front porch just then. Lyssa recognized him immediately as William, the Texas Talent Show announcer. In one hand William held a wireless microphone and, in the other, several pieces of a beat-up, silvery drum kit. There was a thin line of sweat on his forehead.

"I'm going to have to ask you all to leave the stage now," he said, addressing Lyssa and all the other people on the porch in his squeaky, anxious voice. Lyssa grinned despite herself. He didn't recognize her at all! "The performance is about to begin."

As soon as he said the word *performance*, Lyssa got tingly all over, like every single hair on her arms was being pulled at with tiny pairs of tweezers. She followed the Lotus gang and Chloe off the porch, but she crowded in as close as she could to the makeshift stage. The grandmother cat leapt down from the porch swing and curled into a ball next to Lyssa's elbow, purring contentedly.

Penn eased through the crowd next to her, holding two dripping ice cream cones.

"I was looking for you," she said, handing Lyssa an ice cream cone.

"I was looking for you, too," Lyssa said through a mouthful of ice cream. She took another big bite—banana and peanut butter, her favorite flavors.

William straightened the lapel on his tux and raised the microphone to his mouth and started to speak.

"Hello and welcome," he said in a voice that was confident and deep—no longer squeaky or anxious at all. "Please gather round. The Texas Talent Show is about to begin."

Dusty yellow lights flickered on and crisscrossed the stage. Lyssa gasped, whipping her head around to see where they were coming from. There were cars parked all along the street, their headlights aimed right at Lyssa's porch like spotlights.

One by one, the performers took to the porch stage. First was Hank and his trained poodles, who jumped through fiery hoops and rode across the stage on skateboards. Then the dancing cowgirls twirled across the porch in sparkling white outfits. People crowded in close, cheering and clapping.

Lyssa clapped too. It was strange watching the show from the audience. She'd always watched from behind the curtain, fetching water for the artists and making sure all the props were show ready.

It was strange, also, watching these people perform when she knew that her mom wouldn't be walking onto the stage last with her homemade instruments and motorcycle boots. Lyssa looked out across the crowd and realized that the people watching must have noticed her mom's absence, too. Tears glittered on their cheeks, and the sound of sniffling spread across the yard.

Then something flickered at the edge of the crowd: a candle flame. More candles flickered to life and, before long, a cardboard box filled with white candles ended up in Lyssa's hands. She took one candle out and lit it from Demo's before passing the box to Penn.

The sun had begun to set, leaving the day in twilight.

As the sun dipped farther and farther behind distant buildings, more people in the crowd grabbed candles and lit them. Even though the trapezists had taken to the stage—Lyssa's favorite act—she found that she couldn't tear her eyes away from the crowd, from the people gathered to honor her mom and the home they'd made together.

The roots we plant are for life . . .

Lyssa felt tears falling freely down her face. Everything was so perfect that she had to pinch her wrist, just to make sure that she wasn't dreaming. She had found her mom at last.

She wasn't a cat or a bird. She was in the light of a thousand candles. She was in Hank's proud grin when his dogs made it through the fiery hoops and in the sound of the cowgirl's heels clanking against the stage. She was in Lyssa. She was everywhere.

Just as the last performer left the stage, Penn turned to Lyssa, a drip of strawberry ice cream clinging to her chin.

Lyssa caught her best friend's eye and knew that Penn was thinking the same thing she was. Lyssa couldn't honor her mom by hanging back in the crowd. Music was in Lyssa's blood. *Magic* was in her blood. She had to sing. Even if it didn't save her home, even if it didn't stop the demolition, she knew that her mother would hear her, no matter where she was.

"What do you think?" Penn asked. She grabbed Lyssa's wrist and squeezed. "You know you're already a star, Lyssa."

Lyssa waited to feel the butterfly nerves in her stomach, but they were gone. She nodded at Penn. She was ready.

William had just lifted the megaphone to his mouth to announce that the performance was over. Before he could say a word, Penn bounded up onto the stage, turning a cartwheel.

"Wait," she shouted to the crowd. "We have one more performer. Lyssa's here."

Whispers and gasps spread through the crowd like wildfire. Lyssa didn't pay them any attention. It didn't matter if someone called the police now; it didn't matter that they all knew where she was. She climbed up the stairs, every inch of her skin humming.

This was it. Showtime.

CHAPTER TWENTY-THREE

Being with You Feels Like Home

Wind blew across the front porch, rustling William's tuxedo coattails. Lyssa stepped onto the stage.

"Did you feel that?" she asked him, goose bumps racing up and down her arms. William grinned, lowering his microphone.

"The winds of change," he answered.

Just past the porch, the light of a thousand candles winked in the darkness like fireflies. The gasps and whispers of surprise had died down and now everyone's eyes were on Lyssa, waiting for what she would do.

"Are you ready?" William asked. Lyssa just smiled. She *was* ready—ready for everything the wind had in store.

She stepped forward, taking the microphone.

"Hi, y'all," she said, her voice booming out over the crowd. "My name is Lyssa Lee."

People cheered. The sound was like an ocean wave crashing through the still evening air. Lyssa held her breath, certain the water would hit her at any second and all of this would be washed away. Her hands felt slick against the microphone. The butterflies were back. Their wings fluttered silently in her chest.

"I'm here to sing you a song," Lyssa continued. The microphone amplified her voice, making her sound much more confident than she felt. "My mom used to sing it to me before I went to bed."

Lyssa didn't say the last part—that this was the song her mom used to sing in the hospital before falling asleep every night. That it was the last song she ever sang to Lyssa.

Lyssa clenched her eyes shut and held the microphone close to her mouth, picturing her mom's beautiful face. Her throat felt tight, but she forced the song out anyway.

"Once upon a yesterday, I lived so very far away . . . But now that I'm here, I'm here to stay."

Lyssa tried to hold the memory of her mom in her head while she sang, but, surprisingly, she found that it was Michael's face that she saw. Michael making her lunch. Michael tucking her in at night. Michael sitting next to her mom's hospital bed, holding Ana's hand while she slept.

As the memories flooded Lyssa's mind, her voice grew stronger and her nerves disappeared like dandelion seeds in the wind. She forced her voice out, sending it soaring over the crowd like a bird.

"We could go to Tuscaloosa, we could go to Timbuktu. All I need is you. Being with you feels like home to me."

She held that last note, stretching it out until her lungs felt like two balloons that were about to pop.

The audience began to cheer. As their applause swelled, Lyssa thought she heard the rhythmic sound of drums, banging underneath the chanting, cheering voices. Lyssa turned and glanced over her shoulder.

Chloe sat at the silver drum set, beating the drums in a steady, smooth rhythm. Her neon-green hair hung over her face as she crashed a drumstick over a cymbal, her arms a blur of speed. Lyssa had never sung this song fast before. The rhythm of the drums seemed to beat up through her heart. Together, she and Chloe belted out:

"Being with you feels like home."

Next, Lyssa heard the clear, beautiful sound of a flute. Penn climbed onto the stage next to her. She must have run back to her room and grabbed the flute she played in the jazz band at school. Lyssa threw an arm around her friend and together they belted even louder:

"Being with you feels like home."

Demo broke in, spitting and humming into his hands. The people in the audience threw their hands in the air and pumped their fists with his beat. Demo did a front flip onto the stage and then bopped over to Lyssa while the audience below them clapped and cheered. Lyssa joined in. Her voice mingled with the crowd until she didn't know where she ended and everyone else began.

More people climbed onto the porch. The mermaids from the Siren Choir arranged themselves behind Lyssa and started performing a line dance. Their glittery silver dresses gave off their own light, making the mermaids look like dancing disco balls.

Tiresias came next. He glided up the stairs with such grace it looked like he was floating several feet off the ground. He'd found another microphone somewhere and started singing backup, his voice deep and throaty.

"Being with you feels like home," they all crooned together.

Standing here, surrounded by Penn and Tiresias and Demo and Chloe and the mermaids, Lyssa thought she could hear her mom's voice. It floated above them all, singing along.

Then something flashed from the street—a new head-light. Lyssa threw a hand over her eyes and squinted into the light, but she couldn't see who—or what—was approaching. Someone stepped in front of the headlight, casting a shadow over the porch. One by one, all of the voices singing along with Lyssa dropped out until it was so quiet Lyssa could have heard a sunflower petal drop. She held her breath as the shadow drew closer. William scurried across the stage and took the microphone from Lyssa.

"I have a very special announcement to make," the man in the tuxedo said. "We have a guest with us tonight, some-one who heard about our protest—"

"I'll take it from here." A woman's voice—deep and rumbling, like thunder—cut him off.

Excitement buzzed along Lyssa's skin and suddenly she felt much too light, like she might float right off this stage and up into the stars. She clenched her hands together in little fists.

No. It couldn't be.

"You think you're slick, but I know your tricks . . ." sang the voice. Just behind Lyssa, Chloe started playing her drums, tapping out a slow, steady beat.

"Ladies and gentlemen," the man in the tuxedo an-nounced, "please welcome, after a year of silence, the one, the only . . . Athena!"

The crowd exploded into roars and screams. It wasn't until their screams and applause started to die down that Lyssa realized she'd been screaming and clapping right along with them. Athena stepped into the light and Lyssa's mouth dropped open.

It *was* Scarlett—and it wasn't. Athena had a platinum-blond beehive hairdo, just like the mermaid from the Siren Choir. She wore rhinestone-covered glasses that were identical to the woman's from the whirlpool. But she had Scarlett's fur coat and the bright pink cowboy boots Athena wore to every concert. The boots had real spurs that clanked against the porch as she crossed over to Lyssa.

Clink, clink, clink.

"Hey there, Ladybug," Athena said. "How's it going? Still nervous?"

Lyssa opened and closed her mouth. She had so many questions, but when she finally found her voice, all she managed to say was, "Nope. Are you?"

Athena smiled wider. "Are you kidding? I have my good luck charm here with me."

"So you . . ." Lyssa started. "You're Athena? Really?"

The singer nodded. "Yup. Crazy world, huh? Now what do you say? Mind if I finish up this song with you?"

The backup music started again. Chloe pounded on the drums and Penn blew into her flute, sending notes soaring up toward the stars. Demo lowered his face to his hands and purred out a beat while Tiresias joined the other mermaids, all humming along.

Athena took her hand as Lyssa lifted the microphone to her lips.

"I'd like to dedicate this to my dad," Lyssa said. "My real dad. I don't think he's here today, but, well, his name is Michael."

She took a deep breath, then sang the last line of her mom's song:

"Whether I sail across the sea, stay on the couch, or climb a tree. Being with you feels like home to me."

Athena squeezed Lyssa's hand, singing the last line with her one more time: *"Being with you feels like home to me."*

The audience roared and clapped. Lyssa felt happy and dizzy and also just a little regretful. She still missed her mom—she knew that she would always miss her mom, even with the magical signs she felt sure her mom would always send her.

But she missed Michael, too. If he'd been there, he would have tweaked her microphone to make her sound clearer, and he'd have been sure to record the entire show. And now that the show was done, he'd have insisted Lyssa go out for a celebratory veggie burger with him at her favorite diner.

Lyssa forced her grin wider, trying to enjoy her moment. But it was like Scarlett had said—it was hard to sing when the most important people weren't there to hear it. Despite all the new friends she'd made, her trip across the country had made her realize that Michael was as important to her as Athena or Penn or even her mom. Michael was her family.

"Lyssa!"

People moved aside until there was a clear path right down the center of the front yard. Lyssa shielded her eyes and stared down the path, dropping her microphone when a bicycle tore down it. The bicycle looked brand new and was covered in gadgets, their screens winking in the candlelight.

Now Lyssa didn't have to force her smile. It was Michael!

His hair was a mess and his glasses were on upside down, but it was him! Lyssa felt like someone had just lit a round of fireworks inside her chest. She jumped off the stage and ran toward Michael. He threw his arms around her. He was wearing a flannel shirt that smelled like pine needles and the fabric softener from the house in Kirkland. *Home,* Lyssa thought, taking a deep breath.

"Your father called when you ran away—he told me you kept talking about some protest, you had to get to the protest." Michael said all of this in one breath. He smiled as he looked down at Lyssa. There were tears in his eyes.

"When I saw you singing up there, I thought I was looking at your mom. You looked just like her."

Lyssa's throat closed up and she knew that any second, she would begin crying. She didn't know what to say—it was maybe the most wonderful thing anyone could have ever said to her. She'd always wanted to be like her mom.

"Your glasses are on upside down," she said finally.

Michael pulled his glasses off and put them on correctly.

"Listen," he said, looking down at his shoes. "I don't tell you this a lot, Lyssa. I'm new at this whole father thing and sometimes I feel like I'm doing a terrible job. But I love you. I do."

Lyssa reached out and grabbed his hand. "It's okay, Michael. I love you, too." She squeezed his stomach, and he hugged her so hard he picked her up off her feet.

The audience was jumping up and down, shouting for an encore. To Lyssa's surprise, it was Michael who started up the stairs. Athena offered him her microphone.

"I have an announcement to make," he said. His voice echoed across the yard and everyone fell silent. He swallowed, tightening his fingers around the microphone.

"My sister, Nora, is a lawyer, Lyssa—that's part of why I wanted to move closer to her," Michael said. He fumbled with his glasses, then glanced down at Lyssa. When he spoke again, he didn't gaze up at the rest of the crowd; he looked only at her.

"We've been investigating the Austin city bylaws and we discovered a loophole."

Lyssa held her breath as Michael continued.

"Back in 1973, Austin passed a law that no family home left to the community in a will can be torn down without express consent from the living descendants. Now, we happen to have the last living descendant of Ana Lee right here."

Michael knelt on the stage next to Lyssa.

"Lyssa," he said. "What do you think? Should we let the Austin Real Estate Corporation. tear this place down?"

"No!" Lyssa shouted. Once again, the audience began to cheer. Michael picked Lyssa up and spun her around the stage. Her wig fell off and her braids whipped out behind her.

A man twice Michael's size in a hard hat stormed up the stairs. He started shouting at Michael, but Michael simply set Lyssa back down on the stage and pulled a crumpled piece of paper from his jacket pocket. He handed it to the man in the hard hat, pointing to a section that Lyssa could see had been highlighted. The bylaws. As the man read, his face grew redder and redder. Finally, he took off his hard hat and threw it on the stage. Michael picked it up and tossed it into the crowd. With more cheers, the people below threw it back and forth, like it was a beach ball.

"All right, Scooting Star," Michael said, turning to Lyssa. "Let's get out of here."

"How did you know about the development company?" Lyssa asked, following Michael down the steps. Behind them, Chloe started in on the drums again and Athena began singing Lyssa's favorite song, "Tricks."

"I've known about it for months," Michael said. "That's what I've been doing in my room every night. Searching the bylaws, looking for a loophole. You didn't think I'd let them take away your mom's garden, did you?"

Lyssa started to get that firecracker feeling inside her chest again. She had no words for what she wanted to say to Michael. She could only reach out for his hand and squeeze.

Together they wove through the cheering crowd and walked back into the garden. Lyssa led them back to the rickety bench that she and her mom had built themselves. She leaned over to study the right leg, quickly finding the heart she and her mom had carved on the back. She traced the lines with her finger.

"How did you know I'd be here?" she asked, sitting back up. Michael laughed.

"Penn. She admitted that you found out about the

demolition, and I knew you'd find some way to make it back here. You're a lot more like your mom than you'll ever know.

"Besides," he added, pulling a newspaper out of his back pocket. "I had this trail to guide me to you."

Frowning, Lyssa took the newspaper from Michael and stared down at the pictures. Four pictures showed tomato plants growing in the strangest places: up and down the marina in Kirkland, behind a motel whirlpool, along the side of a salty lake.

"You must've been leaking seeds everywhere you went," Michael said, pointing to the photos. "People have been discovering your tomatoes all along the west side of the country. You're inspiring people, Lyssa. Just like your mom always did. It's all right here in the story."

Lyssa felt her smile stretch ear to ear. "Maybe we can plant some more when we get back to . . . when we get back home."

Michael cleared his throat, then slipped off his glasses and wiped them on his T-shirt. It was the first time Lyssa had ever called his house in Kirkland home. She liked the way it sounded.

"We could do that," he said. For a moment they sat together in silence. Lyssa reached up and slipped her hand into Michael's.

"Your mom isn't going anywhere, Lyssa," he said. He looked up at the sky. "And if there's anything I can do to help you remember her, you just let me know."

The grandmother cat jumped onto the bench. It stretched its neck, rubbing its face on Lyssa's arm. She scratched the cat under her chin.

"You could get my grandmother some coffee," she said finally. Michael glanced down at the cat, then leaned over and rubbed her behind the ears.

"Right. Let's go, then." Michael folded the newspaper article up and started to put it in his back pocket.

"Wait," Lyssa said. "Can I keep that?"

"Sure." Michael picked up her backpack and unzipped it, pulling out the school journal Lyssa had been writing in for the past several days. "Oh, hey!" he said, flipping through the pages. "You finished your school project."

"What? No I . . ." Lyssa started to say, but she let her sentence trail off when she looked down at the journal. All her letters to Penn added up to a story of how she'd spent her summer. Plus, there was the recipe for peanut butter and banana brownies and Circe's PB&J, and the receipt from the costume shop, and a bus ticket stub from her ride to Oregon. Stuck to a few of the pages were the last of the tomato seeds. It was like a big scrapbook of all her adventures.

"Wow, Lyssa. This is very creative." Grinning, Michael placed the newspaper article between the last pages and snapped the journal shut. "I think your teachers are going to love it."

He handed the journal back to Lyssa and she tucked it, carefully, inside her backpack. Lyssa picked up the cat and, together, she and Michael headed to the house. Not too far in the distance, she heard a thousand voices coming together, singing.

Everything was perfect. Everything except . . .

"Hey, Michael," Lyssa said. She shifted the grandmother cat's weight in her arms. "I forgot to tell you. Zip . . . I mean, you know my scooter?"

Michael raised an eyebrow over his glasses. "Yeah?"

"Well, it's just . . . it's kind of broken."

"Do you want me to help you build a new one?"

"Actually," Lyssa said, giving the grandmother cat an extra squeeze, "I was thinking you could help me build a bike. A yellow one. Maybe it can be my birthday present."

"I think we can work that out." Smiling, Michael put a hand on Lyssa's shoulder, giving it a squeeze. "We can even race each other around the lake—after you're done being grounded, of course."

Ana Lee's Homemade Granola

4–6 cups oats

1 cup each of:

Powdered milk	Shredded coconut
Soy flour	Wheat germ
Sesame seeds	Honey
Sunflower seeds	Oil
Slivered almonds	

Pour oats into a very large bowl and add remaining dry ingredients. Add oil and honey. Mix well by hand and pour onto 4 cookie sheets in shallow layer. If Grandmother Cat is nearby, have her taste. She always knows when to add more coconut.

Bake at 250° F for 1 to 2 hours, until golden brown. Stir occasionally.

Acknowledgments

Thanks to Lauren Oliver, for plucking me out of the submissions pile and seeing the humor in comparing mountains and trees to tacos. I don't think I'd have found Lyssa's voice without you. Also, a resounding thanks to Lexa Hillyer and Rhoda Belleza and the entire team at Paper Lantern Lit for everything that they've done to bring Lyssa's world to life. You guys rock my world! Also, thanks to Stephen Barbara, who found *Zip* the absolute perfect home.

More thanks to Laura Arnold, who's been a dream to work with and who turned every new revision into a scavenger hunt of "Now how can I make this even better?" I can't even really picture what this book was before you.

Now on to my fabulous first readers: A big, sloppy thanks to my very good friend Lucy Randall, who proofread chapters for me and loved *Zip* from the beginning, and made me feel like the world's biggest rock star when I sold it. More thanks to Jon VanZile for trading e-mails with me in the early days and for telling me that maybe I just needed to make the whole thing "bigger." Big enough yet, Jon?

I've been lucky beyond belief to find critique partners who've read, loved, and challenged my writing. Many of them haven't read *Zip* yet, but the advice they've given over the years has stuck with me as I've worked to bring this book to life. So Andrew Stoute, Tim Fletcher, Jon VanZile (again!), Leah Konen, Anna Hecker, and Micol Ostow's entire YA Advanced Writing Class, thank you!

Lastly, thanks to my amazing family. To say that you've been supportive is such an understatement. I wouldn't have made it this far without you guys. And, finally, thank you to Ron, for all of the things I won't ever be able to put into words.